P9-DHN-166

ALSO BY DONNA GRANT

THAT
COWBOY
OF MINE

DONNA GRANT

St. Martin's Paperbacks

This is a work of fiction. All of the characters, organizations, and events portrayed in this novel are either products of the author's imagination or are used fictitiously.

First published in the United States by St. Martin's Paperbacks, an imprint of St. Martin's Publishing Group

THAT COWBOY OF MINE

For information, address St. Martin's Publishing Group, 120 Broadway, New York, NY 10271.

www.stmartins.com

ISBN: 978-1-250-82028-0

Our books may be purchased in bulk for promotional, educational, or business use. Please contact your local bookseller or the Macmillan Corporate and Premium Sales Department at 1-800-221-7945, ext. 5442, or by email at MacmillanSpecialMarkets@macmillan.com.

Printed in the United States of America

St. Martin's Paperbacks edition / May 2022

10 9 8 7 6 5 4 3 2 1

Chapter 1

Hill Country Texas
June

The distinct sound of metal snapping loudly before cracking back into place jerked Cal awake. He knew that sound. *Everyone* knew that sound. His heart hammered in his chest with the knowledge that someone had just cocked a shotgun.

And he was pretty sure it was at him.

He blinked rapidly against the bright sunlight that pierced his eyes like laser beams. In the next second, he realized that he was lying on the ground. Cal raised his hand to block the sun. That's when he saw someone standing five feet from him. His gaze moved from well-worn boots, up slim, jean-clad legs, to the red plaid button-down, unbuttoned to reveal the white tank top underneath. It wasn't until Cal's eyes locked on the woman's face that his heart skipped a beat.

She was stunning. Utterly exquisite. Powder blue eyes that reminded him of a clear, summer sky glared at him with annoyance. Wavy brunette locks gently ruffled by a soft breeze fell from beneath the straw Stetson. Her delicate, heart-shaped face, pronounced cheekbones, and slim neck gave her a fragile, almost vulnerable appearance.

But there was nothing weak about the gun aimed at him.

He wanted to know her name and everything about her. He couldn't wait to hear her voice. With one look, he was captivated. It was a good thing he was already on the ground. He was *that* struck by her. Cal couldn't remember the last time a female had left him so dumbstruck. Then again, he had never encountered such a woman before.

He hadn't known that someone could feel this way just by looking at another. Someone should've warned him.

"What are you doing on my land?" she demanded.

Damn. Her voice was just as sexy as he imagined it would be. If her voice was that good, how would her laugh be? He swallowed in an effort to collect his thoughts, but his mouth felt like cotton. What he wouldn't do for some water. But he wasn't stupid enough to ask. His head throbbed mercilessly, made worse by the sunlight. He held both hands up, palms out, showing her that he wasn't a threat.

"I asked you a question."

The way she held the shotgun told him that she knew how to use it—and she wouldn't hesitate. Once again, he attempted to swallow before saying, "I . . . don't know."

"You don't know?" she repeated doubtfully. "You don't know why you came onto my land and stole a horse?"

"What? I-I would never steal a horse. I swear. I don't know how I got here," he hastened to say as he searched his fuzzy memories. "I . . . well, I had a bad day yesterday. At least, I think it was yesterday." He tried to remember, but it was all a haze.

She blew out an irritated breath. "I suppose that *bad day* is why you reek of alcohol?"

He nodded, which was a mistake since the pain in his head doubled.

"My guess is that you were so inebriated, you were unsuccessful in stealing one horse, but you did open the gate to another."

Cal glanced at the barrel of the gun she still had aimed at

him with steady, sure hands. "I apologize, ma'am, for being on your property, but I'd never steal a horse. The last thing I remember is being in town at Ike's."

"That bar is not only in a seedy location, but the clientele is questionable, as well."

"I wasn't exactly thinking clearly. My name is Cal Bennett. I'm a bull rider. Or, at least, I was. I didn't qualify at the Bandera rodeo this past weekend to move on to the next round."

"Forgive me if I don't cry in my beer," she replied as she lowered the gun so it pointed at the ground instead of at his chest. "Get on your feet and off my land. I've got a horse to find. And you can tell whoever sent you that my answer hasn't changed."

Cal sat up, the movement causing his head to feel as if hundreds of tiny jackhammers drilled into his skull. He squeezed his eyes shut, though her last words confused him. To the point where he felt compelled to say, "No one sent me."

"I don't want to hear it. I've heard enough lies recently to last a lifetime."

His stomach roiled violently. The last thing he wanted to do was get sick in front of this woman. As displeased as she was—with reason—he feared she just might shoot him. He swallowed, praying that his head stopped pounding, and his stomach would ease long enough for him to get to his vehicle. "I'll be happy to leave. Just point me in the direction of my truck."

She glanced away as she murmured, "You've got to be kidding me." Then her blue eyes locked on him. "I haven't seen your truck."

"Then . . . how did I get here?" he asked in confusion.

She glared at him for several tense seconds. "I. Don't. Know. What I do know is that I want you gone. Immediately. If I see you on my land again, I'll shoot first and ask questions later."

"Understood," he said as his stomach roiled again. He parted his lips, breathing through his mouth.

"You can't even stand up, can you?"

He heard the frustration and exasperation in the sigh that followed her words. Cal had done several idiotic things in his life, but trespassing was a first. "I . . . just need a moment."

When she didn't demand that he get to his feet, Cal lay back on the ground and closed his eyes. His stomach eased enough that he wasn't worried about getting sick, but he knew from past experience that his headache wouldn't ease for hours. His mind drifted as he fought to sober up. The ground was hard, and the morning sun was already warm and rapidly headed toward sweltering—and the day would only get hotter.

How in the hell had he ended up on a ranch? The last memory he could dredge up in his hazy mind was sitting at the bar at Ike's, doing his damnedest to drink his cares away. Apparently, he had succeeded. It didn't bode well that he couldn't remember anything. It had been ages since he'd drunk so much that he blacked out.

And given how he felt, this was likely the last time he'd do it. He was getting too old for such idiocy.

"Come on."

Cal's eyes jerked open for a second time when he realized that her voice was nearer. He found her squatting beside him.

"I've got work to do. Do you want help getting to your feet, or should I let you attempt it on your own?" she asked icily.

"Honestly, I'm not sure," he replied. "You were just pointing a gun at me."

"I could still shoot you."

He found his lips curving into a smile, and damned if he didn't see a grin pull at her mouth as well before she turned her head away. He took her outstretched hand. From his vantage point on the ground, she didn't look that tall or strong enough to be able to do much. He soon discovered that he was wrong.

She not only got him to his feet in one movement, but she also steadied him by taking most of his weight. Her arm wrapped around his waist while her other hand held the shotgun. The top of her hat barely reached his chin. That was when he realized that his Stetson was missing.

He wanted to ask her name, but he wasn't sure if he should push her if she weren't willing to offer it up. Her comment about someone sending him was troubling. He hadn't been sent.

Or had he?

Cal couldn't recall how he had gotten to the ranch, much less why. Then there was the case of him supposedly trying to steal a horse. That in and of itself was enough for her to shoot him over. Horse stealing was never taken lightly. It didn't matter what century it was.

He had to lean most of his weight on her as she began walking. The world tilted and swam before his eyes. It took all his concentration to put one foot in front of the other. He didn't want to fall. He'd already made a fool of himself. The least he could do was remain standing. It was by sheer will alone that he didn't allow his wobbly legs to buckle. He desperately wanted to act proper and be a gentleman. Maybe because the last person who'd looked at him with such disapproval had been his grandmother, and she had demanded those things in him.

Cal wanted to rejoice when they finally reached her enclosed, six-seater Polaris Ranger 1000 UTV. Not only because he was able to get out of the sun to shade his eyes, but also because he could sit. She reached into the back and grabbed something.

"I suppose this is yours?"

He opened his eyes long enough to see his favorite black Stetson. It was dirty and covered in dust, but it was once more in his hands. "It is. Thanks."

She said nothing as she started the UTV and put it in gear. He slumped in the seat and closed his eyes. The drive back to the ranch was bumpy as they headed up and down the hills. Cal had a few close calls where he feared he might vomit. Somehow, he managed to keep whatever remained of his battered dignity.

When the vehicle slowed, he cracked open his eyes. He expected to see a house or barns. But they were still in the middle of nowhere. The woman put the UTV in park before she got out. Cal watched through cracked eyelids as she walked to the nearby creek and squatted to inspect something.

Suddenly, the birds got quiet. *Too* quiet. The hairs on the back of Cal's neck rose. He slowly sat up, fully alert while his gaze moved around the dense growth of trees and brush that surrounded them. He didn't see anything, but he didn't need to. The animals had warned him. Cal's gaze returned to the woman as a soft gust of wind ruffled the foliage. She was out in the open with nothing to shield her.

No sooner had that thought gone through his head than he heard the *pop*. Without thinking, he jumped out of the vehicle and rushed up behind her, wrapping his arms around her and taking her to the ground as a second *pop* followed. As they fell, Cal looked to where she had been and saw the bullet ricochet off the rock.

"Are you hit?" he asked in a whisper.

She shook her head.

When he glanced at her, he saw that her face was pale, and she was shaking. His attention returned to the spot next to the creek to see what she had been investigating. He spotted a horse halter that looked as if someone had cut it.

"Do you have hunters on your property?"

She shook her head again.

Unease filled him. Was he still drunk, or had he just witnessed someone attempting a murder?

"We need to get back to the UTV," he told her. "It'll offer us some protection. Can you walk?"

"Of course," she snapped.

He didn't take her sharp words personally. He would probably do the same if someone had just tried to kill him. Cal released her. Together, they got to their feet and hurried to the vehicle. Her hands shook when she started the engine and put the UTV in drive. Cal searched the area where he thought the shooter had been as they sped away, but he didn't see anything.

Whether he wanted it or not, he was now sober. His head still hurt, and his stomach needed food to soak up the alcohol, but he was well and truly clearheaded.

They rode in silence until he spotted roofs in the distance. When they reached the homestead, he noted how well-maintained the fences, corrals, and barns were. The house was older but impressive with its rustic beams and columns around the porch. The white limestone found so prevalently in the area gave the domicile a grand appearance. He particularly loved the wide porch that included rocking chairs and even a swing. Cal could imagine how nice it would be to sit on the porch as dusk settled over the land.

The UTV jerked to a halt. His head swung to the woman to find her blue eyes focused on him.

"Thank you," she said.

"I'm glad I was there."

She held out her hand. "I'm Dillon. Dillon Young."

He shook with her, the feel of her skin against his like a punch to the gut. He blinked, trying to discern what had just happened, and gave her a nod. "Nice to meet you."

"I don't know if you just happened to stumble onto my land, or if you were sent. Regardless, you saved me today, and I owe you."

"I wasn't sent," he replied, holding her gaze so she knew he meant every word. "You owe me nothing. I did what anyone would do."

She glanced away. "Hardly."

"Has someone shot at you before?"

She shook her head and gripped the steering wheel tightly. "He did shoot at me, didn't he?"

"Yes, ma'am, he did."

"Dillon?"

Her head turned at the sound of her name. Cal spotted an older man striding toward them. He was bowlegged with wrinkled skin that looked like old leather from years out in the sun. The hair peeking out of his brown Stetson was solid white, matching his bushy eyebrows. His light brown eyes were clear and intense. He sported a handlebar mustache that matched his hair and completely covered his upper lip. Despite his obvious age, he moved like a young man, covering ground quickly.

"What happened?" he demanded as he reached Dillon. There was concern on his face as he looked her over. "You're pale."

Then the man's gaze slid to Cal and lingered for a moment. When Dillon shook her head as if she wouldn't answer, Cal took it upon himself to do so. "There was an incident. Someone shot at her."

"Dillon," the old man admonished and removed his hat as he shook his head in shock.

"I'm fine," she answered woodenly.

But it was obvious she wasn't.

Cal cleared his throat and held out his hand across Dillon to the man. "I'm Cal Bennett. Apparently, I got drunk last night and wandered onto the ranch. Dillon found me passed out this morning."

"Emmett Perkins," he replied as they shook. "I've worked at the Bar 4 Ranch since I was fourteen. Worked my way up to ranch manager," he replied with a smile. "I'm honestly surprised Dillon didn't shoot you."

"It was close," Cal said with a grin. He glanced at Dillon to find her staring off into the distance. His smile faded as he thought about what could have happened had he not pulled her out of the way.

Emmett cleared his throat as his gaze darted to Dillon. "How close was it?"

Cal didn't need to ask for clarification. "There were two pops. I didn't see where the first landed. Most likely, it went into the water. There was a shift in the wind, and I think that's the only reason it missed. The second ricocheted off the rock where she had been."

"Had been?" Emmett asked with his shaggy eyebrows raised.

Dillon replied. "Cal jerked me out of the way."

"These things can't keep happening," Emmett said.

Cal frowned. Keep? Had Emmett just said *keep*? He didn't want to ask since he was a trespasser on the ranch, but he couldn't help but feel involved after witnessing things first-hand.

"I'm fine," Dillon said and climbed out of the vehicle.

"You wouldn't be," Cal said as he followed suit and walked around the front of the UTV. "You were out there by yourself. If you had been shot, who's to say you would've been able to get back? Who's to say that whoever was there wouldn't have stayed to finish the job?"

"He's got a point," Emmett said.

Dillon put her hands on her hips and faced Cal.

Before she could reply, he said, "You need someone to patrol."

"That's a fine idea," Emmett said. "You up for the job?"

Cal blinked. He had no money, nowhere to go, and nothing

to do. But did he want to get involved in whatever was going on? He looked into Dillon's powder blue eyes and recalled how she had shaken in his arms after being shot at. How the mere touch of her had run through him like lightning. There was no way he would walk away. Not after finding someone like her.

"Yes," Cal answered.

Chapter 2

The last thing Dillon wanted to do was hire someone that could be responsible for opening Legacy's gate so the stallion could get out. However, Cal had saved her life. She might have said she was fine, but she was anything but.

Dillon could have dismissed the *accidents* around the ranch lately as simply that, but she couldn't with this. Someone had shot at her. Actually, fired at her with the intention of ending her life. There was no doubt in her mind.

And she knew who was responsible—Hank Stephens.

No matter how scared she was, she couldn't show fear. Not to anyone. Not even to those working for her that she trusted. People like Hank Stephens could sniff out fear like a shark smelled blood. The only way she would survive was to carry on much like a man would. Because she was in a man's world. As much as she wished it otherwise, it was a fact.

"We've lost two workers in the last week," Emmett said, bringing her back from her thoughts.

As if she had forgotten. She didn't need Emmett broadcasting such things. But she knew why he'd said it. He used it as a reason to hire Cal.

Everyone was afraid. She was, too, but she wouldn't be forced off her land. She didn't blame any of the workers for leaving. They owed her nothing. They were protecting themselves and their families. She would have done the same in their positions. However, that left her in a bind. She, Emmett, and Dusty were doing double the work. If the ranch lost another worker, she wasn't sure how they would continue.

Dillon found herself staring into Cal's gray eyes. They reminded her of the clouds in the afternoon that would cover the summer sky before unleashing violent thunderstorms. His gaze was just as penetrating and direct. He had dirt on his right cheek from where he had been sleeping when she found him. His dark blond hair needed to be cut and was in disarray from his wild night under the stars.

He had sharp cheekbones and hollowed cheeks that she found appealing—even though she didn't want to. She tried not to notice his strong jawline or the fact that he had a chin dimple. His white button-down shirt was filthy, but it allowed her to see his broad shoulders that tapered to a trim waist with an impressive belt buckle and then down long legs.

Handsome? Oh, yes, he was definitely that and more. If she were in the market to date, she would flirt. Not that it would take much. He had an easy way about him, a calming vibe that drew her like a moth to a flame. His crooked grin made her stomach flutter. His strong arms as he tackled her to the ground had been firm but gentle. She wondered what it would be like to be kissed by him.

Her thoughts halted when she realized that some of the dirt covering his shirt and jeans was from saving her. All thoughts of romance fell away as anxiety took hold. Odd things had been happening around the ranch, but this was the first time someone had taken a shot at her. It had shaken her. She shouldn't have been on that part of the ranch. She'd assumed that Cal had left the gate open when he came through, but now she wondered if that were true. There were two other places much closer to the road where Cal could've gotten onto the ranch rather than coming to the house and opening the gate so the horses could get out.

If he hadn't left the gate open, that meant someone else had. Someone who wanted to make sure she was on that part of the ranch. Someone who'd left the halter near the creek so she would see it and stop—giving them a perfect shot at her.

"It's true," she told Cal. "I could use some help, and you did tell me you didn't qualify for the rodeo."

He shifted his feet. "I did."

Dillon didn't know him, and she certainly didn't trust him. But it had been hell trying to find someone to work for her. She was desperate, and desperate people did desperate things. "Are you up for the job?"

"I am," he replied as he settled his hat atop his head.

"You can stay in the bunkhouse if you'd like."

Emmett made a sound in the back of his throat. "If he's going to be your bodyguard, shouldn't he stay in the house?"

"Bodyguard?" she asked, taken aback. For just a moment, the thought of him by her side all day didn't sound half bad. He was nice to look at. Too nice, actually. "I never said he would have such a position."

Cal shrugged. "It seems like you need someone to watch over you. Or do I need to remind you how close that bullet came?"

"I don't need reminding," she snapped. Damn, if her thoughts didn't take her back to how it'd felt to be in his arms. She inwardly shook herself, angry that her mind kept drifting to places it had no business going. Then she took a deep breath and tried to get control of her emotions. She didn't like that she was now scared to be out by herself. Would it really hurt her pride to have someone watching out for her? "I'll be fine alone in the house."

Emmett scratched his head before replacing his Stetson. "I disagree, but you're the boss. I'd advise you never to be alone. Not even when you head into town."

It was on the tip of Dillon's tongue to argue that was taking things too far, but she could still hear the retort of the gun in her thoughts. Her vanity wasn't so great that she couldn't admit when she needed help.

Even when it meant trusting a stranger.

She caught Cal's gaze. "If I find out you were sent to harm me, anyone on this property, or to take my ranch from me, I'll hunt you down."

"Understood," he replied.

Emmett flashed her a smile. "I don't know 'bout you, but I feel better. Now, I take it you didn't find Legacy?"

She shook her head. "There were no tracks, either."

"I'll head out with Dusty and see what we can find," Emmett told her.

Dillon wanted a few minutes alone so she could fully process what had happened that morning between discovering her stallion gone, finding Cal, and being shot at. But it didn't look like that would happen. She could've told Emmett that she would take his spot, but she didn't want to be back out there just yet. For all she knew, the shooter was lying in wait for her.

She blew out a breath, her gaze returning to Cal. A shiver took her when she found his eyes locked on her. She wished she knew what he was thinking. And she really wished she could stop remembering being in his arms. "Shall we head to Ike's to see if your truck is there?"

"I'd appreciate that."

Dillon eyed him. He looked better than he had when she first found him, but not by much. "You aren't going to vomit in my truck, are you?"

"I should be good."

"Do you need food? Water?"

"If you don't mind."

She motioned for him to follow as she made her way to the house and up the two porch steps. Dillon opened the back door and removed her hat to hang it on the hook near the door. She then went to the sink and washed her hands. A smile tugged at her lips when she spotted Cal looking around the kitchen.

"This was my aunt's place," she told him. "It has been in the Young family since 1863. She left it to me when she passed away a little over a year ago. She was what most people would call an eccentric." Dillon shut off the water and dried her hands. "The truth is, she liked her independence. She also liked doing things her way. Some men can't stand taking orders from a woman."

Cal glanced at her. "Times have changed."

"Have they?" She knew for a fact that wasn't entirely true.

"This place is beautiful."

"Aunt Dolly liked nice things. She kept the house updated, and she loved to splurge on a few items that would be conversation pieces." Dillon hung up the towel as she smiled, thinking of her aunt. "She was my favorite person. I loved her style and her flair for doing whatever she wanted. She never cared what anyone thought."

"She sounds like a wonderful person." Cal turned to her. "She didn't have any kids?"

"You think there's a disgruntled family member angry that they didn't get the ranch? That would be easy. Dolly never had any children. I have cousins, but none were even remotely interested in the ranch, and she left each of them sizable monetary gifts. Trust me, they think I got the bad end of the stick. I was the only one who ever showed an interest in the ranch, but even so, I never thought she would leave it to me."

Cal shot her a flat look. "You expect me to believe that?"

"I do. She never asked if I wanted it. I never said I did.

I worked for a bank in Fort Worth. I came here often. For me, it was a vacation. Even after I graduated college, I still visited as often as I could." Dillon motioned to the stools at the island. "Have a seat. I'll see what I can find in the fridge."

"Do you mind if I wash up?" he asked.

She leaned back to look at him around the fridge door. "Take the hallway. First door on the left."

Dillon set out bread, roast from the night before, cheese, and some condiments so Cal could make a sandwich. When he took longer than expected, she sliced the roast and set about making it for him. She ate a slice of meat herself before putting everything away.

"You didn't tell me I had dirt on my cheek," Cal said as he returned.

She smiled, shrugging. "Oops."

He made a sound as he removed his hat and set it on the island. "Is that for me?"

For a second, she couldn't answer. Not only had he cleaned the dirt from his face, but he had finger-combed his hair. He'd been handsome in a hungover kind of way. Now . . . well, *now* she was faced with how it might have been had she met him some other way. The way her stomach fluttered told her that she certainly wouldn't have been demanding he leave. His stormy gray eyes watched her closely, causing her to clear her throat as she tried to remember what they had been talking about.

"Yes," she said as she caught sight of the meal. "That's for you."

"Thank you."

He didn't ask what it was, simply lifted the sandwich and began eating. He scarfed it down in record time, causing Dillon to wonder if she should've made two. When he finished, he wiped his mouth with the napkin and put the plate in the sink.

"Would it be too much trouble for some coffee?" he asked.

Dillon motioned to the single-serve coffee maker so he could choose whatever flavor he wanted. After he had prepared his coffee and put the lid on the paper cup, he put his Stetson back on his head and gave her a nod.

She grabbed her keys and hat and left the house, silently urging herself to stop thinking about him. Once they were in the truck and headed into town, she became conscious of their confinement. Of how close he was. Of how close he had been earlier when someone had shot at her. Of how she hadn't wanted him to let her go.

"When did it start?"

Dillon jerked at the sound of Cal's voice. She had forgotten that he was in the vehicle with her. "Sorry? What?"

"When did things begin happening around the ranch? To you?"

"About five months ago. An offer to buy the ranch came through a law firm acting as a go-between. I declined and told the firm that I wasn't interested in selling. A week later, the second offer came. I declined four in total, all of them doubling in price by the end. It was way too high for the property."

Cal let out a whistle. "That much, huh? I suppose that made you suspicious."

"Yep. But, really, it came down to the fact that I'm happy there. It's the only place I've ever felt myself. No amount of money in the world could make me give up the ranch."

"By the way things have turned, I'm guessing the buyers have realized that, as well."

Dillon gripped the steering wheel tighter at his words. "If I die, the ranch passes to another family member."

"You said yourself, they aren't interested. How likely are they to sell?"

"They wouldn't hesitate."

Cal grunted. "That's what I assumed. Why does this buyer want the ranch so badly?"

"I have no idea," she said as she glanced at a fence along the main road.

"Do you know who it is?"

She snorted. "Everyone does."

"And who would that be?" Cal asked.

"Hank Stephens. He owns the Ivy Ridge Ranch that surrounds mine. He tried to get Dolly to sell for years."

Chapter 3

Cal frowned at the mention of the Ivy Ridge Ranch. "Do you really think a man like Hank Stephens would resort to shooting you just to get your ranch?"

"When you put it like that, no," Dillon admitted. "He's an ass, but I don't think he's a killer."

"Then again, he has let it be known he wants your place."

Dillon didn't respond until she had taken a left turn and straightened the wheel. "The Bar 4 is only fifteen hundred acres. Hank's place is four times that size. Though, he has been buying up other ranches and property in the area for years."

"I should tell you I know Hank."

"Of course you do," Dillon said with a roll of her eyes.

Cal turned his head to her. "Just because I know him doesn't mean I'm helping him or whoever is after your ranch. I'm not. I give you my word."

"I don't know you, Mr. Bennett."

"And yet, you hired me."

A beat of silence passed before she said, "So, I did."

"If I were working for someone else, would I have saved your life this morning?"

Dillon shrugged and blew out a breath. "I don't know."

Cal let the topic drop. It was obvious that Dillon was weary and scared, though she hid it well. If he hadn't witnessed the shooting, he probably wouldn't have believed the situation was so serious. Individuals and companies tried to acquire huge swaths of land all the time. Few millionaires and billionaires *didn't* own land. Cal could well see Hank trying to purchase the Bar 4. But Hank wouldn't try to kill Dillon for it.

"What else has happened?" Cal asked.

Dillon glanced at him, a frown furrowing her brow. "What?"

"Besides the attempt on your life, what else has transpired? Emmett referenced that things couldn't keep happening."

They reached the edge of town. Dillon slowed when she came to the stop sign and waited for her turn before continuing through town. "Small things."

"Like?" Cal pushed.

Her nostrils flared, showing her irritation. "The gate being open sometime last night and the prized quarter horse stallion I just purchased—Legacy—getting out. A feed container I inspected the day before and found clean filled with rats. Fences that had just been checked ending up cut with cattle getting loose."

"Do you think it's someone working for you?"

"What?" she asked incredulously, jerking her head to him. "No. Absolutely not."

"You said you lost a couple of workers. Could they be to blame?"

She shook her head. "I saw the letters they received. Whoever sent them told the men to stop working for me or their families would be harmed. They didn't want to take the chance, so they quit."

"They could have written the letters themselves."

"It's a possibility I've considered, but they aren't the only ones who received them. Everyone who works for me got one."

Cal rubbed his right temple. "It sounds like someone is trying to make it impossible for you to run your ranch."

"That's exactly what they're doing. I've sunk a lot of money into the new stallion. My aunt founded a breeding program that has sustained the ranch far better than cattle ever did. I'm continuing it. Without that stallion, I can't recoup the money I invested."

"Not to mention losing two workers, getting rid of the rats, and constantly fixing fence that was purposefully cut."

She slowed again and put her blinker on to pull into the parking area in front of Ike's. "Exactly."

Cal pointed to his ten-year-old black Chevy Z71, the only vehicle in the parking lot. He waited until Dillon parked beside it before saying, "Whoever wants your ranch must not want to wait for you to throw in the towel. That's the only reason I can think of for things to have escalated to the shooting this morning."

"I wasn't supposed to be in that part of the ranch. I was there looking for Legacy," she said as she met his gaze.

"You think someone let the stallion loose so you would look for him?"

"I do."

"How would they know where you would go?"

She shrugged and rested both hands on the steering wheel. "I'm the one who found the gate open. The horse would've had to go through two pastures to get to the other side of the ranch. It was a clear shot to where I went, which is why I chose it. I called Emmett to let him know what was going on."

"But you told him you didn't see any tracks."

"I saw them leading toward the area you were in. After that, nothing."

"So, that's why you said I attempted to steal a horse."

She twisted her lips. "Oh, you definitely did. Your mistake was trying to take Houdini. No matter what we've used to secure his stall, he always gets out. We leave it open if he wants to go in, but he prefers to remain in the pasture at night. I should also point out that he's not let anyone ride him since Dolly died. Somehow, you managed to get a bridle on him and a saddle out."

"Well, hell," Cal said as he looked away, embarrassed. Her words jogged a faint memory of him struggling to get a halter on a horse. "I thought for sure that was a dream. Every time I put the saddle blanket on the horse and turned to get the saddle, I'd turn back around, and it would be on the ground."

"That's Houdini."

He inwardly grimaced. "I've never stolen anything in my life. I've also never been that drunk. Please accept my sincerest apologies."

She faced forward and sighed. "You don't have to return to the ranch."

Cal was shocked by her words. "But you just hired me."

"Because Emmett was making a big deal of things."

"I was there, Ms. Young. It *was* a big deal."

Her head swiveled to him. "Call me Dillon. And it doesn't matter who is around or where I am. If someone wants to kill me, they're going to do it. You and I both know that."

Anger sliced through Cal. "The hell they will."

"You're one man. What are you going to do?"

"Keep you safe."

Her powder blue eyes watched him for a long moment. "It's fine to say you need the money."

"I do, but that isn't the point. Call it Fate if you want, but something made sure I was at the Bar 4 today so you'd find me, and I'd be there to save you."

"How do I know you didn't let Legacy out?"

He'd been waiting for her to ask that question. Despite

knowing that she would, he didn't have a response. Not one that would cause her to believe him, anyway. "I was raised with livestock. I know how important locked gates are. I would never willingly open one."

"I hate to keep pointing out the obvious, but you trespassed on my land and attempted to steal Houdini."

"If I did, it was for a reason."

She licked her lips, her gaze telling him that she didn't believe a word he said.

"I may not remember last night, but I'm not the type of man who leaves someone in a bad situation if I can help," he told her.

Dillon turned her head to look out her window, her shoulders sagging. "I may be new to running a ranch, but I'm not stupid." She turned back to him. "I don't know you. And while I do need help, I'm not sure hiring a stranger is the right way to go."

"I can track," he said suddenly. Cal wasn't sure what had prompted him to blurt the words. All he knew was that he wanted—no, he *needed*—to stay with Dillon. Because if he didn't, he knew she would be dead in a matter of days.

Her blue eyes narrowed on him. "What?"

"Let me come back to the ranch. If I can track Legacy, let me stay to work and protect you."

She studied him for a long minute.

He saw her waffling. "My daddy taught me well. I can find the tracks. I can find your stallion."

"All right," she said. "You've got a deal. Find Legacy, and I'll hire you."

He smiled, not sure why he was so happy. "You won't regret it."

"I'd better not. I'll meet you back at the ranch."

"I'll follow you," he told her.

Cal didn't think about keys until he went to open his door. He felt his front jeans pockets, and, thankfully, found the set.

He fished them out and climbed into the cab. In seconds, he started the truck and pulled out behind Dillon.

On the drive back to the ranch, Cal kept thinking about what Dillon had told him. The things happening at the ranch had seemed relatively small, but they had leapt forward significantly this morning. He couldn't help but think that more had been happening that Dillon hadn't shared. Not that he blamed her. She didn't know who to trust. Not to mention, he was a stranger. Why would she open up to him?

Cal needed to talk to Emmett. It was obvious the old cowboy cared about Dillon. If anyone would tell him the complete story, it was Emmett. With that sorted, Cal shifted his mind to the missing stallion.

His head felt measurably better, and his stomach was finally sorting itself out. Getting on a horse should be the last thing he did, but he would do it anyway. A broken collarbone hadn't stopped him from riding in a rodeo. A hangover headache certainly wouldn't now.

He leaned to the side while driving and pulled the leather bag onto the seat from the floorboard. It had belonged to his grandfather and his father. The leather had a beautiful patina from use to go along with its soft, pliable texture. He unzipped it with one hand and dug into the side compartment for a bottle of ibuprofen while never taking his eyes off the road.

Cal hooked the bottle with his left thumb and forefinger while the rest of his hand held the wheel, then opened the cap with his right hand. He dug out three pills that he tossed into his mouth and swallowed before closing the bottle and returning it to his bag. If he were lucky, the medicine would dull his headache.

Back at the ranch, he had Dillon show him what had occurred that morning when she found the stallion gone. She took him through all of it, step by step, pointing to the southwest. Cal walked along the pasture's fence, searching for any clues. The ground was dry, firm, and trampled enough from others that it made it hard for him to determine tracks. But he did find some. He climbed the fence and jumped inside the pasture. He stayed close to the fence as he let his gaze slowly move over the grass.

"What do you see?" Dillon asked.

"I count two horses. One outside the paddock. One in." He pointed to a spot in the middle of the paddock near the gate where the grass had been flattened. "The stallion circled there several times before running out."

Dillon met his gaze. "Legacy had only spent two nights here. He was learning the ranch."

Cal studied the area near the gate that still stood open. He made his way to it and knelt to analyze the impression of a boot heel in the grass. It was deeper on the outside. Unfortunately, that was the only print he found. The stallion had covered anything else during his run.

"You don't happen to have security cameras, do you?"

Dillon walked around the pasture to the gate. "There hasn't been a need before now."

Cal didn't point out that she hadn't answered his question. He reminded himself that she had no reason to trust him, and every reason not to. He straightened and adjusted his hat as he squinted against the bright sun and looked into the distance. "We need to go now. The longer we wait, the harder it'll be to track."

"Let's go."

His head swung around to see Dillon already headed to a paddock. Cal followed to see her lead out a female with a shiny black coat, four white fetlocks, and a white star on her forehead. Dillon tied the horse to the fence and began brushing the mare.

"Take your pick of horses," she told him.

Cal strode into the barn, impressed by the design and the attention to detail. Dillon hadn't been joking when she said the quarter horses made the ranch more money than the cattle. It was obvious by the barn. Since quarter horses were used in many aspects of ranching, not to mention rodeos, he wasn't surprised.

He gazed over the impressive animals available until he found himself looking at a sorrel gelding. The horse stared at him. He had a suspicion it was Houdini. As much as Cal wanted to get to know the horse after his encounter, now wasn't the time. Instead, Cal chose a bay and led the gelding outside.

After the horses were brushed, he and Dillon got saddles and bridles from the tack room and readied their mounts. The minute his foot hit the stirrup, and he swung his leg over, a smile pulled at his lips. It had been entirely too long since he had been on a horse. The anxious feeling that had been with him for most of his life lessened. He couldn't explain it, and he didn't want to try.

He used the reins and turned the gelding. The rolling hill country stood before him, and somewhere, hidden in the picturesque landscape, was someone out to harm Dillon—something he had no intention of allowing to happen.

Chapter 4

"I missed," Freddy said as he hung his head.

Isaac Gomez puffed on the fat cigar, making smacking sounds with his lips as he turned the stogie in his fingers. He leaned back and put his feet up on his desk, the walls covered with proof of his many accomplishments, including pictures with presidents and Texas governors. "You had one job, Freddy. One job."

Freddy removed his cowboy hat, holding it by the brim and turning the straw Stetson around and around. "The wind prevented the first bullet from finding its mark. But . . . someone was with her."

"Who?" Isaac demanded, his dark eyes locked on Freddy.

Freddy shrugged, fear making his eyes go round. "Cal Bennett."

Isaac started laughing. Things couldn't be more perfect if he had planned them himself. Oh, wait. He had.

"He's the one who pulled her out of the way," Freddy hurried to say.

"Don't worry about him."

Freddy frowned. "So, he's with us?"

Isaac's dark eyes glared at him. "I said not to worry about Cal."

"Yes, sir."

"Go. I'll send for you when it's time to fulfill your promise."

Freddy nodded and hurried out of the office. The minute the door closed, Isaac lowered his feet to the floor and turned his head when a side door opened. Isaac's career as a lawyer had been a good one. He'd worked hard and played even harder. He and his wife—as well as his numerous girlfriends—had enjoyed the many benefits his connections had sown.

He liked money. The more, the better. He'd always had expensive tastes. It was what had led him to be an attorney. Not to mention, he had an affinity for learning laws—and discovering how to bend them to suit his purposes. It was a win-win situation.

No matter how much money he had that gave him a very comfortable living, he always wanted something else. And once he coveted something, he didn't stop until he had it. Which had put him in his current situation.

"He missed? What the fuck did he mean?"

Isaac held his cigar between his first two fingers and put his elbow on the arm of the chair so his hand dangled as he stared into Hank Stephens's bright blue eyes. Hank was tall, charismatic, and a ladies' man. "Your tactic was taking too long."

Hank ran a hand down his face and turned away before he spun back to Isaac, his hands braced on the back of one of the two chairs before Isaac's desk. "You tried to kill her?"

"*I* didn't do anything."

"You hired that man," Hank stated, poking his finger on the desk to accentuate each word.

Isaac shrugged and took another puff of his cigar.

Hank dropped his chin to his chest. "Dammit, Isaac. I told

you we had to be careful. I didn't want to be connected to anything with the Bar 4 or Dillon Young. Not after I tried to buy the ranch."

"You sent her offers," Isaac said with a wave of his hand. "People do that all the time. That doesn't make you a murderer."

"Perhaps. But if she comes up dead, I'm the first person the police are going to look at."

Isaac grinned. "It's why you hired me. Don't worry, Hank. Everything will go our way."

"Not if you have her killed," he said in a low whisper.

"We tried things your way. She's not budging."

"Those things take time. She's hanging on by a thread. I can't believe you made a decision without discussing it with me."

Isaac clenched his teeth as rage rolled through him. "You were quick to take my suggestions when she wouldn't consider any of your offers to purchase the ranch. You were looking for any way to get that land. So much so, you took me on as a partner in this. Nothing is going to happen to you. Because if it does, it happens to me."

Hank was quiet as he considered Isaac's words.

"Besides," Isaac said, "she was hit with a double dose this morning."

"What did you do?"

"There's a stallion waiting for you on your ranch."

Hank's face went white. "You didn't."

"I didn't."

"You know what I mean!"

Isaac quirked a brow. "The more problems she has, the more money she loses, and the quicker she'll sell."

"Do you have any idea what will happen now? Horse thefts aren't taken lightly."

"As if you need to worry. Bill will do whatever we want."

Hank's nostrils flared. "One of these days, the sheriff isn't going to do what we want."

"You know as well as I do that Bill is an imbecile. Stop worrying."

Hank shook his head in anger. "You're doing all of this without talking to me. But worse than that, you're putting the heat on me."

Isaac sat forward, leaning his forearms on his desk. "Do you know how much money we're going to make once that land is ours? Remember that when you're second-guessing my decisions."

"Do you think she knows what we're after?" Hank asked.

Isaac made a sound in the back of his throat. "No."

"But you can't be sure."

"Go ask her, then. Shit, Hank. You've never acted like this before."

His nostrils flared again as he stood straight. "We've never taken such drastic . . . action . . . before."

"Fine," Isaac said, throwing up his hands. "You win. We'll go back to your plan if that's what you want."

Hank nodded once. "It's what I want."

"If she discovers what we're after, she'll fight tooth and nail."

"Then let's make sure she doesn't find out."

Everyone thought Isaac could pull shit like this out of his ass. He couldn't guarantee that Dillon Young wouldn't discover why Hank Stephens was so keen on getting her land.

Hank turned to go, then paused and looked at Isaac. "What is Cal doing at the Bar 4?"

"I thought you knew."

"Isaac, I'm not in the mood to be fucked with."

Isaac rolled his eyes. "So testy. You can't even take a joke. Let's just say he was a little drunk last night, and I had some friends help him onto Dillon's land. He'll be aiding us."

"Why?" Hank asked with narrowed eyes.

"Don't worry. Cal will be fine."

"*Why?*" Hank demanded a second time.

Isaac sighed heavily. "He's spying for us."

"You knew I'd never allow you to bring Cal into this."

"Stop worrying. Cal was all for it once I mentioned your name."

Hank let out a long breath. "I hope you're right."

"Oh, please," Isaac said with a roll of his eyes. "No one will suspect Cal. I thought you'd approve."

"I promised Cal's father I'd keep an eye on him, not put him in the middle of our scheme."

Isaac fisted his left hand. He was used to getting what he wanted, and he hated when anyone tried to tell him what to do. Hank was a client, and though that technically meant that Isaac worked for him, that was never how Isaac saw things. Besides, they were partners at the moment. Hank needed to realize that he wasn't running things anymore.

"Cal Bennett is a grown-ass man who can make his own decisions. He doesn't need anyone looking out for him."

"Shouldn't he be going to the next town with the rodeo?" Hank asked.

Isaac raised his brows. "Wow. For someone keeping a promise to an old friend, you don't know shit about Cal. He didn't qualify."

Hank's shoulders lifted as he took a deep breath, stretching the confines of his button-down. He put his hands on the large belt buckle proclaiming him a rodeo champion from twenty-three years earlier.

"I don't want Cal mixed up in this."

"Too late. He's in."

Hank's blue eyes were hard and unyielding. "No more decisions without discussing them with me. That's what we agreed on."

"Cal is on Dillon's ranch. He was the one who got her out of harm's way. You should be thankful I sent him there."

"If you won't pull Cal out, then I'll go see him myself."

"You do what you have to do. But remember, the longer it takes for us to get the land, the more time it gives Dillon to figure things out."

Hank left without another word.

Isaac stared at the door well after it'd closed behind his long-time client. He'd always considered Hank a friend, but if the man got in the way, Isaac would do whatever was necessary to secure the land.

Slowly, he sat back in his chair, contemplating not sharing the profits with anyone. He might pursue it, but Hank had the documents secured at his ranch. Which meant that Isaac had no choice but to keep Hank as a partner. Just as Hank had to keep him.

Isaac rose from his chair and went to the windows. He parted the blinds and looked into the parking lot to see Hank getting into a white Ford King Ranch pickup. Hank sat in the driver's seat for several minutes, staring out the window before starting the engine and driving away. Isaac breathed a sigh of relief.

His years with Hank had allowed him to read the rancher. Hank was calculating and manipulative, but he wasn't an idiot. He knew a good deal when he found it. Despite Hank's aversion to killing Dillon, or Cal Bennett being on the ranch, he wouldn't interfere.

Isaac walked to the bar cart in his office and poured himself a bourbon. When he looked up, he stared into the mirror. He smoothed his hand over his clean-shaven face. Unremarkable brown eyes stared back at him. He kept his brown hair trimmed neatly. He wasn't handsome, but that didn't seem to matter once he acquired wealth and power. His gaze lowered to his trim physique that he worked hard to maintain. As a child, he'd sworn not to have a potbelly, and he had kept that vow.

All in all, he looked healthy. The signs of the cancer eating away at his body weren't visible. He still felt good, but he wasn't going to take chances. It was why he had upped the stakes with Dillon Young and the Bar 4 Ranch.

He had time scheduled in the next few weeks that would take him to Houston for treatment. He would beat the disease. He had no doubt. Simply because there was a lot of money nearly in his hands that he wanted to enjoy. Once the Bar 4 was theirs, he would shut down the law practice and leave the area forever. Isaac didn't know where he would go, but it was time for a fresh start.

His office door opened, and Stella walked in. She flashed him a bright smile and leaned against the closed door. He turned to eye her hourglass figure, the way her blouse clung to her large breasts, and her pencil skirt highlighting her small waist and wide hips.

"Damn, woman. You are beautiful."

Her red lips curved upward. Then she crooked a perfectly manicured finger at him, her long nails painted crimson. He set aside his bourbon and strode to her. Isaac groaned as he gripped her hips and ground himself into her.

"From the moment you walked into my office two years ago, all I wanted to do was fuck you."

She giggled as she wound her arms around him. "We had sex in the middle of the interview. I'll never forget that."

He kissed her, loving the taste and feel of her. She was a unique woman. He'd never known anyone who liked sex as much as he did, but Stella did. Half the time, he couldn't keep up with her. He'd kept their affair going because she'd never asked for a relationship. Never wanted to know what they were. She simply allowed them to enjoy whatever it was they had.

He ended the kiss and pulled back to look down at her. "What's wrong?"

"I came to ask you that," she said as she fixed his bolero at his neck. "Hank left looking rather annoyed, and I heard raised voices. Everything okay between the two of you?"

"It'll be fine. Just a difference of opinion."

"Anything I can help with?"

It wasn't the first time Isaac had considered sharing what he and Hank had planned with Stella, but he decided against it once more. Stella had shown her loyalties, but Isaac knew what money did to people. Greed was a powerful force. He should know. He'd lost against it his entire life.

He shook his head as he kissed her. "I've got it."

She pulled out of his arms and walked to his desk. Then she turned and pulled her skirt up to show her thigh-high stockings before sitting on the desk, her legs spread. "Then perhaps there's something else I can do," she said in a sultry voice.

"Definitely," he replied as he began unbuckling his belt.

Chapter 5

It wasn't that Dillon didn't trust Cal. . . . Actually, that was a lie. She absolutely didn't trust him. That's why she hadn't let him go looking for her stallion alone. He had saved her, and she would never forget that. However, that didn't mean he got an immediate pass to being her best friend—or even someone she trusted.

She glanced over at him as they rode side by side. He had a smile on his face, and the contentment and pleasure took her aback. She was so shocked by it that she found herself looking at him again. This time, his stormy gray gaze met hers.

"Something the matter?" he asked casually.

Dillon shook her head and looked ahead. She managed to go all of a minute before glancing his way again. And, dammit, he was staring at her.

"Something is definitely the matter," he said. "And don't you dare tell me it's nothing."

She tugged hair out of her eye and tucked the strand behind her ear, hoping it would stay there. Her hair never did what it was supposed to. "I'm just surprised to see such happiness on your face."

"Ah." He was quiet for a moment as the *clip-clop* of the horses' hooves filled the silence. "It's been some time since I've gone riding. I grew up with horses, see them all the time at rodeos, but . . ."

"They weren't your focus," she finished for him.

Gray eyes met hers as he nodded. "I didn't realize how much I missed riding until now."

"Why bull riding?" she asked, unable to help herself.

His lips twisted as he shrugged. "Followed in my father's footsteps. I'm not sure if my mother will ever forgive me for that."

"She's your mother. She forgave you the minute you made the decision."

Cal snorted, though he had a smile on his face. "You don't know my mother."

Dillon found herself returning his grin. "When is the last time you saw your parents?"

"I'm ashamed to say it's been too long since I've seen Mom. I call her. Check in as often as I can."

"Bullshit."

His head jerked to her, and his brows furrowed deeply. "Excuse me?"

"You don't go because you don't want to see the disappointment in her eyes, and you don't call as often as you should because you don't want to hear her tell you all the different things you could be doing instead of bull riding."

Cal looked forward, a muscle clenching in his jaw. "Mom would like you. You don't hesitate to state things just as they are. She's the same."

"She might not be on your side, but your father is. How does he feel about the situation with your mom?"

"I'm sure he'd be pissed. There isn't much he can do, though, since he died when I was ten."

Dillon closed her eyes, hating that she had let her mouth way with her. "I'm sorry, Cal. I didn't know."

"It was a long time ago," he said with a shrug. "Bull riding is a dangerous sport."

She didn't say more, even though she wanted to ask. Some topics were off-limits, and Dillon had touched on one. She drew in a deep breath and released it, making a mental note to stay away from talk of Cal's parents.

"Dad's death nearly killed Mom. She had been begging him to stop for a long time. He'd suffered several injuries already, had a couple of surgeries, but nothing could keep him from getting back in the chute and on the next bull. He was a good rider, but talent can only get you so far. You have to draw good bulls. And, sometimes, that doesn't happen. You stop winning, the funds dry up, and a choice has to be made: Take what little you have left and give it to the family to pay bills and put food on the table, or . . . use the money for a hotel in the next town on the circuit. Bull riding was an addiction for my father. It's kinda a tradition in my family."

"Are you addicted?" Dillon asked.

Cal met her gaze and shrugged. "I don't know. Some might claim I am. I know my mother would. Dad and I spent hours together training when he was home from the circuit. I didn't realize it was in secret. Mom had apparently told him that if he trained me to ride bulls, she'd divorce him."

"I can't say I blame her."

"Me, neither. I was just happy to be with Dad and doing something he adored. That last year on the circuit, I remember the times he called Mom. I heard their arguments and her begging him to come back so we could be a regular family. We had about thirty acres. Nothing huge, but it was hard work for Mom and me to take care of with her also working a full-time job. She ended up having to sell most of the cattle as well as her horse. I still remember hearing her crying in her bedroom after she'd loaded her mare onto the trailer for the buyer. My father had given her that horse."

Dillon could well imagine Cal's mom's anguish.

He made a sound that was half-laugh, half-snort. "Dad was having the best year of his career. He'd brought in a lot of money. That eased some monetary stress for Mom, but her fear and worry over him getting hurt—or worse—never let up. He called her right before he was about to ride. Told her there were two more rodeos in the circuit, but he had qualified for the semi-finals in Vegas. He told her that no matter if he won or lost in Vegas, he would retire so they could have the life he'd always promised. Mom hung up the phone, happier than I could remember seeing her. That was the last time they talked."

Dillon looked at Cal, but he was staring straight ahead.

"He'd drawn the best bull at the rodeo. Dad was all but guaranteed to win that night. Years later, I saw the ride on tape. He did everything right. It was like he could sense which direction the bull would twist and spin, so he never lost his balance. It was the best ride of his life." Cal paused, his shoulders rising as he took a deep breath. "When he tried to dismount, everything went wrong. His hand got hung up in the rope. It happens. Bullfighters are always ready when something like that happens. Three immediately went to help my father, but they weren't fast enough."

Chills raced up Dillon's arm. She wasn't sure she wanted to hear any more.

But Cal continued. "Whatever connection he had with the bull ended when he tried to dismount. The bull twisted and bucked, sending my father's legs flying while hi and was still strapped to the animal. He came down on   o of the bull's head and was flung again. Sometime during that, Dad's arm got pulled out of its socket. A bullfighter grabbed the bull's horns in an attempt to prevent him from goring my ther while the other two loosened Dad's strap. Then   hing went to shit. The bull's horn speared one of the   . Just as Dad's hand slipped out of the strap, the bull   nd butted him, throwing him into the air like a doll.

Dad landed on his head, breaking his neck, and killing him instantly."

Dillon couldn't find words. She stared at Cal, wondering why he would've watched his father's last ride, but she knew the reason. Because she would've done it, as well.

Cal suddenly pulled back on the reins to halt his horse and dismounted. He knelt beside something, but all Dillon could think about was his father and the horrific way he'd died. There were proper words to say to someone after learning of such an event, but for the life of her, Dillon couldn't think of them.

"The horses came through here," Cal said. "And they weren't alone. There's a third horse with them. By the depth of the tracks, it had a rider."

"Cal, I'm terribly sorry for what happened to your father."

He flashed her a quick smile before he remounted and clicked to the gelding to start walking. "You couldn't have known. Besides, it happened eighteen years ago."

They rode for several minutes in silence. Dillon wasn't sure what to say, and she decided it was better not to speak. For the next thirty minutes, Cal impressed her with his tracking skills. Some of the places he found, she would've overlooked completely. In fact, she had. But he showed her the outline of the horse's shoe as proof. Either he was a really good tracker, or he had been in on it.

Dillon had smelled the alcohol emanating from him when she'd found him. It hadn't been spilled liquor on his clothes. It'd come from his skin—proof that he had drunk that much. If he had been in on the stallion's release, he would've slowed them down for certain.

"You still think I'm part of this, don't you?"

She glanced at him. "I didn't say that."

"You didn't have to. I'd be thinking it. A stranger shows up on your property the same night a gate is opened, and a stallion gets out? Hell, I'd probably have a gun trained on me."

"I already did that."

He chuckled as he glanced her way. "It was certainly a first meeting I'll never forget." His smile faded. "I'm not helping whoever did this. I can keep telling you that, but you have no reason to trust anything I say. So, I'll prove it to you."

"Why do you want to help?"

Cal reached up and adjusted his Stetson. "Let's just say that I don't have any other pressing obligations at the moment. I also feel responsible because I was trespassing. Not to mention, hearing and seeing how close that bullet came to you this morning. Truth be told, I don't think I'd leave now even if you asked me. Someone opened that gate, knowing how much you depended on that horse. And two riders took the stallion somewhere."

"The only place they could've taken them is Ivy Ridge. Hank's property flanks mine on all sides. And there's only the one road between us. Everything else is fence line."

"Hank is a good man. I can't imagine he'd take part in this."

That was the second time he had spoken about Hank. "How do you know him? Did you work for him?"

"Nothing like that, though I'm sure he would've hired me had I asked. He and my father were on the circuit together and became good friends. Dad used to talk about how talented Hank was at bronc riding, but Hank didn't have rodeoing in his blood like Dad did. Hank was in it only for the money to buy his ranch. The minute Hank got the cash, he quit. But he and Dad remained friends. Dad asked him to keep an eye on Mom and me if anything were to happen to him."

Dillon guided her mare around a fallen limb. "And did Hank?"

"He came to the house several times, asking Mom if she needed anything. She's a proud woman. She doesn't like handouts."

"Not even if it would have helped her child?"

"I never went hungry or without. We had family, and she

leaned on them for everything but money. Over the years, Hank stopped coming by. Instead, he called. Eventually, I was the one he talked to. Mom allowed me to go to his place for a few weeks every summer. He was the one who gave me the last fifty dollars I needed for the rodeo membership so I could begin the circuit."

Dillon wrinkled her nose. "I bet your mother wasn't happy about that."

"Not in the least. But I would've gotten there eventually. Hank just shortened my wait time."

"When did you see Hank last?"

Cal shrugged. "It's been a few years." He glanced at her, a knowing grin on his face. "I've not spoken with him, either."

"So, I'm supposed to believe that you just happened to be in the area and that you just happened to get onto my land?"

"Like I said, I plan to prove to you that I'm a man of my word. I swear I'm not helping anyone or in league with anyone to harm you or take away your ranch."

Dillon wanted to believe because she could use someone like Cal on the ranch. He had a confidence that drew her, and a smile that made her breath quicken each time he flashed it at her. Something about him kept pulling her attention, but damned if she could pinpoint what it was.

The problem was, she wasn't sure she could bring herself to believe him. Yet, her future and her life were on the line. Somehow, Cal was to be a part of that in some way. All she could do was hope that he was there to help her.

Chapter 6

Cal was under no illusions that Dillon would trust him in the near future. He couldn't shake the feeling that there was more going on at the ranch that she hadn't told him about, and the sooner he spoke with Emmett, the better. But for now, his attention was on locating the stallion.

He'd told her that Hank wasn't involved, but even Cal had to admit that it didn't look good for his friend. Cal wanted to talk to Hank and hear what he had to say for himself. That conversation wouldn't take place on the phone, though. It would be a face-to-face so Cal could see Hank's expressions. People could say all the right things, but the truth was generally in their eyes and face. The problem with his plan was that if he told Dillon he wanted to talk to Hank, she would think that Cal was working for him.

And bringing Dillon with him would get Cal nowhere. Hank wouldn't drop his guard as long as he had someone with him. That put Cal in a precarious position.

His thoughts halted as he lost the tracks. Cal kicked free of the stirrups and dismounted. He kept hold of the horse's reins as he backtracked and scanned the nearby ground, searching for any sign of the stallion. Whoever had been leading the horse had purposefully taken him over terrain that would be difficult to track.

Cal squatted and moved dead leaves, but there was nothing to see. "We need to retrace our steps to where I last saw the tracks."

Without hesitation, Dillon turned her mare around and nudged her into a gallop. Cal quickly mounted and followed suit. In no time, they were back where the horses' tracks were clear. The sun beat down on them relentlessly. The heat did little to help his head. He heard a whistle and looked up in time to see Dillon toss him a bottle of water.

Cal caught it and nodded his thanks before drinking the liquid. He needed about a gallon more. He crumpled the plastic bottle and put it in the saddlebag as he jumped to the ground. When he came around his gelding, Dillon held out another bottle.

"You need this a lot more than I do. Besides, I packed a few since I knew you would need them," she said.

He tipped his hat to her. "Thank you."

As he drank the second bottle, slower this time, he surveyed the ground. Upon first glance, it appeared as if the horses had run right through the space. But now that he took a closer look, he saw that the animals had circled the small area a few times. The section of packed earth was one that Dillon and her employees regularly used for the UTV and riding from one pasture to another, causing it to look like a road.

"What's near here?" he asked.

Dillon shook her head. "Pasture. This section is one of the largest. It allows the cattle to graze freely. Occasionally, we let the horses in here."

"How far is the creek?"

"Half a mile that way," she said, pointing to her left.

Cal followed her finger. There were large trees, providing plenty of cover for anyone lying in wait. The brush was tall, and the ground dense and dry. The area they stood in was relatively open, the trees about thirty feet away in small clusters. Cal walked to the nearest tree and studied the space. He wasn't surprised to find some cigarette butts on the ground.

Dillon walked up beside him and stared down at the remnants of the smokes. "Someone was waiting."

"Or the person who steered the stallion here waited for someone. It would explain the area where the horse tracks are so numerous. They stood there long enough to walk around that section several times."

Her blue eyes met his as she tipped back her head. "Can you find the tracks from here?"

"The horses didn't just vanish. There are no tire tracks other than your UTV's, so no one brought a trailer and loaded them up."

She said nothing more as he went back to the area the horses had been and began to analyze the ground, searching for anything that could show him where they had gone. Then he found it.

"Here," he called to Dillon.

She rushed to him so he could show her the ground as he pushed some dead leaves out of the way. Half a hoof print was visible. They had moved off the road and onto the grass. The breeze had shifted the leaves just enough to cause Cal to miss the transition, but now that he knew their direction, he would be more careful.

Instead of getting back on the horses, Cal tugged his gelding after him by the reins so he could be closer to the ground. Dillon remained slightly behind him. He wasn't sure if it was to give him space or study him. And, honestly, he didn't care. He would find the stallion and prove that neither he nor Hank had any part in the theft.

But if Hank had . . .

Cal didn't want to think about that. Hank was a link to his father, and Cal would hate to sever it. But he wouldn't associate himself with anyone who went to such lengths to acquire property the owner didn't want to sell.

He glanced up, noticing that the stallion had been led in the opposite direction from which Cal had been found. If he were a suspicious person, Cal might think that he had been a decoy to prevent Dillon from seeing where the horse had really been taken. The only way to clear his name was to find the stallion.

They had gone about a mile when Cal halted and looked back at Dillon. He took off his hat and wiped the sweat from his forehead with his sleeve-covered forearm before replacing his hat. He then rolled up his sleeves and pushed them over his elbows to allow his skin to cool.

Sweat dripped down Dillon's face, and she wiped at it with a cloth. "What is it?"

"They've not deviated from the straight path yet. What's ahead?"

"The fence between my land and Hank's."

Cal had been afraid she would say that. He looked in that direction and saw more trees. At least they would get a little shade as they searched. He continued on for about another hundred and fifty feet when the tracks shifted to the right.

"There's an old hunting cabin ahead," Dillon told him as they turned. "And a small corral where the horses were put at night."

"A perfect place to keep a stallion," he said as he met her gaze.

"I didn't even think of that." Dillon shook her head in agitation. "I've not been out there since Dolly died."

"Who else knows about it?"

She lifted one shoulder in a shrug. "Everyone who works for me."

"They may change directions again. I'd rather follow the tracks than ride straight there."

"Or we go to the cabin in hopes of getting to them before they move Legacy."

Cal had to admit that was something to consider. "How close is the cabin to the fence?"

"A ways."

"So, no one could back up a trailer, cut the fence, and load up a horse?"

She shook her head. "It would take more than that."

Cal jerked his chin to the horses. "We'll move faster on them."

"You'll see better on foot."

"The goal is to find the stallion and catch whoever did this. We need to move quickly."

Dillon turned and mounted. Cal did the same. She stayed behind him as he rode, his gaze moving from the tracks to the distance and back again, constantly looking, constantly searching. And all the while, making sure he didn't lose the tracks again.

Once more, the tracks headed in a straight line. They didn't roam. Didn't stop to graze. And that proved again that someone had been leading the stallion. Forty minutes later, Cal spotted a structure through the trees. He looked back at Dillon, who nodded, letting him know that it was the hunting cabin. He motioned for her to go around as he went in the other direction. If anyone was there, either he or Dillon would see them.

Cal kept sight of Dillon until they reached the trees. He decided to stay on his horse in case he needed to chase someone. Suddenly, the gelding's ears pricked forward.

"You hear something, boy?" Cal whispered.

The horse's attention remained on the cabin. Cal guided him close, keeping an eye on the windows to see if anyone was inside. There was no vehicle or horse at the front of the house, and as he moved around the side, he spotted the corral—also empty.

Dillon sat atop her black mare, gazing at the empty space, the ground inside churned up by the horses. "They were here. We're too late."

"We tracked them this far. We can keep tracking them."

Cal spun his horse around and returned to the front of the house. Years of dirt and debris on the porch had been disturbed from someone walking to and from the door. Cal dismounted and made his way to the entrance. He turned the knob and pushed open the door. It banged against the wall, kicking up dust. A quick look inside showed that it was empty. The only other room was a bathroom, and Cal could see straight inside.

He spun on his heel and grabbed his horse's reins as he walked to the corral. The ground in the area was damp from the cover of the trees. Algae grew plentifully and showed him exactly which way they'd taken the stallion.

Dillon rode up beside him. "Let's go."

"We're not armed. If we catch up with them, they could be," Cal cautioned.

"I can't wait for the sheriff. Cell service out here is spotty at best, and I'm not taking the time to return to the house. Besides, who said I wasn't armed?"

Cal couldn't contain his smile. "You are one impressive lady."

"I know," she replied with a grin.

He chuckled and mounted before they followed the tracks. Whoever had led the horse no longer seemed to try and hide the hoof marks. When Cal spotted the deepening of the tracks and the spacing that showed the horses in a gallop, he knew they had to move quickly.

Before he could say anything, Dillon clicked to her mare. The horse leapt into a run, and Cal leaned low over his gelding, urging him to match her speed. Quarter horses were known for their quick bursts, beating nearly all other horses in a quarter-mile sprint—hence their name.

He and Dillon kept pace with each other, the ground fly-ing beneath them as the horses ate up the distance—until they came to the fence.

Cal dropped his heels and pulled up on the reins. His geld-ing jerked up his head and slid on his back haunches as he came to a sudden stop. Cal looked at Dillon, seeing her face filled with fury as they both saw the horse tracks leading from her land right to Ivy Ridge Ranch.

Chapter 7

Dillon had known Hank Stephens had taken her stallion, but that didn't make her feel any better about the situation. Violent, forceful fury surged through her like hot lead. She couldn't remember ever being so livid in her entire life.

Her gaze slid to Cal. Shock and dread lined his face. Was it a ruse? Frankly, Dillon didn't know. She liked him. He had a relaxed personality, and he was certainly easy on the eyes. Too easy, in fact. If it had been any other situation, she wouldn't have hesitated to . . . She halted her thoughts. Now wasn't the time to think about what might have been. Not when she had a stolen stallion to get back.

She tugged on the reins, turning her mare in a tight circle. Before she could click the horse into a run, Cal shouted her name.

"Don't do it."

"Do what?" she demanded, knowing full well what he meant.

Cal walked his horse to her. "Let me talk to Hank."

"Oh, I don't think so."

"I'm not working with him," Cal stated firmly.

She raised her brows. "I just met you this morning. Drunk.

Remember? The same morning my stallion went missing. And you want me to take your word?"

"Shit," he murmured as he removed his hat and hooked it on the saddle horn before raking his hands through his dark blond locks. "All I have is my word. And that means nothing to you."

"That's right."

"I promised I'd track the stallion."

"You could be in on it with them."

He blew out a breath. "I'm not. Let me prove myself. Let's go see Hank together."

She was about to nix that idea. Yet the more she thought about it, the more she realized that she might be able to see some kind of signal or gesture that could verify her suspicions. Of course, there was always the chance that she wouldn't see anything. Regardless, she would rather have Cal with her so she could keep an eye on him.

"Fine," she replied.

Cal nodded once and put his hat back on his head. There was a determined look in his gray eyes. Dillon squeezed her knees twice, and her mare set off in a gallop. Normally, she enjoyed riding along the rolling hills, enthralled by the ranch that was now hers. She'd always felt connected to the land, which was why she had visited Dolly so often. She loved her aunt, but they had bonded over the land, allowing them to become even closer throughout the years.

It had been Dolly and the Bar 4 that Dillon had retreated to after her five-month marriage crumbled. Between bouts of tears, Dillon would take one of the horses and ride the fence line, stopping to repair it wherever needed. The time alone did wonders for her—mentally and emotionally. To this day, Dillon knew that Dolly and the ranch had helped her dust herself off and continue with her life.

Now that the Bar 4 was hers, Dillon was determined to make it work. Dolly had struggled in life, coming up against men who thought they could do things better. Dillon believed that things had changed, but perhaps not. Maybe ranching was still very much a *men's club*.

But they were about to learn that she was prepared to fight back.

Her shirt flapped against her as the mare quickened her pace. The horse wanted to run, and Dillon loosened her grip on the reins to allow the animal its head. Dillon didn't look behind her to see if Cal was there. She didn't care at this point.

By the time the homestead came into view, she slowed the mare into a gallop, then a trot, and finally a walk before stopping at the rear of the barn. Dillon dismounted at the same time Emmett walked around the building.

"I know that face," he said.

Cal had his gelding by the reins when he said, "We tracked the stallion to Hank's."

"Sonofabitch," Emmett swore, shock clouding his aged face.

Dillon usually got a kick out of Emmett making one word out of the phrase, but she wasn't in the mood. She hooked the left stirrup on the horn and released the cinch straps at the mare's belly. Dillon hoisted the saddle, with the blanket beneath, and stalked to the tack room to return it to its rack.

As she walked out, Cal met her at the door with his saddle. Their gazes met, but she quickly looked away. She wanted to believe him. His willingness to help was a blessing. Maybe. But the fact that he knew Hank made her suspicious—even when she wanted to believe him. Worse, being near him confused her because her body felt one thing while her head felt another. And it was playing havoc with her emotions.

Dillon grabbed the halter and lead rope as she returned to the mare, furious that she was attracted to Cal. That muddied the waters when she needed them clear. Once the bridle was off and the halter in place, Dillon clipped the lead rope beneath the mare's throat and tied her to the hitching post. She then brushed her down.

When Cal walked out, she told herself not to look his way, but damn if her gaze didn't go right to his cute ass. She'd gotten many looks earlier. But, apparently, she needed one more. Why did he have to be so handsome? And why now, of all times, had someone come into her life that she was attracted to?

Emmett leaned against the side of the stables, remaining in the shade. "You heading to the Ivy Ridge?"

"Yep," she answered as Cal glanced at her over his horse's back.

Emmett grunted. "Is that a wise decision?"

"It is." Her ire rankled even more when she saw Emmett and Cal exchange a look. "What?" she demanded of them.

Cal threw up his hands and went back to brushing his horse.

It was Emmett who pushed away from the building and walked to her. "All Hank will do is deny it."

"He can't refute the tracks."

"He'll say you put them there and cut his fence."

Dillon turned from the mare and glared at him. "What do you want me to do? Stand back and let him take my horse?"

"Of course, not," Emmett hastened to say.

"Call the sheriff."

Dillon and Emmett swung their heads to Cal. She had been too angry to think of that. Once more, Cal had come to the rescue. If she weren't so irritated, she might grin. "It is a crime."

Cal rested his arms on the horse's back and grinned. "Yes, ma'am, it is. They'll send someone over and see the proof."

Dillon handed Emmett the brush and pulled her cell phone from her pocket. She had noted Cal's cool head when she first met him, and she was thankful for it now. She would tell him later. Once she knew that she wouldn't do something stupid like flirt.

It didn't take long to connect with the sheriff's department and report the crime. Within fifteen minutes, a deputy named Bobby Jo Smith arrived. As much as Dillon wanted to confront Hank, she wanted the crime documented.

She, along with Cal and Emmett, drove the deputy in the UTV from the paddock where Legacy had been let out to where he had been taken onto Hank's property. Cal pointed out the tracks he'd found, making sure the deputy noted the deeper imprints of a horse with a rider. The deputy took lots of notes as well as pictures.

Dillon felt better having everything documented. She found herself staring at Cal, hoping he was on her side. Because in the short time he had been on the ranch, he had proven how capable he was. She was now glad that she had been the one to find him that morning. Without him, not only would she not have found what'd happened to Legacy, but she likely would've been shot and would possibly be dead. Maybe she needed to go easier on him.

His gaze slid to her, causing goose bumps to rise on her skin. She hastily looked away. Cal worked for her. She needed to remember that. Getting involved with the help would be a foolish move—regardless of how sexy he was.

On the drive back to the ranch, she asked Deputy Smith, "What happens now?"

"This will be a case for the TSCRA."

Dillon frowned, not having heard the acronym. "The what?"

"The Texas and Southwestern Cattle Raisers Association," Cal told her. "They're special rangers commissioned through the Texas Department of Public Safety, and the Oklahoma State Bureau of Investigation to investigate agricultural crimes in both states."

The deputy nodded in agreement. "I'll forward everything

I've documented today to the TSCRA. They'll get in contact with you. Probably by phone first, but I'm sure they'll want to head out here and see things for themselves."

"I know where my stallion is," she insisted.

The deputy shifted in his seat. "You don't have proof. For all we know, the horse was taken through the Ivy Ridge Ranch and onto someone else's land."

It was bullshit. All of it. But Dillon didn't say any more. When they reached the stables, she shook the deputy's hand in thanks. He handed her a card for the TSCRA before getting into his patrol vehicle and driving away.

Dillon turned on her heel and strode toward the house, where she grabbed her keys. When she came out onto the porch, Emmett and Cal stood there, waiting for her. "What?" she asked.

Cal shook his head. "Just waiting on you to head out."

"I don't like this," Emmett told her.

Dillon jerked her chin to Cal. "I'm not going alone."

She walked past Emmett and climbed into her truck. Before she had closed her door, Cal was in the passenger side and his seatbelt buckled. Why did a little thrill go through her at being alone with Cal again? She started the engine and waved to Emmett as she drove away.

Neither she nor Cal said anything on the ride to Ivy Ridge. Dillon wasn't sure what she would do if Cal were working with Hank. What *could* she do, really? If there was even the tiniest suspicion, she would fire him—and report him to the sheriff as well as the TSCRA.

It annoyed her that she needed Cal to work. If her two ranch hands hadn't quit, she wouldn't have had to hire him. And if she hadn't, there was a real possibility that she never would've found the tracks leading to Hank's. The entire situation gave her a headache. The future of the ranch lay with the stallion. If she couldn't get him back, then it would only be a matter of time before she had no choice but to sell.

She had worked herself into quite a fit by the time she pulled up in front of Hank's sprawling house. It was beautiful, though a bit on the pretentious side for her tastes. She turned off the engine and unbuckled her seat belt.

Her gaze met Cal's. "Remember, I'm doing the talking."

"Of course," he replied.

They exited in unison. Dillon didn't make it to the porch before one of the twenty-foot wooden double doors opened, and none other than Hank Stephens stepped out. For a man in his mid-fifties, he was still handsome. He had a head full of black hair just beginning to gray at the temples. His clean-shaven face showed an impressive jawline, and he had a smile that always captivated people. Hank's blue eyes were dark like the ocean, and those attributes, along with a toned body, caused women and men alike to fall all over themselves to get his attention.

His money didn't hurt, either.

"Dillon," Hank said with a smile. "What brings you to my door?" His gaze moved to Cal before she could answer.

She saw the surprise and the genuine happiness that spread over Hank's face at the sight of Cal.

"Damn, son. You're a sight for sore eyes," Hank said as he embraced Cal.

Dillon watched them closely. She could see Cal's face, but not Hank's, so she couldn't be sure that Hank hadn't passed a message on to Cal.

"How've you been?" Cal asked when he stepped back, a smile curving his lips.

Hank shook his head and put his hands on his waist. "The same. I didn't know you were in town. When did you get in?"

"The other night."

"Why didn't you come see me?"

Cal glanced at her. "I was otherwise occupied."

Hank's black brows shot up as his blue eyes landed on her before returning to Cal. "I see."

Cal shrugged. "These things happen."

"Don't I know it," Hank said with a chuckle. "Come inside, you two."

Dillon narrowed her eyes on Cal after Hank had turned his back to them.

"*Trust me*," Cal mouthed.

If he said those words one more time, Dillon might just scream.

Chapter 8

It had been a long time since Cal had been at Ivy Ridge. The grand house always made him feel like he needed to take off his shoes and remain standing lest he dirty or scuff something.

While Hank had looked sincerely surprised by his appearance, Cal wasn't fooled. Hank had known that he was in the area. It was in the subtleties someone who didn't know Hank wouldn't catch. Like how the shock didn't quite reach his eyes, and his voice hadn't risen. Little things Cal would have probably missed himself if he hadn't been looking.

But how much did Hank know about Cal's association with Dillon? They had been extremely close at one time, but as Cal had gotten older, the phone calls and visits had decreased significantly.

"You should've told me you were in town," Hank said as they walked through the house to a living area, where he motioned to the leather furniture for them to sit. "I would've come to see you at the rodeo."

Dillon didn't hesitate to take a seat.

Cal remained standing. He still had dirt on him from that

morning and even more after his ride through the pastures while tracking. Since rodeos were usually where Cal and Hank caught up, his comment didn't seem out of the ordinary. Cal shrugged. "I didn't final, which gave me the time I wanted."

"I see," Hank said with a smile as he glanced at Dillon. "When did the two of you meet?"

"About six months ago," Cal replied with a shrug. "I never expected to meet someone like her through internet dating."

There was real surprise in Hank's eyes—and something that looked a little like fear. "I never took you for someone who would turn to the internet for dates."

"You know for yourself that rodeoing brings certain kinds of people. I was looking for something different. Once I met Dillon, we hit it off and have been seeing each other as often as my time allows."

Cal felt Dillon's eyes on him. He didn't look her way. Instead, he held Hank's gaze.

Finally, Hank nodded, his lips twisting. "What does this mean for your rodeo career?"

"We've not had that conversation," Dillon said.

Cal hid his smile when Hank jerked his attention to her as if he had forgotten she was there.

"Of course. Of course," Hank said with a nod.

Cal crossed his arms over his chest. "I wish our visit was a social one, but Dillon is here on business."

"Oh?" Hank asked as he sat up, propping his forearms on his knees. "What might that be?"

Dillon lifted her chin and looked straight at Hank. "The theft of my stallion."

"Theft? I hope you called the sheriff as well as the TSCRA. In case you didn't know, they handle situations like these."

Cal noted that Hank said all the right things and appeared affronted by Dillon's news. Nothing showed that he might be behind it. It had been a longshot, but one Cal had counted on.

"I know about the TSCRA," Dillon told him. "A sheriff's deputy has already been out to the Bar 4 to take notes and pictures of evidence of my horse being taken right through to your property."

Hank snorted and shook his head as he sat back. "I knew you would accuse me. Just because my land surrounds yours doesn't mean I'm to blame for everything that happens to you."

"Then who is?" Dillon demanded. "The fence was cut. The tracks lead right to your property."

Hank threw up his hands in defeat. "I don't know what to tell you."

"Let us search the area where I found the tracks leading from the Bar 4," Cal suggested.

Cal saw a flash of anger in Hank's blue eyes when he looked his way. "I don't take kindly to being called a thief."

"Letting us search would clear your name. If you aren't involved, that is," Dillon said.

Hank got to his feet and smiled, though there wasn't a shred of benevolence in it. "I think it's time you two left. And, Cal, I'm disappointed. I thought your father taught you better than this."

"My father—and mother—taught me to be a good man. I'm doing exactly that."

Dillon stood and waited until Hank looked her way. "I hope you aren't involved in the theft of my horse, but if you are, I will find out. And I'll make sure charges are brought against you and anyone who helped."

"Why would I steal your horse?" Hank demanded. "I have enough money to buy as many as I want."

Dillon shrugged, her lips twisting. "Why do you want my ranch so badly that you made four attempts to buy it, offering twice as much as it's worth?"

"I like land," Hank replied.

Dillon's blue eyes went hard. "There's plenty of other land. Besides, don't you have enough?"

"No."

Cal walked to Dillon and put his hand on her lower back, giving her a little nudge. Thankfully, she started walking. He guided her out of the house to the porch. That's when Cal paused and looked behind him. Hank stood at the door. For the first time since Cal had met him, Hank no longer exuded an open, friendly demeanor. Cal's visit might have ruined a friendship, but if Hank had stolen a horse, he didn't want Hank as a friend.

Dillon didn't talk until they were in her truck, and she was driving away. She looked in the rearview mirror. "He's still watching us."

"I'd probably do the same."

"Why did you tell him we were dating?"

Cal had known she would ask, and he didn't have a good answer. "I don't know. It just came to me."

"He didn't believe it."

"Does it matter?" Cal looked her way to see her shake her head.

Dillon turned and started toward her ranch. "What did you think?"

"I think anyone being accused of theft would be upset."

"That's not what I asked."

Their gazes met briefly as she glanced his way. He sighed as he faced forward. "It's difficult to say. I've known Hank for almost twenty years. Something was off."

"Like?" she urged.

"He knew I was in town."

Dillon propped her elbow on the door and leaned her head into her hand, steering with her other. "Hmm. You sure?"

"Oh, yeah."

"So, he didn't buy your story of us dating?"

Cal shrugged. "He might have. I can't be sure."

"What are you sure about?"

He ran a hand over his jaw. "That I saw a man I thought I knew, acting in ways I've never seen."

"How often do you see Hank in a year?"

"Depends. I saw him a lot when I was younger. Even when I first started on the circuit—he came to a lot of rodeos. We each had a life, which meant we didn't see each other as much as before. Why?"

She briefly looked his way. "Because people change. He isn't the man you once knew. And you aren't the man he once knew."

"Why do you think he wants your land?"

Dillon let out a bark of laughter as she turned into the Bar 4 drive. "He told you why."

"I think it's more than that. Like you said, there is plenty of other land."

"Not near his ranch. He's bought everyone out that he can. He's butting up against some housing developments now."

Cal shook his head. "Land is land. Sure, it's better if the ranch is all connected, but many large ranches are broken up into pieces. It's nothing new."

"Why do you think he wants it?" she asked as she parked the truck and turned off the ignition.

He looked into her eyes and lifted his shoulders in a shrug. "I don't know."

But he was determined to find out. Cal didn't know why he felt such a need to help Dillon. She was a capable woman who was more than able to take care of herself. Yet, there was no denying he *wanted* to help her.

Dillon got out of the truck, and Cal followed. She walked slowly around to the front of the vehicle before looking at him. The way she stared told him that she had been studying his interaction with Hank.

"Well?" he asked.

Her brows snapped together. "Well, what?"

"Have you made your decision about me?"

She bit the left side of her lower lip as she looked toward the barn where Emmett and another ranch hand were talking. "I've not."

"Fair enough."

Powder blue eyes met his. "It's after lunch. You had a tough night, and a pretty rough morning. Why don't you take an hour and grab some lunch? Then see Emmett. He'll tell you what to do."

"You're letting me stay?" He hadn't expected her to give him the job.

She shrugged. "I need the help, and we made a deal. You fulfilled your end of the bargain. I'll uphold mine."

Cal nodded and watched as she walked into the house. Once she was out of sight, he walked to Emmett. As soon as the old man spotted him, he sent the young cowboy off and faced Cal, glancing toward the house.

"She inside?" Emmett asked.

Cal nodded.

"How did things go?"

Cal moved into the barn so Dillon wouldn't see them. "As good as you could expect. Hank was affronted that we suspected him of stealing. I asked if he would let us check his property, but he refused."

"Bastard," Emmett murmured as he shook his head. "Dolly never had an easy go of things running this ranch by herself, but she persevered. Dillon has that same strength."

"But?" Cal asked when Emmett paused.

The man sighed, shaking his head. "Dolly didn't have anyone stealing her livestock or shooting at her."

"We're going to have to make sure Dillon is safe."

Emmett's smile was wide as he asked, "You stickin' around?"

"I am. And I should let you know that I told Hank I met

Dillon through an online dating service six months ago, and that we've been seeing each other off and on since."

Emmett chuckled. "That should get the tongues wagging in town as well as give you a reason for always being with her. I wasn't jokin' this mornin'. I want you by her side constantly. Why aren't you with her now?"

Cal couldn't hold back his smile. "I'll be with her as often as I can, but there will be times when I can't. She needs some time alone, and she sent me to get food, which is perfect because I wanted to talk to you."

"About?"

"What else has happened around the ranch that she didn't tell me about?"

Emmett looked away and turned to pet one of the horses that stuck its head over the stall door. "Little things."

"Yeah, she already told me that. I need specifics so I know what to look out for."

Emmett sighed loudly. "The brake line was cut on the tractor she favors. She managed to turn it toward a tree to stop the tractor before it wrecked any fence or harmed anyone. Her tires were also slashed in town one night."

"All four?" Cal asked, shocked.

Emmett nodded. "There was a letter in the mail threatening her. It didn't go through the post office. Someone drove to the ranch and placed it in the mailbox."

"Damn. Financially, how is the ranch?"

"She doesn't talk to me about that."

"Dillon said she sank a lot of money into the stallion and that the loss could be detrimental."

Emmett shrugged and hooked his thumbs into his belt loops. "The stallion is from prime stock up near Dallas. He cost a lot more than Dolly ever paid for any horse, but Dillon has a keen eye. She learned from Dolly, and Dillon knows where she wants to take the ranch."

"But she needs that stallion to do it."

"But she needs the stallion to do it," Emmett agreed.

Cal looked at the house. All these years, he'd thought the hardest job in the world was bull riding. He was coming to realize that he might have had it easy. Because the mystery surrounding Dillon and her ranch would take everything he had—and probably mean calling in every favor he could.

Which wasn't many.

Chapter 9

The second the door closed behind her, Dillon leaned back against it and turned the lock. She had never locked the door during the day, but after everything she had experienced that morning, she had reached the end of her rope.

Her hands shook, and her breath came in ragged gasps like she had been running. How she had held it all together until that point, she'd never know. She had refused to break down in front of anyone, especially Hank Stephens. But it had been close.

So very close.

Dillon didn't have the strength to walk. She slid down the door until her butt hit the floor. Once it did, it was like something snapped inside her. She covered her face with her hands as she let out a silent scream. She sobbed, allowing the emotions that she had kept bottled up to pour out of her.

She didn't know how long she cried. When she was finally able to lift her head, her face was soaked, and her eyes burned. Dillon curled up on her side and closed her eyes in an effort to stop the pain. To her surprise, Cal's face popped into her mind's eye. She didn't want to think about him. Not his sexiness, how he had come to be on the ranch, or if he was someone she could trust.

The cool tile felt good on her heated cheeks. She sniffed, sleep pulling her. She needed water to replenish her body of all it had lost by sweating and crying, but she couldn't make herself move just yet. Her mind drifted to Cal again and again, and each time, she forced the thoughts away. Because every time she thought of him, she wanted to trust him.

And she couldn't take that chance.

Dillon's thoughts then turned to Hank Stephens. Dolly had often spoken of him when she was alive. Though her aunt never told her specifics, Dolly hadn't liked Hank.

"People need to look past his charm and money to see the snake he really is."

The sound of her aunt's voice in her head made Dillon smile. How she wished Dolly was still alive. Not just to talk about what was happening now but because her aunt had been a trusted confidante. Dillon wished she had gotten specifics about Hank before Dolly's death so maybe she would know how to handle her neighbor.

It was no good to wish for what couldn't be. This was Dillon's mess, and she would sort it out. Somehow. She just wasn't quite sure how yet.

She wanted to crawl into bed and sleep with every fiber of her being, but there wasn't time for that. She had to find her stallion. Dillon took a deep breath and pushed herself into a sitting position. No matter how much Hank or anyone else wanted her land, she wouldn't be put into a position where they forced her to sell.

Dillon climbed to her feet and went to the sink. She splashed water on her face and washed her hands. Her gaze lifted to the wide window and landed on none other than Cal. He was at one of the paddocks with a mare and her newborn foal. The mare took a carrot from his hand. The little filly tentatively walked to the fence, inching closer to him.

Cal slowly squatted down and held out his hand for the foal to smell.

When she finally brushed her nose against his fingers, she then turned around and ran off a few steps before spinning back to face him. Cal let out a laugh. Dillon was surprised to find that she was smiling, too. She told herself it was because of the filly's antics, but she suspected that Cal's booming laugh might have contributed.

She turned off the water and dried her hands. As she hung up the damp towel, she spotted her hat on the floor. She hadn't realized it had fallen off. Dillon bent over to retrieve it, but instead of putting it on and heading outside, she hung it on the peg and walked into the office to work on the budget.

Years in the corporate world had taught her how to budget for any business. She was always conservative in her estimates because it was better to have more come in than expected rather than vice versa.

She sank into the office chair and looked around. Dillon had changed very little in the office when she took over. Partly as an homage to Dolly, and partly because she would rather spend money on the ranch instead of furnishings that she hadn't brought with her. However, the more time that passed since her aunt's untimely passing, the more Dillon realized that she needed to leave her mark on more than just the ranch. She needed to make the house—and the office— hers. It was what Dolly would have wanted—and expected.

Dillon shifted in the uncomfortable chair. It was the first thing she would replace, but that was for later. She turned to the computer and logged in. Dolly had always kept it password-protected, and Dillon had followed suit. Though her aunt had never said she didn't trust her employees, it was simply a matter of being proactive.

For the next hour, Dillon looked over spreadsheets, calculating totals and moving around expenses to another month if they weren't a necessity for the ranch. When she finished, she sat back and looked at the total. The loss of the stallion would cut deeply into the final revenue. Dillon would have to dip into her savings even more to keep the ranch afloat, but she would do it in a heartbeat.

She sat back and rested her elbow on the arm of the chair as she propped her hand against her face. Her gaze moved to a stack of mail on the right side. That's when she saw an envelope from the insurance company. Dillon had forgotten that she had called an equine insurance company and had gotten a policy on the stallion as soon as the sale had been finalized—and before Dillon had put the animal in the trailer to bring to the ranch.

Dillon reached for the envelope and tore it open to pull out the papers. In her hands was the stallion's policy. She scanned the pages until she found the section on mortality/theft. There, in black and white, it stated that if the horse were stolen, she would be reimbursed for the insured value of the animal.

She breathed a sigh of relief. She recalled the agent telling her about that part of the policy, but she had never thought someone would steal her horse. Yet she hesitated to call the insurance company. It might be suspicious for her to file a claim after just purchasing the stallion a few days before.

"Dammit," she said and tossed the papers down.

The money would help cover the cost of the horse, but the simple fact was they needed another stallion for the ranch. One way or another, she would have to replace this one if they couldn't find him.

Dillon then recalled the business card the deputy had given her. She pulled it out of her back pocket and called the Texas and Southwestern Cattle Raisers Association. After talking with a man who picked up the phone and answering a lot of questions, they transferred her to a ranger named Chet Thompson.

She answered more questions as well as going over everything that'd happened from the time she'd picked up the stallion until now. Then the ranger asked her another set of questions. She rested her head against her hand with her elbow on the desk and her eyes closed since they felt like sandpaper.

Just when she thought they might be wrapping things up, Chet put her on hold. Dillon had no choice but to wait. Fortunately, he didn't leave her for long.

"Ms. Young?"

"I'm here," she answered.

"My apologies for leaving you on hold. I was reviewing the pictures the sheriff's department sent over. Good call on getting them out there ASAP."

Her eyes opened and she sat up straighter. "I just want my horse back."

"I understand, and I'm going to do everything I can to facilitate that. I'll be at your ranch at eight in the morning. Be prepared to take me through the same route you took the deputy. I want to see things for myself."

For the first time, she had hope. Dillon knew there was no guarantee that she would get the stallion back, but it was a step. "I can do that."

"Oh, and Ms. Young? One more thing."

"What's that?"

"Don't go to Mr. Stephens and accuse him of the theft."

Dillon squeezed her eyes closed and wrinkled her nose.

"I see," Chet replied in a flat tone. Her silence must have given her away.

She was immediately defensive as her eyes opened. "That stallion is a three-time world champion. He's coveted across the country, and I paid top dollar for him. Not just to breed my mares, but to put him out for stud, as well."

"I'm aware how that works."

"I can't do any of that without him," she said, close to tears again.

He sighed, the sound coming through the phone. "The fact that there's an agency dealing with stolen livestock and ranching equipment should tell you how often this happens."

"That doesn't bolster my hope."

"You're in the right hands, Ms. Young. We'll talk more in the morning."

She hung up the phone and slumped in the chair. Dillon shifted it slightly to look out the window. The Bar 4 had another stallion. Cupid, as Dolly had named him, was an even-tempered sorrel who had proudly sired dozens of beautiful foals. He had been a champion cutting horse, and ranchers from all over had paid handsomely to use him as a stud.

Dillon had no intention of getting rid of Cupid, despite his age. He was a good horse, but she wanted to bring in new blood—and a new revenue stream. She had looked long and hard before she finally found Legacy. Cupid was a ranch stallion, which meant they didn't keep him in a stall and pampered. He worked—sometimes harder than anyone else.

When Cupid wasn't out working cattle, he was in the pasture with a small herd of mares ready to go into heat. Cupid was one of the most well-behaved stallions Dillon had been around, and she was determined to bring another just like that onto the ranch. She had found that in Legacy, who wasn't just a beautiful champion horse but had also made a name for himself by siring phenomenal offspring that matched his unusual champagne-colored coat. It was a win-win for her, which was why Dillon hadn't hesitated to drop that kind of money on him.

She rubbed her eyes and flipped to another spreadsheet that listed the mares and their calculated due dates, appointments for checkups, and estimated costs for feed and the vet. There was also a column with names of individuals looking for specific young horses to bring into their breeding programs. Once the foals were born, Dillon would alert the potential seller, who would make multiple visits to check on the mare and her foal to see how it was. Six months was the average time that it took for a foal to be weaned from its mother. During that period, Dillon and her employees worked with the foal in stages to get it used to being touched as well as being around humans. It was a long process, but one Dillon loved.

Two foals were coming up on their sixth-month mark in three weeks. They had made great progress, but she wasn't surprised. Both mares were excellent mothers. Dillon had only marked one sale in the spreadsheet, on the off chance that both weren't bought next month. Even though she knew that both would sell, she couldn't make herself change the spreadsheet to reflect that.

She pushed away from the desk and stood. Her eyes were crossing from looking at the same numbers again and again. There was nothing more she could do, and staring at the spreadsheets was only making things worse.

Dillon strode to the kitchen, where she got her hat and un-locked the door. She left the house, heading to the paddock with the newest member of the ranch. Being with the foals always put her in a good mood. Their antics, their excitement and curiosity, as well as watching them learn how to use their long legs was always fun. Observing the foals learn the *horse* language was truly awe-inspiring.

But so was gaining their trust and how much love they had to give.

Chapter 10

The afternoon went quickly. It had been a long time since Cal had been so worn out. It was a different kind of feeling, but one he didn't mind. His entire body ached—partly from imbibing the night before, and partly because of the work he'd done. But it was a good pain. The kind that caused a man to feel as if he had made a difference in the world.

"When's the last time you put in such a hard day's work?"

He turned at the sound of Dillon's voice. Cal had kept his eye on her throughout the afternoon, but she had managed to sneak up on him when he was putting away the feed buckets. He grinned at her. "Too long. It feels good, though."

Her brows shot up on her forehead. "Oh?"

"Don't look so surprised. My momma used to get me up at dawn to help her muck out the stalls before I got ready for school in the mornings."

Dillon chuckled. "This was a little more than mucking stalls."

"It was. I've moved muscles I haven't used in years. No doubt I'll be sore tomorrow, but this is a sight better than being thrown off a bull and wondering what bones I'll break when I land."

"I can't promise you won't break bones working here."

"But I won't have a bull chasing me." He frowned then. "Or will I?"

Dillon laughed, an open-mouthed one that hit him straight in the chest. "We have two bulls. Caesar and Brutus. Dolly raised both from calves. They're the tamest bulls you'll ever meet. The only time you see them move quickly is when they're randy."

This time, it was Cal's turn to laugh. "I can't wait to meet them."

"A ranger from the TSCRA will be here in the morning."

"That's good, right?"

She nodded and leaned against the stable wall.

He frowned at her defeated look. "Things are just getting rolling. You need to give the authorities time to track down the stallion."

"I know where he is."

"We can't prove it."

She shrugged one shoulder before putting her fingers in the front pockets of her jeans. "Maybe we don't have to. Hank stole Legacy from me. I can get him back."

"I wouldn't advise that."

"Why not?"

"You know why. Hank has security cameras everywhere. He would be able to see every inch of his ranch with a push of a button. He'd see you coming before you got two feet on the property."

Dillon's response was a slow smile.

Cal was more confused than ever. "What?"

"Hank has cameras."

"So?" Cal asked with a shrug.

"Then he can show the ranger the area where the fence was cut. Where Legacy was stolen."

Cal shook his head, amazed at her thinking. "He sure can."

But his smile didn't last. "The problem is whether Hank will allow the ranger to look at the footage."

"If Hank has Legacy on Ivy Ridge, then the ranger will need a court order to see the footage. If he doesn't get it before he visits Hank's, the footage will likely be erased."

"If it hasn't been already."

Dillon dropped her head back and shifted so her back was to the wall. "Perhaps going to accuse Hank wasn't the best decision."

"I would've done the same thing. The proof is there. It didn't help that he refused us access to check his property for ourselves."

"He has a lot of land. Legacy could be anywhere on Ivy Ridge. We'd never be able to check it all."

"Maybe we don't have to."

Dillon's head lifted as she met his gaze.

An odd sensation filled his stomach when hope flared in her blue depths. He quite liked the feeling.

"What?" she asked.

"Hank won't let us search, and he'd hear a helicopter from miles away. But he'd never hear—or see—a drone."

"Why are you helping me? Hank is your friend going back decades."

Cal looked away briefly. "It began as a way to pay you back for me trespassing. When I heard those gunshots and knew the bullets were meant for you, it changed everything."

"You don't know me. Nor do you owe me anything."

"Someone is trying to hurt you. Any person who would turn their back on someone in need isn't someone I want to associate with."

Her powder blue eyes searched his. "You feel this way, even though I still don't trust you?"

"I do. I'll earn your trust."

She pushed away from the wall and dropped her arms to her sides. "Did Emmett show you where the bunkhouse was?"

"He didn't." In fact, Emmett had ordered Cal to stay in the house with Dillon, but Cal knew that wouldn't happen.

"I can take you."

"You can point me in the general direction."

Emmett came around the barn, shaking his head. "Dillon, you need someone in the house with you."

"I'm fine," she stated.

It looked like Emmett might be pressing his lips together, but it was hard to tell with how thick and long his handlebar mustache was. "Want to come to dinner?"

It took a second for Cal to realize that Emmett was asking him. "Thanks, but I'll pass tonight."

"Suit yourself," Emmett said as he walked away.

Dillon grinned as she watched the older man. "He's been a fixture on this ranch for as long as I can remember. He is rather set in his ways, though."

"That's generally what happens to everyone."

"I always thought he had a thing for Dolly."

Cal couldn't imagine a young Emmett. "Did they?"

"I have no idea," Dillon said as she looked at him. "I asked Dolly once. She rolled her eyes but never answered."

"Did you ever ask Emmett?"

She twisted her lips. "I haven't. Figured it was none of my business. He's never spoken of a wife or children. Maybe my young brain imagined something that wasn't there."

"Or it could've been. Would explain why Emmett has been so loyal."

"Maybe. Come. I'll point you in the direction of the bunkhouse."

He could smell the stink on himself and desperately wanted a shower. "I'd appreciate that."

Cal followed her out of the barn and saw her pointing toward a distant dirt road.

"That last road. There's nothing down there but the bunk-house and Emmett's place, though his is farther down. The bunkhouse will be on the right."

"Thanks," he said as he turned to go to his truck.

"Um . . ."

He halted and looked at her over his shoulder. "Everything all right?"

"I know Dusty already went to town, and Emmett just left. I'm not great at it, but I'm cooking tonight. It's difficult to make meals for one."

Cal waited for her to finish. When she didn't, he asked, "Are you inviting me for dinner?"

"If you want to come. But you probably want to get to town."

"I don't," he hurried to say. Cal couldn't explain why the thought of sharing a private meal with her excited him as it did.

A lot.

"Okay," Dillon said.

He glanced at his truck. "Mind if I get out of these clothes and perhaps shower?"

"Definitely shower," she said, not bothering to hide her smile.

Cal laughed. "Clean clothes would be good, too."

"I would recommend that."

They shared a smile. When he found himself staring at her as the silence lengthened, Cal cleared his throat and motioned to his truck with his thumb. "I'd better get going, then."

"Indeed." Her smile widened as she started toward the house.

Cal couldn't remember the last time he was so excited—giddy even—about anything. He'd spent years putting his body through hell, chasing a dream that wasn't even his. He'd ignored anything that even came close to normal because he'd thought the circuit was what he wanted. Over the last few years, he'd begun to question what he wanted. The problem he encountered was that he didn't have an answer. It was easier to keep doing what he'd always done rather than step outside the box and see what else was out there.

Not qualifying for the rodeo gave him no choice but to face the future. His response had been to get drunk. Not exactly his finest performance. He still had no idea how he'd gotten onto the Bar 4 property, but he was glad that he'd found his way to Dillon's ranch. The day had shown him what it was his soul had been hungering for. What he had denied himself for years.

He got into his truck and started driving to the bunkhouse. The work was honest and hard, and he was looking forward to tomorrow. Being with the animals and putting effort into the ranch made him feel as if he had a purpose. As if he were doing something worthwhile. The thought of getting back on a bull and putting his life on the line again was no longer appealing.

Maybe he'd followed in his father's footsteps out of some attempt to connect with a man he'd barely known. He'd thought he had the same love for the sport that his dad did, but Cal was beginning to suspect that he'd idealized bull riding because it was what his father had done. But it was also something he'd had to do.

Just as he was working his future out now.

He spotted the bunkhouse and pulled up in front of two hitching posts that stood before the building. Cal parked the truck and grabbed his leather bag before getting out. When he walked inside, he was surprised to find a main living area with a sofa and a loveseat, as well as a large television to his right. To his left sat a small kitchen with a table. He spotted two bathrooms as he walked through the house. Then he found the bunks.

Cal looked at the six beds, three on each side, and noted that the farthest one on the left had been claimed. He dropped his bag on the first bed on the right and pulled out his toiletry bag and some fresh clothes. He planned to enjoy a nice, long shower to work out the kinks in his sore muscles.

Chapter 11

"What the hell did I just do?" Dillon asked herself as she walked to the house.

She glanced over her shoulder to see Cal driving toward the bunkhouse. After going out of her way to say that she didn't trust him, she had invited him to dinner. That wasn't exactly a smart move. No matter how many times she tried to understand what she had done, Dillon couldn't come up with an answer.

Emmett was like family, and yet they rarely ate together. She had never invited any of the other employees to a private dinner. Sure, there were special celebrations where they all ate together throughout the year, but nothing like this.

"I think the stress is getting to me. It's the only explanation."

Right. And you don't think it could be the fact that you like Cal's smile?

Dillon ignored her inner voice. It was pointless to argue with herself. Instead, she made her way upstairs to her room. She got out of her clothes and into the shower to scrub off the sweat, dirt, and horse smell from the day. With that done, she toweled off and stood in front of the large bathroom mirror.

She looked at her reflection, lifting the wet strands of her hair to let them fall haphazardly. At one time, she had religiously gotten her hair cut and colored every six weeks. The highlights had been the first thing she'd stopped. Then, it became harder and harder to find the time to get to her stylist. The last time had been three months ago, and she had requested a cut that could sustain her for several months. However, now that she looked at herself, she realized she had waited too long. There wasn't anything she could do about it now, though.

Dillon rubbed some product between her hands and spread it evenly through her tresses. She wasn't sure why she'd gotten out the blow-dryer. It had been ages since she had done more than let her hair dry as she slept. But tonight, she was making an effort.

"It's for me. This has nothing to do with Cal."

Her subconscious issued a loud snort.

She quickly shut off her mind regarding anything to do with Cal. It lasted all of two minutes before she thought about him again. It was incredibly frustrating. She didn't want to think about him. To wonder about his past.

And hope that she could trust him.

Everything inside her urged her to believe him. Dillon wanted to have faith in her intuition, but she wasn't sure she could trust it right now. She worried that her brain might be getting confused by a handsome face and ignoring the truth.

Dillon turned off the blow-dryer and put it away before going into her closet. It was a hot, sticky night, and she didn't want to put on another pair of jeans. She chose a simple, white, sleeveless maxi dress and brown sandals. When she turned to look at herself in the mirror, she stopped, shocked by her reflection.

She couldn't remember the last time she had worn anything

but jeans, yoga pants, or sweatpants. Her life was the ranch. She didn't regret it, but she had let little things fall by the wayside. Like getting her hair cut.

"Oh, no," she said as she leaned forward to look closely at her eyebrows.

Without hesitation, she rushed to her vanity and dug through the drawer until she found a pair of tweezers to start plucking her brows into some semblance of shape. How could she have forgotten about her eyebrows? Well, that answer was easy. Because she hadn't cared. The horses and cattle certainly never looked at her brows. Dolly had kept herself up. Dillon had thought she would, as well, but the facts were staring her in the face—and she didn't like what she saw.

By the time she'd finished, the skin around her eyebrows was red. She rushed downstairs, got an ice cube from the freezer, and rolled it over the skin to take the swelling and redness down. When she returned to her vanity, the effects of the ice had begun to kick in. But it wasn't enough.

Dillon sighed as she looked into her eyes. It had been so long since she'd put on makeup, she wasn't sure if she remembered how. The last thing she wanted was for Cal to think that she had done this for him. But what else would he believe?

She settled on some mascara and lipstick as a compromise. When she finished, she was quite pleased with the outcome. The mascara made her eyes look bigger, but it also kept the casual look she wanted. Still, she gave in and added a hint of bronzer to her cheeks, nose, and forehead.

Dillon put everything away and ran her hand through her hair before getting to her feet. As she turned to leave, her gaze landed on her jewelry box. She walked to it and opened the lid. Dolly had left her everything, including her jewelry. Much of it hadn't been to Dillon's tastes, but she had fallen in love with the turquoise set. The necklace was three strands of stones and silver beads. The earrings were sterling silver chain drop with a turquoise bead. But the real beauty of the set was the turquoise bracelets that ranged from beaded styles to five thin cuffs accented with the beautiful stone set in different ways.

She clasped the necklace into place and put on the earrings. Then she divided the bracelets to cover both wrists. The blue-green stone popped against her white dress. The more Dillon stared at herself, the more she remembered what it was like to get dressed up—even if it *was* only for herself.

"I've got to do this more often."

The problem was that she was usually bone-tired by the time she returned to the house for the night. Many times, she ate beef jerky and chips and drank a Coke for dinner. It wasn't the healthiest of meals, but it was better than skipping a meal altogether. But when you were too tired to think, the last thing a person should do is get out knives or use hot pans for cooking. For her safety, she opted out.

And yet, she had said that she would cook tonight—after a horrendous day full of so many ups and downs that it made her stomach clench just thinking about it. She shook her head, putting aside the turbulent thoughts and what troubles lay ahead. For the moment, she had done all she could, short of sneaking onto Hank's land herself. She would've done it, too, had Cal not warned her about the cameras.

She had known about them. Everyone in town did because Hank had told everyone and made a big show of detailing the expensive system he'd had installed and the crew that had come to set it all up. It was a good thing that Cal had stopped her. Otherwise, she could've ended up in jail, and that definitely wouldn't look good for her in her case with Hank.

A knock at the door startled her out of her musings. She turned off the lights and went downstairs, seeing Cal through the glass window of the back door. This time, he wore a blue plaid button-down. As she neared, she noticed that he had shaved his two-day growth of beard. She wasn't sure if she liked him better clean-shaven or with that five o'clock shadow.

She opened the door with a smile. "Come in."

"Wow," he said as his gray eyes looked her up and down. "You look amazing."

Inside, Dillon beamed, but she kept her smile neutral. "Thanks. Make yourself comfortable. Would you like a beer?"

"Ah . . . I think I'm going to pass."

They shared a chuckle. "Probably a smart move."

"Don't let that stop you," he said.

"I'm not fond of beer, though I always keep some for guests."

"What do you drink?"

She shrugged. "Wine, gin and soda, or Chambord and soda. My go-to is Chambord."

"I thought for sure you were going to say bourbon."

Dillon laughed as she walked to the fridge. "The only time I can stomach it is when it's fixed in a hot toddy, and I'm sick."

"What can I help you do?" he asked when she took some steaks out of the fridge.

"Can you grill?"

He shot her a crooked smile. "Yes, ma'am."

"Perfect. You're in charge of the meat. The grill is outside if you want to get it ready."

Cal nodded and walked outside. The sun was sinking into the horizon, casting long shadows, but it would still be another hour or more before it was dark. Dillon loved summer. She didn't even mind the heat too much. The animals even found the shade some days, but she had gotten accustomed to being outside for the majority of the day for the most part.

She went to the sink to rinse off the broccolini. Without meaning to, her gaze went to Cal. He had rolled up his sleeves and bent over to look at the grill, giving her a great view of his ass. Dillon smiled because there was just something about a cowboy in jeans. She hastily turned away when she thought Cal might look her way.

Dillon then got out the new potatoes and sliced them accordion-style, careful not to cut all the way through. After setting them on a baking sheet, she brushed a mixture of olive oil, garlic, and butter over them and popped them into the oven.

While the potatoes cooked, she got the broccolini ready by cutting off the hard ends and brushing them with olive oil before adding salt and pepper. She placed them on another baking sheet and set them aside. Next, she put the steaks on a plate and seasoned them on each side. It wasn't long before Cal returned for the meat.

"Grill needs a little longer to heat up," he said.

She leaned back against the counter behind her as she wiped her hands on a towel. "How did you find the bunkhouse?"

"It's nice. More than I expected."

"Good."

Cal glanced away and rocked back on his heels. "I, ah, I appreciate the meal."

"You've not tasted it yet. You might be heading into town to fill your belly."

"I doubt that."

"You don't even know what I'm cooking."

He shrugged. "My momma raised me to eat whatever was put in front of me. I can't remember the last time I had a home-cooked meal."

"You saved my life today. I figured I owed you."

"You gave me a job."

Dillon lowered her gaze to the floor for a moment. "I needed the help."

"You won't regret it."

There was such sincerity in his gaze that Dillon found

herself believing him. She cautioned herself, but the damage had already been done. She was staring, and yet she couldn't stop. What was it about him that made her forget reason? She wasn't sure if she liked it or not.

Cal jerked his chin to the steaks. "Why don't I see if the grill is ready?"

"Sure."

He reached for the plate. "I'm betting you like your steaks medium-rare."

"Impressive."

"It's a gift," he said with a bright smile before walking out.

The timer went off for the potatoes. Dillon turned her attention to them, giving them another brush of garlic, olive oil, and butter before returning them to the oven. She then turned on the second oven to heat it for the broccolini. It wasn't long before the veggies were in the oven and roasting.

Dillon got out some plates and utensils. Though the dining table was free of clutter, she realized that it hadn't been used in a long time. After wiping it down, she then set it. As she walked to the kitchen, the timers went off just as Cal returned with the steaks.

"That's timing," he said with a grin.

She smiled and pointed to the dining room. "You can put the steaks on the table."

Her attention returned to the oven as she took out the broccolini first, dumping it into a dish. Then she removed the potatoes and carefully placed them on a flat platter before carrying both to the table.

"Wow."

"Don't be impressed. It's simple potatoes, steak, and veggies."

He shrugged and met her gaze. "Too bad. I'm impressed."

"Ah . . . what would you like to drink? I've got tea, Coke, and water."

"Sweet tea?"

"Of course," she replied with a grin.

"That sounds perfect."

She got the pitcher and two glasses and brought them to the table, pouring the tea. It wasn't until she sat down and found herself looking across the table at Cal, their eyes meeting, that she noticed he had removed his Stetson. The last meal she'd had with a man had been her ex-husband.

And now, she was sitting across from a man who made her feel things she didn't ever think she would feel again.

Chapter 12

Cal couldn't stop staring at Dillon. If he'd thought her attractive holding that shotgun with her tank top, open plaid shirt, cowboy hat, and jeans, she was drop-dead gorgeous in her white dress.

He'd wondered all day what her hair looked like down, and now he got to see it. The shiny brunette locks were cut in layers that gave the thick tresses beautiful, large waves. Her hair was parted to the side, and she kept shoving away the shortest layer that fell into her eyes.

And those eyes. *God*. They were so vivid, they competed with her turquoise jewelry.

He swallowed and watched as she reached for a plate of food to fill for herself before handing one to him. Her dress was sleeveless, allowing him to see her trim arms—not that he needed more proof that she worked hard.

Cal took the broccolini from her and dished some onto his plate, then they exchanged bowls. His stomach growled at the delicious smells. Once they each had their steak, he watched as she cut into her meat and took a bite.

Her eyes widened. "This is cooked perfectly."

"Thank you," he said with a nod.

For the next few moments, they ate quietly. The potatoes were some of the best he'd ever eaten, and he also liked the veggies. He didn't know why she had invited him to dinner, but he was glad she had. He'd needed a home-cooked meal. He'd discovered a lot about himself today. He probably would've learned it a lot sooner had he taken the time before, but he hadn't until forced.

"What?" he asked when he caught her staring.

She swallowed her bite and wiped her mouth with her napkin. "You're smiling."

"I was thinking about today. It seems odd that I've known you for less than twenty-four hours, but at the same time, I feel as if I've been here for months."

Dillon's brows rose. "Is that bad?"

"Not at all. I thought my life was over when I didn't qualify at the rodeo. I've lost so much over the years. A couple of failed relationships, my home, and even what little belongings I had to my name—all in the name of getting on that next bull." He set down his utensils and sat back as he took a long drink. "I thought I had hit rock bottom last night. That's what drove me to the bar. I figured I'd drown my sorrows and work out something the next day. Then I woke up here."

"With a gun aimed at you," she said with a grin.

He chuckled and glanced at his plate. "Today showed me all the things I've been missing. It also showed me that I didn't know what I wanted or needed. I've been following a dream, but it wasn't mine."

"Meaning?" she urged.

"I think I'm pretty lucky to have gotten out of the circuit now without too many injuries—as well as my life. Getting on the horse this morning freed something within me. Something I hadn't known was there. The work here is hard, and I'm sure it'll only get harder, but this is what I want to do."

Dillon's powder blue eyes held his. "For how long?"

"I can't answer that because I don't know. I have no intention of leaving anytime soon."

"Well, don't get used to these meals because this was a one-time offer," she said, though there was a smile on her lips.

He laughed and nodded once. "Yes, ma'am."

"Have you called your mom?" Dillon asked after a brief pause.

"I will tonight. She'll be thrilled."

"Which is why you shouldn't wait to tell her."

Cal took another few bites before setting his fork down again to say something that had been bothering him. "I hadn't planned that lie I told Hank about us. Otherwise, I would've talked it over with you."

"It doesn't matter," she said with a dismissive wave of her hand. "I'm sure he isn't thinking twice about it."

Cal wasn't so sure, but he didn't point that out.

"Besides," she continued, "you know Hank better than I do. You told him that for a reason."

"I wanted to see his reaction."

"What did you see?"

Cal sighed. "I think he's lying."

"Most people would stand with their friends versus a stranger. Do you understand now why I'm hesitant to believe you?"

"I do. I know not everything is black and white. The world is full of grays. But sometimes a person innately knows when things are either right or wrong—like what is happening to you."

Dillon finished the last of her steak. "I could have stolen my own horse for the insurance money."

"You could have, but you don't strike me as that kind of person."

"How can you say that? You don't know me."

He lifted one shoulder in a shrug. "When you're around as many people as I am, you learn to see things quickly. Like deceit. And honesty. Besides, someone who stole their own stallion wouldn't be as riled to confront Hank about it as you were. Then there was the attempt on your life. You aren't going to tell me you could've done that, too, are you?"

Her eyes dropped to the table as she shook her head. "No. No, I'm not."

"Do you have any idea who it might be?"

She shook her head again, causing the brunette waves to move with her.

"You really should have some type of surveillance on the ranch."

"I didn't think I needed it with Hank's land around mine and his cameras. I guess I was wrong."

Cal wanted to reach across the table and cover her hand with his, but he held back. "I can try to talk to Hank again."

"That will only make matters worse. Chet, the TSCRA ranger, told me not to accuse Hank."

"Oops."

Dillon laughed as she shoved the hair out of her face again. "That was pretty much how I responded."

"We'll get the stallion back."

"I don't see how. He's very recognizable."

Cal frowned since this was the first time he'd heard this. "What do you mean?"

"He's champagne in color."

"Shit," he murmured.

The champagne color was only present in some horse breeds in North America and was a highly sought-after attribute. The gene dilution acted on black and red hair pigments, making the coat appear champagne. It was a stunning color.

Dillon raised her brows and nodded.

"Shit," he said again, louder this time. "If Hank has him, he'll have to keep the stallion hidden. He'd never be able to sell him."

"Hank could keep Legacy forever, and I'd never know."

"Someone would say something because he'd want everyone to know he had such a stallion. Hank can't help himself. He loves to show off."

Dillon rolled her eyes and pushed her plate away. "I feel like I'll never see the horse again."

Cal had to agree with her. Because the only way Hank could get out of this situation without charges being brought against him was if he got rid of the stallion. He couldn't sell him, and he wouldn't be able to hide him, so that left one option—killing the horse.

Whether Dillon wanted him to or not, Cal was going to talk to Hank again.

"I didn't mean to put a damper on dinner," Dillon said.

Cal shook his head. "You didn't. Not at all. It's an important matter that needs to be discussed."

"That's difficult when I can't do anything right now to recover Legacy."

"You've done all the right things."

She made a sound in the back of her throat as she got to her feet and took their plates. "Let's hope the authorities can do their jobs now."

Cal helped her clean the table and put away the leftovers. He rinsed the plates and handed them to her to load into the dishwasher.

When they finished, Dillon wiped her hands on the towel and nodded through the kitchen window. "Looks to be a beautiful sunset. Want to join me?"

"I would."

He grabbed his hat and followed her out of the house to the back porch and two rocking chairs. The setup reminded him of his grandmother and how she would sit out on her porch every night after dinner.

"Being on the ranch has brought back a lot of memories," he told her.

She turned her head to him. "Good ones?"

"Yeah. I've missed a lot of things over the years."

"You can make it up to everyone now."

He wrinkled his nose. "There are some things you can't make up."

"Did you cheat?"

The way she asked the question made Cal instinctively aware that someone had cheated on her. "No," he said with a shake of his head. "But I was never around. I chose the rodeo over relationships. Any relationships. Not just romantic ones."

"Yeah, that one might be hard to make up for. Or maybe not, if there can be a second chance at something."

Cal chuckled and shook his head. "Definitely not. It's not easy balancing the rodeo with romantic relationships."

"Relationships aren't easy, in general."

"Some are."

She shot him a skeptical look.

"Seriously," he stated. "I think they can be. If both people are in the right places in their lives when they meet."

"The odds of that are slim."

"I take it you were hurt?"

Her shoulders lifted as she drew in a deep breath and then slowly released it as she looked into the distance. "It was a whirlwind relationship. Everything happened really fast. We met through mutual friends, went out the next night on our first date, and within a month, he had moved in with me. Three months later, we were married. Five months after that, I got a package in the mail full of pictures of him with a blonde. She was his ex-girlfriend. As far as I knew, they had broken up. Apparently, she came back into the picture shortly after we got married. He kept telling her that he would divorce me. She got tired of waiting, so she made sure I knew what was going on."

"You divorced him?"

Dillon's head turned to him. "She got what she wanted.

He didn't have the balls to end things with me. Instead, he strung both of us along."

"Are they still together?"

"I don't know, nor do I care. After I signed the divorce papers, I came here to spend time with Dolly. She died less than a year later. Those few weeks with her got me back on my feet."

Cal noted there was no pain on her face when she talked about her ex, but it had apparently been a horrible experience. "I'm sorry you went through that."

"I'm not happy it happened, but I'm glad I didn't waste years with him. In the end, I came out so much better," she replied with a smile. "Look at this place. All the stress I had while living in Dallas and working melted away once I quit and took up the reins here. There's still stress, but it's a different kind. I don't feel like I'm being run into the ground, either."

He nodded, understanding. "It's rewarding work."

"Very," she agreed with a grin.

The rays of the setting sun lit up her face, bathing it in red and orange and giving her hair a burnished appearance. Cal smiled, truly happy for the first time in a very long while.

Chapter 13

Fury—and a healthy dose of panic—assaulted Hank Stephens as he looked at Isaac over the rim of his tumbler. His legs shook, threatening to fold and drop him to the floor. He lowered the glass, his heart thudding loudly. "What?"

"My contact at TSCRA confirmed that Dillon filed a report," Isaac replied from his position on the plush leather couch.

Hank's chest hurt. He set the glass on his desk and leaned a hip against the corner in a bid to stay upright. Why wasn't Isaac freaking out? He had as much to lose as Hank did. There must be something Isaac knew that he hadn't yet shared. At least, that's what Hank hoped.

"How worried do I need to be?" Hank asked.

Isaac snorted, his brows raised as he crossed one leg over the other. "I'd say very. The ranger is Chet Thompson. From what my contact said, he's a by-the-book cowboy. If you try to bribe him, it'll only make things worse."

"Me?" Hank said, anger surpassing the apprehension. "I'm not in this alone. Or do I need to remind you?"

Isaac eyed him dryly. "Don't be so dramatic."

"A ranger from the TSCRA isn't coming to your place of

business to investigate a theft. I can be as fucking dramatic as I want."

Isaac lifted one of his hands, palm out. "Whatever you say."

He hated when Isaac patronized him. It made Hank want to punch him in the nose. For all his bluster and strutting around town, Isaac had never been in a real fight. He didn't know what it felt like to have his kidneys punched or his nose broken. Maybe it was time that happened. As much as Hank wanted to give in to the impulse, he also knew Isaac would press charges because that's just the kind of man he was.

Come hell or high water, they were in this debacle together. Somehow, they would have to find a way out of it. Because Hank wasn't going down on his own. If he were charged, he would turn on everyone in the group and alert the authorities to everyone's role in things.

Isaac uncrossed his legs and leaned forward, setting his empty glass on the table before him. "I'm not leaving you hanging out to dry."

"You're damn right, you aren't. I told you it wasn't smart to take the stallion."

"How the fuck was I supposed to know it was such a rare-colored horse?" Isaac snapped, finally losing his temper.

Hank bit back his smile. Isaac prided himself on keeping his cool. To see him rattled for anything was an event that always pleased Hank. They grated on each other's nerves, which had been acceptable when they had little association except for business. Despite their differences, they had somehow become friendly through the years. Hank wouldn't necessarily call Isaac a *friend*. He really didn't know what Isaac was, but he knew enough to watch his back. Isaac looked after one person first and foremost—himself.

"Sell the damn horse," Isaac ordered as he sat back with a huff.

Hank dropped his arm, thankful that his chest had stopped hurting. He straightened and shook his head. "I can't. Nor can I keep him here. Every hour the horse is here, there's a chance for one of us to see him and tell someone."

Isaac's dark eyes were cold and merciless as his attention turned to Hank. "Then you only have one other option. Kill it."

Hank had seen the stallion with his own eyes. He was one of the most magnificent animals he'd ever seen. He would bring in tens of thousands of dollars in profit. The thought of ending the horse's life didn't sit well with him.

Then again, neither did being charged with a felony or going to prison.

What most people didn't realize was that, in the eyes of the law, a horse thief was the same as someone who stole cars.

Isaac must have sensed Hank's indecision. "You've got to be fucking kidding," Isaac said as he stood, his lip curled in a sneer, and disgust darkening his face. "If you allow that horse to live, you're on your own."

"You can't walk away from this. We're both in too deep."

Isaac laughed, a confident smile curving his lips. "Do you want to test that theory? Let's see who ends up in jail, and who ends up getting the Bar 4 Ranch." His smile vanished. "Kill the goddamn horse and save your ass."

Hank watched Isaac stride out of his office and then the house. It wasn't long before he heard the roar of Isaac's Mercedes Benz S-class starting and then driving away. He remained standing, going over the conversation in his head.

While he might not be the smartest man in the county, he was far from stupid. He had built a ranching empire with his blood, sweat, and tears. He'd known what he wanted from an early age, and he hadn't let anyone or anything stop him. Not bull riding, not women, not ethics. He'd had a chance at love once, but he had given it up for his dream. *Nothing* had stopped him from achieving what he wanted.

Dillon Young, the TSCRA, and Isaac weren't going to start.

Stealing the stallion hadn't been Hank's idea, but now that he'd seen the horse for himself, he wanted it. Since he couldn't offer Dillon money for it without alerting her that the stallion was on his property, he'd just have to be creative about where he housed the animal. The fact that Ivy Ridge was so large would give him plenty of time to move the horse around when the ranger asked to search. Of course, he'd allow the ranger to search. Denying it would only cause more issues and raise suspicions. The ranger would get a search warrant and force the situation anyway.

Hank sighed as he thought about the TSCRA. If things had stayed at the local level, he could've swayed things in his direction. Campaign contributions went a long way to create ties with the sheriff. He and Bill went back a long way, too. He'd helped Bill out on many occasions. Bill had a hard time keeping his dick in his pants when it came to pretty, young girls. Fortunately for the sheriff, those instances occurred on Hank's ranch and away from the general public's eyes—and Bill's wife.

It also meant that Bill owed Hank.

Why hadn't the sheriff stopped his deputy from contacting the TSCRA? If Bill had, then Hank wouldn't feel as if everything he'd worked so hard for was shifting uneasily beneath his feet.

A knock at the door interrupted his thoughts. Hank didn't answer it, preferring to allow his housekeeper, Nancy, to do the chore. Hank listened, nonetheless. As if his thoughts had conjured him, Bill's voice reached Hank. Hank walked around to his desk and sat just as Nancy poked her head through the open doorway.

"The sheriff is here to see you," she said.

Hank nodded. Nancy stepped aside to allow Bill into the office. Their gazes met. Hank noted that Bill looked apprehensive. A part of Hank wanted to let Bill stew in his juices, but time was of the essence. Besides, there still might be something the sheriff could do.

"I'm sure you've heard," Bill said.

Hank motioned to a chair before his desk. "Right down to business, is it?"

"I thought you'd prefer it that way."

"I do. Tell me what happened."

Bill sighed as he sank into one of the chairs. "It was Bobby Jo Smith. He gave Ms. Young a business card to the TSCRA after documenting the crime. Deputy Smith also filed the report in our office and then sent the pictures to the TSCRA. Dillon Young called the TSCRA before I had a chance to talk to her."

"It wouldn't have done any good. Thanks to your deputy being so . . . accommodating, the TSCRA was already notified."

A frown marred Bill's aging face. "He was doing his job, Hank."

"I thought we had an understanding."

The anxiety was back, causing Bill's gaze to drop to the floor. "We do. I know you've helped me keep my office."

"And your marriage."

Bill nodded and dropped his chin to his chest as he folded his hands in his lap. What Bill hated more than his wife was that her family's money paid for his campaigns. Without it, he never would've been able to run for sheriff. Bill might be a decent police officer, but he was worthless with money.

"What do you want me to do?" Bill asked as he met Hank's gaze.

Hank slowly let out a breath. "I've never been involved in one of these investigations. Do you have any insight?"

"These special rangers are about as thorough as the Texas Rangers. They run solo or with another of their team. They don't like—nor want—outside involvement. None of that should matter if you're innocent."

Hank smiled. "Exactly. But we both know how authorities can zero in on culprits. I assume you read the report."

"I did."

"And?"

Bill shrugged half-heartedly. "The ranger will see the cut fence and the tracks going onto your property."

"Do you think I did it?"

Bill opened his mouth and blinked, but no words came out.

Hank nodded and smacked his lips. "I see. Did it ever occur to you that Dillon Young and her employees could've staged all of that? She's still angry that I wanted to buy the Bar 4."

"You still want it," Bill stated.

Hank drew in a sharp breath at the direction the conversation was going. "What do you mean?"

"What?" Bill asked with a forced chuckle. "Everyone who knows you knows that once you set your sights on something, you don't back down until you have it."

Son of a bitch. Hank clenched his teeth in an effort not to lose the last shred of his calm and bellow to the heavens. "So, I do."

"But I know you. You'd never steal livestock," Bill added quickly.

Hank forced a smile. Maybe he'd made a dreadful mistake in taking Isaac on as his partner. Not only was Isaac making decisions without talking to him, but he'd also brought in others to do different jobs.

Every time Hank thought about Cal, he wanted to punch something. Cal was the closest thing to a son he would ever have. Isaac had known that and had used it against them. After Cal had shown up earlier with Dillon, Hank wasn't sure which side of things Cal would fall on because it looked as if he were completely taken with Dillon.

Hank needed to talk to Cal. He needed to know if Cal was playing a part or if he was going against him. Because if Cal sided with Dillon, Isaac wouldn't hesitate to kill him.

Chapter 14

Dillon was up before dawn. She'd barely slept, her thoughts drifting between Legacy's theft, the arrival of the TSCRA ranger, and Cal. She had tossed and turned for hours before finally giving up and deciding that if she was awake, she might as well get some work done.

She spent a couple of hours in her office. When she got tired of that and still wasn't sleepy, she did a chore she hated more than anything—cleaning toilets. Then she found herself back in the office, taking down pictures and other items of Dolly's to make room for her things. It seemed wrong in a way, but she knew her aunt would have wanted her to make the place hers. That was the only reason Dillon was able to remove the items.

When the first rays of dawn streaked across the sky, she'd already had breakfast and was leading the horses out of their stalls. Once the horses were out, she grabbed the wheelbarrow and a rake and started mucking the stalls.

"Didn't sleep?"

The deep timbre of Cal's voice caused chills to race across her skin. She glanced over her shoulder to find him standing outside the stall. "Not really."

"I'm sure other things need your attention. Want me to take over?"

She shook her head as she returned to her work. "I'm good. Thanks."

When several seconds passed without a reply, she glanced behind her to find that he was gone. A part of her was relieved. She didn't want to talk to anyone. And yet . . . another part, the one that had invited him to dinner, dressed up, and asked him to sit on the porch, wished he had stayed. Dillon wasn't sure what to make of that other side of herself.

Sure, she got lonely. Who didn't? But there was so much to do on the ranch that most nights she didn't think about it. Still, other nights . . .

Dillon paused, her breathing harsh as she rested her arm atop the rake. It wasn't that she had closed herself off to the possibility of a relationship. Rather, it had to do with logistics. She spent most of her time on the ranch. The few times she got out usually had something to do with Bar 4. The handful of other times? Well, she'd never had men beating down her door, asking her out.

She'd never gone through that long of a dry spell, either. Some of it had been self-imposed. She'd needed time to get over her divorce and the consequences of what had happened there. After that, she dove fully into the ranch. It had given her a purpose, a reason to wake up each day. It had been enough for Dolly, so she thought it would be enough for her.

Now, she wondered if she had been wrong.

All because of Cal's arrival. Dillon didn't want to find him attractive. She didn't want to like him. She certainly didn't want to feel that tingling in her stomach when he laughed or have her skin prickle at the sound of his sexy voice. But she couldn't stop herself from reacting to any of it.

She blew out a tired breath and moved on to the next stall, though her thoughts didn't stop whirling. Part of her wanted to take her problems and hand them off to someone else, but she couldn't. She wouldn't. No matter how tempting it was. She had known that things would be difficult at times on the ranch. This was one of them. And if she wanted people to take her seriously, she had to prove her worth—not just to everyone else but to herself, as well.

Dillon finished with the stalls and took the wheelbarrow to a site she had dedicated for the waste. The minute she'd read that there was a market to sell horse manure, she'd instituted proper disposal procedures on the ranch. It was another revenue stream that had, surprisingly, done very well. Which was great because there was a lot of manure.

On her way back, she spotted Cal, Emmett, and Dusty going about their daily jobs. She returned the wheelbarrow to its spot and checked her phone for the time. She still had another hour before the ranger was due to arrive. Dillon pocketed her cell and began spreading new bedding in the stalls. The next time she looked up, Cal was on the other side of the stables, filling those stalls.

She finished the last stall and closed the door. When she turned around, Cal flashed her a smile. "Thanks."

"I—" he began, but the sound of a vehicle door closing interrupted them.

Dillon hurried out of the barn to see a tall, middle-aged man standing beside a Ford F-250 truck. She caught the flash of a badge hanging around his neck. He wore a white Stetson, a simple white button-down over his extended stomach, Wranglers, and boots.

"Now it begins," Cal said as he came up beside her.

She turned her head to him.

Cal grinned. "Ready?"

"Absolutely."

She started toward the ranger, her blood moving like ice through her veins. She was, in turn, nervous, anxious, and frightened about what the outcome would be. Her gaze took in the older gentleman.

He was in his sixties, his long face wrinkled with time and sun exposure. He was tall, giving an air of authority, but at the same time, his brown eyes were direct and kind. She sensed that he wasn't quite so pleasant when facing perpetrators.

"Mr. Thompson?" she asked.

"Chet, please," he said as he held out his hand, his jowls wiggling slightly as he spoke. "I take it you're Dillon Young?"

She shook his hand and smiled. "I am."

"Nice place here," he said as he looked around in admiration.

Dillon couldn't hold back her happiness. "I love it."

His brown eyes met hers. "Shall we get down to business?"

"Absolutely." Dillon looked around for Emmett. She saw him near one of the paddocks and called him over. Then, she looked at Cal near the barn and motioned for him. "This is Emmett Perkins, my ranch manager. And Cal Bennett, the one who tracked the horses."

Chet shook their hands, nodding in greeting. Then he pulled out a tape recorder. "Okay. Start from the beginning. Tell me everything that happened before the theft, all the way through this morning."

Dillon took a deep breath and began the story. She didn't leave anything out, including how she'd discovered Cal. The ranger gave Cal a brief look, but Chet kept his emotions behind a wall, making it impossible for her to decipher what he was thinking.

"Hold on," the ranger stopped her when she mentioned the bit about Cal saving her. "Are you telling me that someone shot at you?"

"Twice," Cal said before she could answer. "The second would've struck her."

Chet's lips flattened. "Things have taken a turn I didn't expect. You left that out yesterday."

"Not on purpose," Dillon quickly replied. "A lot happened

yesterday. Trust me. I was rattled by the attempt. I still am."
When he said nothing more, Dillon returned to her story.

Chet nodded when she finally finished. "All right, then.
Now, go through all of it again, but this time walk me
through your steps, starting from when you discovered the
stallion gone."

A bead of sweat ran down Dillon's back, making her
tank top beneath her shirt stick to her back. She retraced
her steps, something she had done numerous times in her
mind, trying to discover if she had missed something. They
walked through the barn, looked at the empty paddock, and
then climbed into the UTV and drove to the area where she
had looked for the stallion but had found Cal instead.

Chet took notes and lots of photos with his phone as well
as continued to record. He didn't speak. Not even when she
stopped at the creek, and she and Cal demonstrated what had
happened.

"Sonofabitch," Emmet murmured when Cal pointed out
how close the bullet had come to striking her.

Chet walked the area, bending to inspect the rock that
the bullet had ricocheted off. He studied the space for a long
time before looking over his shoulder. The three of them
waited as the ranger rummaged around in the brush.

"Did any of you look for the shooter?" he asked as he
faced them.

Dillon shook her head. "I just wanted to get back."

"I was more concerned with someone firing another bullet," Cal said. "I thought the best thing would be for Dillon
to get away and to safety."

Emmett stood with his arms crossed over his chest. "I
searched this area once Dillon returned to the homestead and
told me what happened. I found some grass that had been
pressed down behind those trees you're at. Figured that's
where the shooter waited."

"It's the perfect cover," Chet said. "Find any shell casings?"

Emmet shook his head. "No, sir."

Chet faced Dillon. "Why would someone want to kill you, Ms. Young?"

"Because Hank Stephens wants her land," Emmett replied. "He's offered to buy it four times, but she won't sell."

"I see. And you think he's responsible for the theft of the stallion as well as the attempted murder?" Chet asked.

Cal lifted one shoulder. "Someone wanted Dillon to come this way."

"You," the ranger replied.

Dillon let out a sigh. "He saved me. If Cal had been part of it, wouldn't he have allowed me to be shot?"

"Good point," Chet said with a grin.

They climbed back into the UTV and returned to the ranch, where Cal went over with Chet, step by step, what he had seen and shown to Dillon about someone letting the stallion loose. Chet compared the deputy's photos from yesterday with what he saw himself, then nodded for Dillon to continue the story. Instead of taking horses as she and Cal had done the day before, they used the UTV.

It was excruciating not knowing what Chet was thinking, but Dillon managed to keep her thoughts to herself. Chet didn't make a sound until they were at the cut fence separating her property from Ivy Ridge. Dillon exchanged looks with Emmet and Cal at the throaty expression, but neither seemed to want to speculate what it meant.

It felt like hours before Chet finally finished his inspection, moving from her property to Hank's. She kept looking for someone from Ivy Ridge to make an appearance, and sure enough, Hank and two of his men rode up in an ATV. Chet straightened and faced the vehicle as Hank climbed out.

"I'm Hank Stephens, the owner of Ivy Ridge. Are you the ranger from the TSCRA?"

Chet shook Hank's hand. "I am. Chet Thompson."

"Nice to meet you, Mr. Thompson. I'm sure we can get this misunderstanding cleared up," Hank said.

Dillon tried not to smile when she noticed that Chet didn't tell Hank to call him by his first name.

Chet smiled at Hank, though it didn't reach his eyes. "Oh, we definitely will. I was going to come see you later. But now that you're here, I'd like to ask you a few questions."

"Of course." Hank's gaze moved to her. "I'd prefer privacy, if you don't mind."

"I do mind," Chet replied.

Dillon looked at the ground and bit her lip to keep from laughing. Hank was used to getting what he wanted. The shock, followed by irritation on Hank's face when Chet refused him, made Dillon want to do a fist pump. But she restrained herself. Again.

"Tell me, Mr. Stephens, do you know of anyone who would shoot at Ms. Young?"

Hank shook his head. "I don't. As I told Dillon yesterday."

Chet crossed his arms over his chest. "It appears the tracks lead right to your property."

"I didn't take the stallion. I don't need to steal things when I have the funds to buy whatever I want. And I don't appreciate being a suspect when it's obvious Dillon did this herself."

Fury shot through Dillon. She took a step toward Hank, ready to blast him, but Cal stepped in front of her.

"Wait," he whispered.

Dillon glared at him before turning her attention on Hank once more. She had detested him. Now, she downright *loathed* him. How dare he blame her for the theft?

"I'd like to take a look around your property," Chet said to Hank. "Since you didn't have anything to do with stealing the stallion, I'm sure you won't hesitate to let me have a look."

Hank's smile was wide. "Of course not."

Chapter 15

The entire event left a bad taste in Cal's mouth. Something was off with Hank. Or was he seeing things that weren't there? Like Dillon had said, people changed. It had been well over a year since Cal had seen or spoken to Hank. Maybe he remembered Hank differently than he truly was.

"I want to be there," Dillon said.

Cal put his hand on her to stop her, and the look she gave him halted him in his tracks. He lifted both his hands in apology and stepped back.

"It'll be better if you stay on your land," Chet calmly told Dillon.

Behind the ranger, Hank smiled as if he had just gotten his way.

"I know my horse," Dillon argued.

Chet motioned for Hank and his men to remain on their side of the fence. The ranger then walked to Dillon, Cal, and Emmett. Chet glanced at all of them before stopping at Dillon. "I understand there's bad blood between the two of you. I don't know who started it, and I don't care. I'm here to find your horse. In order for me to do that, I need to carry out my investigation. That means I need to concentrate on Mr. Stephens, everyone who has access to his ranch, and the ranch itself. I can't do that if I'm pulling the two of you apart every other minute."

"Fair enough," Dillon conceded. "My apologies. I know better."

Chet shook his head, his lips pressing together briefly. "I understand your distress. You're attempting to locate a valuable animal. You have every right to what you're feeling."

"Don't trust him," Dillon warned.

A crooked smile appeared on the older man's lips when he said, "Ma'am, I don't trust anyone."

"We'll return to the house," Emmett said as he climbed into the UTV.

But Cal hesitated. He looked at Chet. "I know Hank. Or, I used to know him. Maybe I should go with you."

"Why?" Chet asked.

Cal glanced at Dillon and then shrugged. "I just explained why. I could help determine if he's lying or not."

"Or you could be working with him." Chet swung his head to Dillon and hooked a thumb at Cal. "Do you trust him?"

Dillon's powder blue gaze slid to him. Cal studied her as she stared at him. He knew she didn't trust him. All he wanted to do was help, but every time he tried, something stopped him. Not that he could blame anyone. But how could he prove his trustworthiness if he couldn't help?

"He saved my life," Dillon finally answered.

Chet made an indistinct sound. "So, he did."

"I'm not sure you should be doing this investigation alone."

"Who said I'm alone?" Chet replied pithily.

Dillon grinned in return. "How will you get back to your truck?"

"Don't worry about me."

She nodded and walked to the UTV. Cal started to follow her when Chet called his name.

The ranger moved close and lowered his voice. "If your truck was at Ike's, how did you get to the Bar 4?"

"I don't know."

"If I were in your shoes, I'd want that answer."

Cal nodded. "I intend to find it and others."

"A lot of unanswered questions involve you. You seem to want to help Ms. Young. Get the facts, son. One way or another, I'll find them."

Cal took the threat to heart and nodded at the ranger before pivoting and climbing into the back passenger seat of the UTV.

"What was that about?" Emmett asked.

Cal briefly met Dillon's gaze as she glanced over her shoulder and started the engine. "He wanted to assure me that he would look everywhere for Legacy."

"I like him," Emmett said. "First time I've ever met one of the special rangers. Hope it's my last."

Dillon said nothing as she drove away. Cal watched Hank and Chet over his shoulder until the vehicle descended a hill and put them out of view. The ride back to the house was silent, which allowed Cal time to think over what the ranger had said. Cal had been so wrapped up in finding Legacy and protecting Dillon that he had set aside something important that he needed to do—find the truth.

There was no way he could've walked from Ike's to the ranch. It was at least five miles from town. Not to mention, he'd been drunk. Unfortunately, he had no memories of most of that night. Blacking out only made things more difficult for him because he couldn't prove anything to Dillon.

Cal had never had his honor or word questioned before. He didn't like that he couldn't provide proof to Dillon to ease her mind. His gaze lingered on the back of her head. She'd tied her brunette locks at the nape of her neck, but he remembered how they had flowed freely the night before.

Dinner had been delightful. The company amazing. The

food delicious. He'd hated when they parted ways because he'd wanted to remain with her. Dillon was witty, and her smile was sublime. She shouldered a lot running the ranch, and she did it effortlessly—even under the current pressure.

When they pulled up to the ranch, all three got out and walked in different directions, returning to their work. Cal kept close to the stables and paddocks where Dillon worked with the foals. All the while, Cal's gaze moved about the property, wondering how someone could have gotten onto the ranch to shoot Dillon. It must not be difficult since *he* had walked onto the ranch without anyone stopping *him*.

Was someone out there now? Were they looking through a scope, lining up the crosshairs with Dillon? The thought chilled Cal.

Why did Hank want the Bar 4 so badly? Why had he suddenly stopped making offers to Dillon? Why would there be so many accidents around the ranch that either potentially hurt Dillon or someone else—or caused the ranch to lose money? Why would anyone want to kill Dillon?

Everything came back to harming her.

The accidents had slowed her down or stopped her, but nothing had put an end to her work. So, drastic action had been taken yesterday. If someone were willing to kill her, they wouldn't stop after one attempt. There would be another.

Cal fisted his hands. He needed answers, but he wouldn't find them on the ranch. He needed to go to town and get them, which wouldn't happen until the day was done. Yet, the thought of leaving Dillon unprotected wasn't an option. Which put Cal in a tough position. He needed to find the truth more than anything because that was the only way he'd untangle the situation around him.

Lunch came and went without any sign of Chet. Hank's ranch was large, with a lot of ground to cover. It could easily take a couple of days before they completed the search of

Ivy Ridge. Dillon was strung tightly, her gaze moving to the drive as she searched for any signs of the ranger.

It was finally nearing the end of another hot day. Cal removed his hat and wiped his forehead with his forearm. As he placed his hat back in place, he saw the glint of sun off chrome a second before hearing an engine start. He lengthened his strides to get a better look at the drive and spotted Dillon driving away.

"Hey!" Cal yelled, but she never saw or heard him.

Emmett was on the porch of the house, glaring at him. "I thought you were supposed to watch her."

"I can't do that if she doesn't tell me what she's doing."

"Son, if you haven't noticed, she has a mind of her own. She's not going to *tell* you anything."

Cal fought to keep his temper in check. "Do you know where she's headed?"

"Town for some supplies."

Cal turned and ran to the bunkhouse to grab his keys and jump in his truck. Once on the road, he pressed the accelerator to the floorboard, but it did no good. He couldn't see Dillon. It wasn't until he crested a hill that he spotted her at the bottom and breathed easier. He let up on the gas and slowed his truck.

When they drove through town, he stared at Ike's. As much as he wanted to return and see if anyone had seen who he'd spoken to the other night, he stayed behind Dillon. She pulled into the parking lot of a grocery store and got out, only to turn and look right at him. Cal parked beside her.

"Are you really following me?" she asked.

He shrugged as he climbed out of the truck. "With everything going on, don't you think that's the smart thing to do?"

"Come on, then," she said with a sigh.

The trip was quick, and they both walked out with bags. Cal put his in the cab of his truck and looked down the street at Ike's flashing sign.

"Go."

He turned at the sound of Dillon's voice. "What?"

"If you want a drink, go."

"I don't want a drink. I want to remember the other night."

She placed her arms on the truck bed frame with a thoughtful expression. "You think you'll find answers there?"

"I won't know until I try."

"Then let's go."

Startled, he asked, "What?"

"You said I can't be alone. And you want answers. We're in town. Makes perfect sense to me," she replied and opened the vehicle door to get in.

Cal had no choice but to climb into his truck and start the engine. He followed Dillon to Ike's, just down the street. Now that he was here, he knew he'd rather do this alone, but he suspected that he wouldn't get rid of Dillon that easily.

She was already at the door of the bar when he slid out of his vehicle. She didn't wait for him to reach her before entering the establishment and walking to a table to sit. Cal looked around as he slowly made his way to her.

"Remember any of this?" she asked.

He shook his head as a country song ended, and another began through the speakers. The smell of stale beer, yeast, and musty upholstery wasn't particular to Ike's, so the smells couldn't help dredge up memories of that evening.

A leggy blonde with a tight-fitting, low-cut shirt over her impressive breasts stood behind the bar. She gave him a nod when she caught him staring.

"Remember her?" Dillon asked.

"Vaguely," he answered and motioned her over.

The blonde approached with a smile. "You're alive. I'm relieved after the other night."

"You remember him?" Dillon asked.

She flashed Cal a dry look. "In my line of work, you remember the ones who get as drunk as you were. I stopped serving you."

"Then how did I get so drunk?"

Her lips flattened in distaste. "Your friends had liquor of their own. You went with them to keep drinking."

"Who were they?" Cal and Dillon asked in unison.

The bartender looked between them. "I don't know their names. Sorry."

"What about their faces?" Dillon asked.

Cal nodded. "Anything."

"Did you kill someone or something?" the bartender asked with a frown of concern.

Cal held her gaze. "I can't remember that night. I have missing time, and I don't know who I was with or how I got to where I was found."

The bartender glanced around the bar to the few patrons before moving closer and lowering her voice. "I don't know their names, but I recognized one guy. He does odd jobs for Isaac Gomez."

"The attorney?" Dillon asked.

"The very one," the waitress replied.

Cal rose and pulled some money out of his pocket to hand to the woman. "Thanks. Is there anything else you can think of?"

"They approached you. You'd been here for a bit. I'd just cut you off and offered to call you a cab when they showed up. They went straight to you as if they were expecting to find you here. They told me they were going to take care of you and that I didn't need to worry about getting you a ride."

Dillon stood and pushed her chair in. "You didn't happen to hear where they were headed, did you?"

"No, but the look they shared didn't sit well with me," the bartender answered.

Cal frowned at her words. "What kind of look?"

"The kind that said they'd found exactly what they wanted."

Chapter 16

Dillon walked from Ike's with more questions than when she went in. Maybe she was a fool, but the more she learned about Cal, the more she believed him. And if everything he'd told her was true, then someone had wanted to make sure that he was on the Bar 4.

"Who is Isaac Gomez?" Cal asked as the door of the bar closed behind them.

She turned to him, seeing his gray eyes filled with apprehension and a healthy dose of worry. "He's a prominent attorney for the county. He rarely loses. He's as well-known as Hank. They move in the same circles."

"And?" Cal asked, his brows rising when she hesitated.

"There have long been rumors that he's not exactly on the up and up."

"Shit," Cal said as he turned away, scratching his forehead. He dropped his arm and faced her again. "Maybe I should talk to him."

She shook her head. "I doubt he'd tell you anything."

"I need to know about that missing time. I have to know what I did."

It suddenly hit her . . . "You believe you let Legacy out."

He stared at her for a long, silent minute. "Those weren't my boot heels around the gate, and I can prove that. I don't think I was directly responsible, but I can't shake the horrible feeling that I was part of it somehow."

Since there was a chance that he could've been, Dillon decided not to reply.

"Maybe I shouldn't be at the ranch," Cal said.

Dillon put her hands on her hips and sighed. "I need the help. Besides, we made a deal."

Cal ran his hand over his mouth and then looked at the ground for several moments. "I'm not lying about any of this."

"I don't know if you are or aren't. What I *do* know is that you saved me and helped me track Legacy. If you were working with Hank, I don't think you would've done that."

His eyes lifted to hers. "Is there a connection between Hank and Isaac Gomez?"

"Yes."

"Dammit," Cal spat as he briefly closed his eyes. "Everything goes back to Hank."

"Yep."

Cal walked to the front of his truck and braced his hands on the hood as he watched the passing traffic on the road. "I need to get to the bottom of things."

"Maybe you shouldn't."

His head swung to her, and his brows furrowed. "Why?"

"You might not like what you find."

"I'm pretty sure that's a guarantee." He blew out a frustrated breath and straightened. "Regardless of what you think, I would never willingly help someone commit a crime."

The sincerity in his eyes struck her straight in the heart. "We're not going to find out any more today. Let's head back to the ranch."

Cal nodded and got into his truck. Dillon moved slower to the driver's side of her vehicle. She gave Ike's one last look before driving away. Cal remained behind her, his black truck visible every time she glanced in the rearview mirror. At first, she had been irritated that he'd followed her. Then she recalled the sound of the bullet that had landed near her and had nearly taken her life.

Dillon didn't know if it was someone who worked for her, someone she knew, or a stranger. Every person she came across now, she wondered if they had pulled the trigger—and when they would make another attempt.

Someone wanted her dead. It would be easy to lock herself in her room and allow fear to rule her. But that wasn't who she was. Besides, she didn't want to give those after her the satisfaction of knowing how deep her terror ran. So, she made herself go about her daily routine. But it wasn't easy, and she knew it would only get harder until whoever was after her was brought to justice.

She slowed to turn onto Bar 4's drive. Cal's truck was right behind her, and she wondered how he was doing. She considered herself a decent judge of character. Either Cal was a fabulous actor, or he was in the middle of this, right along with her. While she hated that he was missing time, she was also glad that she had someone who understood a little of what she was going through. Not that Emmett didn't, but it was different with him.

Dillon parked the truck and turned off the ignition. Cal waved to her as he continued on to the bunkhouse. She almost got out and flagged him down to ask him to have dinner with her again, but then decided against it at the last minute.

She walked up the porch steps and unlocked the door. Once inside, she stood at the kitchen island and listened to the silence. The house had been built for a family. When Dillon mentioned that once, Dolly had snorted loudly.

"My dear, the worst thing you can do is follow everyone else's rules about life. Do what you want. What makes you happy."

At one time, Dillon had thought to have a husband and kids. That path had been clear before her. But it had vanished in an instant. It had been the lowest point of her life. Then, Dolly had died. And Dillon was bereft. The last thing she had thought about was the ranch, but Dolly had made sure that everything was in order.

Dillon dropped her gaze to the island and set her hat down. She trudged to the stairs and made her way to her room, where she took a long shower. After she'd dried off, she looked at herself in the mirror and gently ran her finger along the fine lines around her eyes. Dillon inwardly shook herself for being concerned about the signs of aging. She removed the towel from atop her head and combed through the wet length of her hair. Then she gently dabbed some rosehip oil onto her face and eyelids. While that soaked in, she put product in her hair. Once she applied her eye and face creams, she put on a pair of cream lounge pants and a tan T-shirt before heading downstairs.

She opened the fridge and pulled out some leftovers from the night before. While they heated in the microwave, she looked out the kitchen window to Bar 4's rolling hills. The summer sun wouldn't set for another couple of hours. Usually, she used the time to work, but she needed a night to herself. Her gaze moved over the pastures dotted with cattle and others with horses. It was a beautiful place. She understood why others might want it, but just because someone coveted what she had didn't mean they had a right to take it.

The microwave dinged, pulling her out of her thoughts. Dillon took her plate and a bottle of Coke and walked to the living area. She curled up on her favorite side of the sofa and turned on the television. After scrolling through various shows that she usually watched, she settled on an old favorite—*Stargate Atlantis*.

Long after she'd finished the meal and her plate had been

put in the dishwasher, Dillon remained on the couch. She even ignored the need to head to her office and take care of administrative work. The next time she looked up, night had fallen. Dillon paused the show and rose to get herself an adult beverage.

She poured some Chambord into a glass with ice and shifted to add some club soda when the window shattered. Dillon instantly dropped below the counter as her heart slammed against her ribs. Two more shots quickly followed. She covered her head as wood splinters rained down on her.

"Dillon? Dillon, answer me!"

More shots rang out. More glass broke. The sound of Cal's voice growing closer had her crawling to the entryway. She flattened herself against the lower cabinets and glanced out the window on the door. She heard shouts from Emmett and Dusty.

A startled yelp escaped Dillon when a figure suddenly appeared. The instant she recognized Cal through the window, she reached over and unlocked the door. He hurried inside and slammed it behind him as he moved away and flattened against the wall. He took in the kitchen and then lowered next to her.

"Are you hurt?" he demanded.

She shook her head. "I-I don't think so."

"Then where did the blood come from?"

Dillon frowned as she looked behind her and saw the smears of blood. She lifted her hands and saw the glass and splinters embedded in her palms. She hadn't felt anything. When she looked lower, she found that her lounge pants were soaked in blood at the knees where more glass protruded from her skin.

"Shit," Cal murmured as he squatted beside her. "Is there more?"

Dillon shrugged. She was suddenly cold.

"It's okay," Cal told her as he checked her feet before lifting her into his arms. "Emmett and Dusty are looking for the shooter."

He gently set her on the sofa and said something before snapping the curtains closed, but all she could think about was that she wasn't even safe in her own home. How silly she'd been to believe that no one could harm her while she was within the safe confines of her house. How naïve she was. How utterly stupid.

"Dillon."

She blinked and found Cal's face close to hers.

"Where is your first-aid kit?"

She heard his question, but for the life of her, she couldn't form a response.

"It's in here," Emmett said as he and Dusty rushed into the house.

Dusty halted just inside the back door. He was shirtless, his jeans hanging open, but he had gotten on his boots, at least. He held a rifle in one hand, and a flashlight in the other. He stared at the kitchen floor before swiveling his head to her.

"Boss?" he asked worriedly.

Emmett tossed Cal the white box filled with first-aid supplies. Then he turned to Dusty. "Stop your gawking. I need you to call the sheriff."

Dusty snapped to attention and did as Emmett ordered. Then the ranch manager turned to her. Emmett's head of white hair was in disarray. He had on a white sleeveless undershirt and jeans that he had managed to buckle, but he was only in his stocking feet.

"I need a bowl," Cal told him. "Warm water and something to wipe up the blood."

Dillon sat quietly. She still didn't feel any pain. The entire event was surreal and as if she were looking at it from far away. She turned her attention to Cal as he took a folding knife out of his pocket and cut her pants so he could get to the glass.

With steady hands, he took tweezers and gently picked out the shards of glass and wood, dropping them into a bowl that Emmett held. Cal was meticulous, making sure he got every sliver and flake. She watched him, absorbed in every movement he made.

The next thing she knew, blue and red lights flashed through every window, and she saw that Dusty and Emmett were with the authorities.

"Look at me," Cal urged her.

She focused on his gray eyes.

He smiled. "Good girl. Don't worry about anything else right now. Okay?"

Dillon nodded. The first stings of pain were beginning to register. She pulled away from it, but there was no running.

By the time Cal finished with her knees, the pain had enveloped her. He took one look at her face and said her name. She heard him as if from a great distance. Nausea set in, and black dots danced on the edges of her vision.

"Cal," she called as she felt herself falling to the side.

Strong arms grabbed her, and she knew without looking that it was Cal. Dimly, she heard him say something, but she couldn't make it out. Her eyes were out of focus, her ears ringing, and she couldn't stop shaking.

Cal held her carefully but firmly. His warmth finally seeped through her icy skin so she could take a deep breath. The ringing gradually lessened, and she cleared her eyes enough to find herself staring into his eyes.

"Almost done," he promised.

Dillon believed him. She realized that she had believed him from the first moment she met him. It was inexplicable why she would do such a thing, but she did. She wanted to tell him. Instead, she watched him gently remove glass and wood from her hands and fingers before dabbing all the cuts with a gauze pad soaked in water. He did another thorough look for any remaining dirt or debris. When he seemed satisfied that the wounds were clean, he applied an antibiotic cream and wrapped the worst of the cuts with a bandage.

Cal didn't look at her until he had put everything back in the first-aid box. "You scared the hell out of me."

His words brought back the events of the night. She swallowed as emotion choked her. Her eyes burned as tears gathered and two fell onto her cheeks.

"Well, Ms. Young," Chet said as he walked up. "This investigation is turning out to be much more than anticipated."

Chapter 17

Fury scorched a trail through Cal's veins. He liked the emotion better than the dread that had assaulted him at the sound of that first shot. He'd never run so fast in his life, and even then, it felt as if it had taken him an eternity to reach the house. When he saw Dillon on the floor with the blood, he'd feared the worst.

"I'd like to ask you both a few questions."

Cal blinked and jerked his gaze to Chet Thompson, who stood over them. Cal realized that the ranger had been speaking to him and Dillon, though Chet's gaze was on Cal. "Of course," he replied.

"Ms. Young?" Chet asked, concern coloring his voice. "Are you up to this now?"

Dillon cleared her throat twice and then opted for a nod.

Cal wanted everyone out of the house so he could go track the son of a bitch who had shot at Dillon *again*. The authorities needed answers first, however. Cal understood that they had a job to do, but so did he. And the quicker the sheriff, his deputies, and the ranger were gone, the better.

"Dillon is still in shock. Let's only make her go through this once," Cal suggested.

Chet held his gaze for a full thirty seconds before nodding and turning on his heel to walk to the group of police officers speaking with Emmett and Dusty.

Cal looked at Dillon. "Do you need anything?"

She tried to smile, but her lips trembled before she shook her head.

Cal rubbed his hands on his jeans, where drops of Dillon's blood stained the denim. "You might not, but I do. Have any liquor?"

Dillon pointed to a cabinet in the dining room. Cal rose and walked to it. When he opened it, he saw that he had his pick of alcohol. He chose a bottle of mezcal and brought it back to Dillon. He opened the bottle and took a drink before handing it to her.

"A small swig might help," Chet told her when he returned.

Dillon looked between them before taking the bottle and bringing it to her lips for a quick drink. Cal took the mezcal and drank another long swig as the sheriff and Deputy Smith from the day before walked up.

"Deputy," Cal said with a nod. His eyes swung to the sheriff, whose name tag read *Sheriff Felps*. "Sheriff."

The sheriff held out his hand. "I've not had the pleasure."

"Cal Bennett," he replied as he shook the sheriff's hand, though Cal had a suspicion Felps knew exactly who he was.

Chet pushed his hat back on his head and caught Dillon's gaze. "May I?" he asked and pointed to a chair.

"Please," Dillon said.

The anger inside Cal tightened at the softness of her voice. This wasn't the Dillon he'd come to know.

Once Chet, Felps, and Deputy Smith had taken seats, their gazes turned to Cal. He wasn't surprised that they wanted to start with him. He remained standing in a bid to calm himself, but it wasn't working.

"Emmett and Dusty said you were the first to the house," the sheriff said.

Cal raised a brow. "As I'm sure Dusty also told you, he was on the phone with a female friend in the bunkhouse, and I didn't want to intrude. I took a walk to give him some privacy and checked on the horses and made sure the gates were locked. I reached the house first because I was the closest. Since more shots were fired *after* I was with Dillon, that should remove me as a suspect. However, I'm also willing to submit to a gunshot residue test."

"You might not have pulled the trigger, but you could've been part of it," Chet said.

Cal gripped the bottle tighter. "I wasn't. No one was with me after I left the bunkhouse and before I found Dillon."

"Where were you exactly when you heard the first shot?" the ranger asked.

Cal swallowed. "I had just double-checked the pasture where Legacy was stolen when I heard the shot and the sound of glass shattering. I looked toward the house and saw the broken window. I ran straight here, shouting for Dillon. I tried to see where the shooter was, but I wanted to make sure Dillon wasn't injured. When I reached the door, it was locked. Three more shots were fired. Between the retorts, I heard Dusty and Emmett, so I knew they were searching for the shooter. The door suddenly opened, and I saw Dillon on the floor with the blood. I quickly got her out of the kitchen to tend to her wounds. Emmett and Dusty arrived soon after, closed the curtains around the open windows, and helped me get Dillon's wounds cleaned."

The sheriff nodded as he wrote in his little notebook. "How many shots were fired?"

"Six," Cal answered.

Deputy Smith asked, "You didn't hear or see anything out of the ordinary?"

"It's only my second night at the ranch. I'm still learning what's normal, but I can tell you that had I seen or heard anything that might have alerted me that someone was trespassing on the ranch, I would've gone to investigate," Cal said.

Chet nodded slowly. "Tell me about your day. What did you do, leading up to tonight?"

"I was with you, Dillon, and Emmett this morning, going through what we discovered yesterday. After we left you with Hank, the three of us returned to the ranch and worked through the day."

"Can anyone verify your whereabouts during the day?" Felps asked.

"I can," Dillon interjected before Cal could.

Chet's dark eyes swung to Dillon. "The entire day?"

"I didn't see him every second, no," she said. "But he was never far from me."

The sheriff frowned. "That sounds a lot like obsessive behavior."

Cal had had enough. "I tackled her out of the way of a bullet yesterday. I was right there with her when the shots were fired. Emmett wanted me hired specifically to be a bodyguard of sorts for Dillon. Plus, she needed a ranch hand."

"So, you took it upon yourself to do both?" Chet asked.

Cal shrugged. "I was attempting to, yes."

Chet motioned with his hand. "Continue with your day."

"Dillon took off for town. I followed and caught up to her at the grocery store. We went in together, and each bought a few things." Cal paused and set the bottle of mezcal down on the coffee table. "I kept thinking about what you said this morning about wanting answers. The last thing I remembered about the other night was being at Ike's. Since we were in town, the two of us headed to the bar to see if we could find those answers."

"Which we did," Dillon added.

The sheriff looked between them. "And?"

"The bartender recognized me," Cal continued. "Said she

cut me off because I was drunk and wanted to call me a cab. Before she could, two men walked in and approached me as if they knew me."

Chet's gaze was intense. "Were you expecting anyone?"

"The only person I knew in town was Hank, and I hadn't told him that I was here. So, to answer your question, no." Cal drew in a deep breath and then slowly released it. "I don't remember the men. Apparently, they told the bartender they would take care of me, and the three of us left."

"And you remember none of this?" Chet asked.

Cal shook his head. "The last thing I remember is sitting at Ike's."

"What about the men?" the sheriff asked. "Do you remember them?"

Cal glanced at Dillon to find her watching him. "I don't. The bartender didn't know their names but said she recognized one guy. She mentioned that he does jobs for Isaac Gomez."

Out of the corner of Cal's eye, he saw the deputy jerk his head toward the sheriff, but the sheriff was making notes, preventing Cal from seeing his face.

"Finding out who that is should be easy," Cal said to get a reaction.

Smith hastily looked away from the sheriff as Felps raised his gaze to Cal. "We'll make some calls."

"What happened after you left Ike's?" Chet asked.

Cal shrugged. "I followed Dillon here. She parked by the house, and I continued to the bunkhouse. I put away my groceries and made a sandwich. I tried to watch some TV, but I was still wound up from what I'd learned. Dusty came in on his phone, and he didn't take kindly to my pacing. That's when I left to check the horses and gates and give him some privacy. You know the rest."

"All right," Felps said. "I don't have any more questions for you right now. Thompson?"

The ranger shook his head.

Their attention shifted to Dillon. Cal noticed that she was still pale, though she looked better every minute. His gaze dropped to her pants that he'd had to cut to get to her injuries. The blood was drying now, turning a rust color. Her hands rested, palms-up, by her sides, the white bandages a stark contrast to the couch's navy fabric.

Cal listened as Dillon went through her day, starting from that morning and going all the way until they returned from town. Then she paused. He saw that she was struggling with the idea of being shot at again.

"I . . . I changed and heated some leftovers," she said, her gaze on the rug covering the hardwood floor. "I watched some TV and then got up to get a drink. I was in the middle of pouring when . . ."

It killed Cal to sit there and watch her battle the emotions. He didn't know what to do or say. He'd never been in such a situation before, and he felt useless. Inept. He was a man of action, yet he couldn't do anything to relieve her of this burden.

She swallowed loudly and lifted her gaze to look at Chet. "The window exploded. Instinctively, I dropped to the floor. Two more shots rang out, and I covered my head with my arms as debris rained down. I heard Cal shouting my name, and I could tell that he was coming closer to the house. I knew he was there to help, so I crawled to the door. I never felt the glass sinking into my skin."

"You couldn't have been certain that Mr. Bennett wasn't the shooter," Felps stated.

Cal fought to keep his mouth shut and stifle the urge to become defensive. He had to remind himself that the authorities were only doing their jobs.

Dillon slid her gaze to him. "More bullets came through my kitchen, Sheriff. And the sound of them firing hadn't grown closer. Common sense told me that Cal was there to help."

Felps, firmly put back in his place, licked his lips. "Do you have any idea who might want to see you dead?"

"You mean other than your good friend, Hank Stephens?" Dillon replied coolly. "No."

Chet rose to his feet. "I think we have all we need for the moment. Don't you, Sheriff?"

Felps nodded and stood. He tipped his hat to Dillon. "We'll be back in touch if we need anything else. I'll have my people searching the area to see if they can find the shooter's location. This is a crime scene now, so they'll continue to gather any evidence they uncover."

After Felps and the deputy walked away to meet with the others, Chet remained behind. Only when the sheriff was out of earshot did the ranger turn to them.

"Two attempts on your life in two days? I don't like this," Chet said to Dillon.

Cal crossed his arms over his chest. "Did you find anything today?"

"Nothing yet." Chet adjusted his Stetson on his head. "I'm good at what I do, and I won't stop until I get to the bottom of this."

Dillon's shoulders sank. "You've got your work cut out for you."

Cal didn't intend to stand by and do nothing. He'd conduct his own investigation. Something was going on, and he didn't like that he had been brought into the middle of it without his consent. But he would get to the bottom of things, one way or another.

Chapter 18

It took hours before the crime scene techs finished gathering evidence. Dillon was emotionally and physically drained, but at the same time, she knew she wouldn't be able to sleep. Her palms and knees throbbed from the dozens of cuts. She stood in the doorway and looked at the kitchen. She was shocked to see that it looked like a war zone. The window over the sink was mostly gone, and several cabinets had holes in them. One cabinet door hung by a single hinge, its contents spilling out onto the counter.

"I'll call the glass company first thing in the morning," Emmett told her.

Dillon squeezed her eyes closed for a moment. She couldn't believe that the night had started out like so many, yet had ended with her nearly being killed. How many more chances would she have before her luck ran out, and her life was forfeit?

Cal came up beside her. He'd walked through the first floor of the house half a dozen times, looking at windows and checking to make sure they were locked. "You shouldn't stay here tonight."

"It's my home," she stated.

Emmett sighed. "He's right. It isn't safe."

"No place is safe for me," she told them.

Dusty paused in his sweeping of the glass. "You can sleep in the bunkhouse with us."

"Now that's an idea," Emmett said, his face brightening.

She turned her head to the ranch manager. "I'm not leaving my house."

"My idea was to have someone here with you." Emmett then looked at Cal.

Cal's gaze moved from Emmett to her before he shrugged. "I agree that you shouldn't be alone. Whether you're at the bunkhouse or here, someone needs to stay with you."

Dillon wanted to appear unaffected by the night's events, but she wasn't. The truth was, she didn't want to be alone. She was relieved by the idea that Cal would be sleeping in the house. "Okay."

"Now, Dillon, don't be—" Emmett halted, confusion on his face. "Did you just agree?"

"I'm not an idiot," Dillon told them.

Cal walked to Dusty. "We'll hurry and finish this so you can get some rest."

The two worked together and did their best to get the glass off the floor and counters. Emmett left, only to return a short time later with a piece of plywood cut to fit the busted window. Once that was in place to keep the mosquitos out and as much of the cool air in, Emmett and Dusty left.

When they were alone, Cal turned to Dillon. "Is there anything you need?"

"You mean besides stopping the lunatic trying to kill me? No, I'm good."

"We will find who it is."

She forced a smile. "There are three spare bedrooms upstairs. Take your pick."

"I'll sleep on the couch."

Dillon frowned and looked at the sofa. "While it's fairly comfortable, I wouldn't advise it when there are beds."

"I'm sleeping down here because I want to hear if anyone tries to get into the house."

"Ah. All right. Let me get you a pillow and a blanket, at least."

Dillon made her way up the stairs to the linen closet in the hallway. She grabbed what she needed and went back down. Cal was waiting for her. They worked together to get the sofa made into a makeshift bed.

Once it was complete, she straightened and looked at him. "Thank you. For everything."

"You don't have to thank me."

"I do. I don't know what's going on, or why someone wants to kill me for the ranch. That can be the only reason. There's no other motive. But as pretty as I think Bar 4 is, I don't know that it's enough to kill for."

Cal's gray eyes held hers. "We're going to get to the bottom of this. I promise you that. And we're going to begin tomorrow."

"Where do you suggest we start?"

"We have several options. Since I'm tied to all of this, we could start with Isaac Gomez, but I don't think we should."

She tilted her head to the side. "Why not?"

"He's friends with Hank. You mentioned tonight that the sheriff and Hank are friendly, as well. If there's even a chance the three of them are in on this in any way, they'll prevent us from discovering the truth."

Dillon stretched her neck one way and then the other as a stress headache began to build at the base of her neck. "Hank is connected to everyone in the county. And anyone in seats of power make it their business to call Hank a friend. Money and power seem to go hand in hand. Dolly once said something about the ties between some of those in power going back decades."

"I don't trust the sheriff. It may be nothing, but I'd rather not let him know what we're doing."

Something about him using the word *we* made her want to cry. She was capable of handling things on her own, but this problem was bigger than any she had ever tackled before, and she was scared. Knowing she had someone to count on, someone who would share the burden, somehow made it easier to carry.

"I've never had dealings with Sheriff Felps before. I thought it was because of tonight, but something about him just didn't sit well with me," she confessed. "I got the feeling that Chet felt the same."

Cal nodded in agreement. "The fact that Chet waited until the sheriff was otherwise occupied to talk to us said a lot."

"I hope I'm not wrong, but I like Chet Thompson. He seems like a decent man. But my opinion might be colored because he didn't let Hank's charm sway him."

Cal's lips split into a wide grin, though it didn't last. "That's understandable. I admit that I'm not sure about Hank. I've known him for a long time, but as Chet pointed out this morning, people change. I've not seen or spoken with Hank in over a year. A lot could've happened."

"Or he may have always hidden the man he really is."

"More often than not, people pretend to be things they aren't, so that wouldn't surprise me."

"Are you pretending?" Dillon was surprised that the words had fallen from her lips, but she was glad that she had voiced them.

Cal's face was serious. "I'm not. It's an exhausting way of life that I don't have any use for. I'm a simple man."

There was absolutely nothing *simple* about Cal, but she decided to keep that thought to herself. All Dillon could do was hope that her gut wasn't wrong about him. She decided to change the subject. "Where do you think we should start tomorrow?"

"Hank wanted the ranch badly enough to offer double what it's worth. I say we find out what it is about this land that interests him so much."

"Dolly had an oil company drill in a couple of places to see if there was oil, but they found nothing."

Cal twisted his lips. "There could be a lot more in the ground that you don't know about. Did your aunt get mineral rights to her property?"

"Actually, she did. Anything belowground on the Bar 4 is hers—I mean, mine," Dillon corrected.

"Then we have a place to start."

Dillon covered her mouth to hide her yawn.

"You should get some rest," Cal told her. "We'll figure things out in the morning."

She nodded, smiling. "Good night."

"'Night," he replied.

Dillon turned and walked to the stairs. When she reached them, she looked back into the living room and halted at the sight of Cal removing his shirt. He had a couple of scars on his back. When he shifted to the side, she saw another long, jagged scar running from beneath his armpit before curving toward his abdomen.

The muscles bunched and moved as he unbuckled his belt. Her eyes took in the wide shoulders down to his waist. When he sat to remove his boots, she inwardly shook herself. She had never spied on a man removing his clothes before. Appalled at her behavior, she silently continued up the stairs to her bedroom.

Once she changed clothes and slipped between the covers, she found herself staring at the ceiling, thinking about Cal shirtless. She wished she had gotten a view of his front. If his back was that corded with muscle, she could only imagine what his chest looked like.

Dillon put an arm on her forehead as her thoughts swirled around Cal. She didn't want to think how things might have gone the past few days without him. Whatever had brought him to the ranch, she was grateful.

The little bit of happiness those thoughts conjured quickly evaporated as she recalled the sound of the shot and the breaking of the kitchen window. She was certain that it would've hit her dead center had she not shifted as she poured the club soda. That was enough to scare her as nothing else had before.

She hadn't let the first attempt on her life stop her from doing normal activities, but this changed things. Cal had saved her the first time. Only a shift in her stance had saved her this time. Would anything or anyone save her a third time? She wasn't so sure she would have such luck. But she couldn't live in a bubble, either. The only way to stop this was to get answers—though she suspected that getting those answers might be just as dangerous.

Chapter 19

The cocking of the revolver in the quiet morning hours halted Freddy in his tracks. His hands flew up by his ears. "It's just me, Mr. Gomez."

A light clicked on, showing Isaac Gomez reclining in his chair with his feet on the desk, and the revolver pointed at Freddy's chest. "I know it's you. Why do you think I got the gun?"

"I-I don't understand. I did what you wanted."

Ice spread through Freddy's veins at the glacial scowl. Isaac put on a show for his clients, appearing congenial and accommodating. But Freddy had always seen another side of Isaac. A side Freddy's momma would've called the Devil before crossing herself and kissing her rosary.

It was that frightening side, that evil side that Freddy found himself staring at now—and he was terrified. From the day he had walked into Isaac Gomez's law office, Freddy's life had gone to hell in a handbasket. No doubt his mother was rolling over in her grave. Freddy had wanted to stop doing Isaac's bidding, but he was in way over his head. The ground beneath him was like quicksand. There was only one way out—down.

"Did what I wanted?" Isaac asked in a calm voice.

Freddy moved his head up and down quickly. "You wanted the Young woman out of the way. You told me to take care of her."

Isaac simply stared.

Freddy's knees started to knock together as fear rose, choking him. "I-I promised I'd make my mistake right."

"Did you?"

Freddy swallowed, the sound loud to his ears. He glanced at the pistol the lawyer still pointed at him. He should've left town. Why had he come here? There was no way Isaac would let him off easy this time.

"I take your silence to mean that you failed. Again."

"She moved at the last minute."

Isaac drew in a deep breath and slowly released it. "Do you know why I'm so good at my job?"

"Because you know the law."

"Anyone can memorize laws. No, Freddy, I'm a great lawyer because I see people's weaknesses and use them to my advantage. Most times, it's against my opponents and their clients."

Most times. Yeah, Freddy knew Isaac never hesitated to use his particular skills on his clients when the need arose.

"Do you know what your weakness is?"

Freddy told himself not to answer, but just like with every other decision he'd made since meeting Isaac Gomez, he couldn't help but obey. "No."

A cold, calculating smile split Isaac's face. "You're spineless. You can't think for yourself. You're a follower."

Each word was like a punch to his gut. Freddy desperately wanted to tell Isaac to go to Hell, but the words stuck in his throat.

"My point exactly," Isaac said.

Freddy glanced at the floor, noticing for the first time that plastic covered it. His stomach dropped to his feet. When he lifted his gaze, he knew he was going to die.

Isaac sighed wearily. "You had one job, Freddy. One job. And you couldn't manage that."

"Give me another chance," he begged.

"Too many people are sniffing around. I can't take the chance of things leading back to me."

Freddy felt tears gathering in his eyes. "I'll leave town and never come back. I swear."

"And why would I take your word for it?"

"Because I'm a coward, and I'm scared shitless of you."

Isaac tsked. "Ah, Freddy. You had an opportunity to get away, but you couldn't do it. And I'm all out of chances."

Hank paced the area in front of his bed. The minute he'd gotten word from his contact at the sheriff's office that someone had taken another shot at Dillon, Hank had been on edge. He didn't know if Dillon was dead or not. He couldn't do anything until he knew one way or another.

He'd brought up Isaac's number numerous times but always decided against it right before he initiated the call. Things had gotten infinitely more volatile with the arrival of the TSCRA ranger. He was sniffing around, making the plans put into place more difficult to carry out. Then there was Cal.

"What the fuck are you doing, Cal?" Hank asked aloud.

He wanted to talk to Cal privately. He needed to know what Cal was thinking—and, more importantly, what he was doing. Hank hated that Isaac had brought Cal into their scheming. And the way Cal looked at him made Hank uneasy. Actually, nothing about any of this was good.

Hank halted and sank onto the bench before his bed. If he could only go back to that day two months ago when he'd vented about Dillon while Isaac had been at the house to finalize some legal papers. If Hank had been at Isaac's office, he never would've mentioned any of it for fear of someone overhearing. But at his house, he hadn't held back when Isaac prodded.

Even after he realized what Isaac had been doing, Hank hadn't been able to help himself and had told him everything. The minute Isaac realized the kind of money they could make, he'd offered Hank a deal he couldn't refuse—one only a fool would accept.

Yet, Hank had. He'd regretted it the very instant the words had left his mouth, but there was no backing out. Isaac had promised to offer assistance when Hank needed it but to otherwise stay out of the situation. When, in fact, Isaac had done anything but.

Isaac's persistence in making decisions without talking to Hank about them first was putting everything in jeopardy. But what was he to do? He couldn't cut Isaac out now. Isaac had too much on him. No doubt the bastard had taped their conversations to ensure that Hank wouldn't try to double-cross him.

"I should've done the same thing," Hank mumbled.

He'd never foreseen things spiraling so out of control as they had. Cal, the ranger, someone shooting at Dillon, stealing the stallion. Each new day brought something more outrageous. At this rate, Hank would find himself in jail. He couldn't spend his money on much if he were behind bars.

There had to be a way out. Unfortunately, the only way he saw was to go to the ranger and tell him everything. Hank would do it in a heartbeat if he knew he wouldn't go to jail, but he knew that probably wasn't possible. He was so close to getting everything he wanted. Why stop now?

His plan would've taken him a year or two. While he disagreed with Isaac's motives, they were getting results. Hank didn't like how he was under the microscope. The only thing that kept him relatively calm was knowing that if he went down, he would bring Isaac with him.

Yet not even that could ease his sour stomach at the idea of Dillon's possible murder. He wanted the land, but he wasn't prepared to take her life for it. The fact that Isaac was, confirmed for Hank everything he'd ever speculated about his lawyer. And it made him look at Isaac differently. It took a special kind of person to willingly take someone's life—whether you were the one who pulled the trigger or ordered the execution. Both were the same in Hank's eyes.

He turned his head to look out his window toward Bar 4 land. He couldn't see anything, but he imagined sheriff's deputies were all around gathering evidence. Whether Dillon was dead or not, Hank would demand that Isaac send whoever had pulled the trigger out of the area. If Dillon were alive . . .

Hank's thoughts halted as his gaze dropped to the carpet. Dillon's death would make it easy to buy the ranch from whoever she left it to. They never had to know anything. It would be much simpler and quicker than his attempts to ruin her so she was forced to sell. Maybe Isaac's idea wasn't such a bad one, after all. Not that Hank condoned murder, but it wasn't as if this were his plan. He hadn't ordered someone to kill Dillon.

In fact, the more he thought about it, the more he realized that his hands were clean. A smile pulled at his lips. Maybe he'd been thinking about this all wrong. Isaac had never steered him wrong in business before. Why would he start now? Especially when they both had so much to gain.

Hank rose and removed his robe, tossing it onto the bench before climbing into bed. He lay on his back and stared at his ceiling, dollar signs flashing in his mind. There was no way the shooter would attempt a second time and miss. Dillon's death would be announced tomorrow, which meant that

Hank needed to act accordingly. He would ensure that he didn't say or do anything that would cause the ranger to look at him suspiciously.

With Dillon dead, there was a chance the ranger would leave. It would take some time for the will to go through probate and for the new owners to take control. No doubt Isaac already had a letter drafted, waiting to be sent with Hank's offer. And with Isaac's connections, there might even be a way to speed up the probating of the will.

All of that meant that Hank could have what he'd been trying to claim for months now.

Chet Thompson sat in his truck in front of the hotel and drummed his fingers on the steering wheel. He'd had some bizarre cases, but this one topped them all. The only one he believed in all of this was Dillon Young.

He lifted his cell phone and placed a call to Marty, another ranger he trusted implicitly. It rang twice before the call connected. "You still up?"

"Kinda hard to sleep with everything going on," Marty replied. "There's been no movement around Ivy Ridge."

Chet flattened his lips. "None that we can see, that is."

"Yeah. I heard the chatter on the scanner about what happened at the Bar 4. Was the shooter found?"

"Not yet."

"This is becoming a shit show. Should we call in more help?"

"No," Chet said, harsher than intended. "I got the feeling Sheriff Felps and Hank Stephens go way back."

Marty grunted. "Something the sheriff said?"

"Just a gut feeling."

"We've been doing this long enough to trust those."

It was Chet's turn to grunt. "Don't remind me about my age. This case isn't going to be what I expected. We need to adjust for that."

"What do you suggest?"

"I'm still working that out."

Marty was silent for a moment. "Ms. Young has been shot at twice now. I doubt they'll miss a third time."

"My job is to find the stolen stallion, not prevent her death."

"Yeah, but we both know what you're going to do."

Chet removed his hat and ran his hands through his thinning hair. "My old bones need some rest. I'll check back in a few hours."

"We're getting too old for this shit, Chet."

Chapter 20

Cal was up with the dawn. He quietly dressed in his clothes from the night before. He hadn't gotten any sleep between thinking of the shooter as well as Dillon above him. In bed. The fear that had been in her eyes when she unlocked the door for him last night was something he hoped to never see again.

He silently left the house and stood outside the kitchen window, trying to get an idea of the trajectory of the bullets. The area the shooter could have hidden in was large. Cal would be searching for hours—if not days—for shell casings or trampled earth from someone lying in wait.

The sheriff's department crime unit would return with the light and start looking for themselves. Cal knew if he went first, he could contaminate the area with his footprints, but if he waited, they might hide the tracks he needed to find.

Cal ran a hand over his jaw and turned to the bunkhouse. He changed and returned to the house. He walked around the perimeter to see if anyone had come close. To his shock and anger, he discovered plants in the flowerbeds with broken stems. Shoe impressions depressed the mulch—one by a living room window, and another at the office window.

"That's a grim face," Dillon said as she walked out onto the back porch with two cups of coffee. She handed one to him. "I didn't know how you liked it, so I left it black."

He smiled in thanks, happy to see her up and dressed, even if she still wore the bandages. Her hair was loose and uncovered. "It's perfect."

"What did you find?"

For a second, he debated lying to her, but if he were in her shoes, he'd want the truth. So, that's what he gave her. "Footprints near the office and living room windows. Plants were stepped on in an attempt to get close."

Dillon nodded and looked out over her land. "Do you think you can track whoever this is?"

"If I can find where they shot from, yes."

Her gaze slid back to him. "But?"

"The cops took as much evidence as they could from the house. I know they had the spotlights on their cars on, as well as flashlights, to find where the shooter was. They'll be back this morning and use the sunlight, just as I would."

Dillon shrugged indifferently. "I still don't understand."

"There's a chance they muddled things last night. Not that I blame them. I wanted to be out there looking, too. If they didn't cover any tracks with theirs, then I can find what I'm looking for."

"But then it goes back to . . . do we wait for them or not?" she concluded.

He sighed, nodding.

Dillon took a couple of sips of coffee as she contemplated his words. Finally, she looked at him. "This is my land. It is my life on the line. I don't want to wait on the authorities because I don't trust them."

"I'm not sure you should trust anyone. Even me."

A soft smile curved her lips. "And yet, I find myself trusting you."

"We don't have answers about the missing time I have."

He glanced at the ground. "A knot in my stomach says I'm involved somehow."

The sound of a vehicle approaching interrupted their conversation. A black truck pulled to a stop, and Chet Thompson got out. He tipped his hat to Dillon and nodded at Cal.

"Good morning," Dillon said as the ranger approached. "Would you like some coffee?"

Chet smiled and shook his head. "I've had my morning quota already, thanks. You've got color in your face this time, I see. Until we can get things sorted I th—"

"No," Dillon spoke over him.

Chet blinked, taken aback. "You didn't allow me to finish."

"I don't need to. You're going to suggest that I remain indoors, huddled in a corner like a scared child."

Cal drank his coffee and looked between the two. He might agree with the ranger, but in the time he'd been with Dillon, he'd come to understand that she was strong-willed. Chet glanced his way, silently seeking help, but Cal shrugged.

Finally, the ranger said, "I would call it being safe. If you don't take precautions, you're a moving target."

"I was a target inside my home," she replied.

Cal took pity on Chet. "I won't leave her side."

The ranger shook his head, his lips flattening in disapproval. "I don't like this. You're needlessly putting yourselves in danger."

"We were just chatting about me tracking the shooter," Cal said.

Chet's aging brown eyes swung to him. "I'd better come with you."

"What about Legacy?" Dillon asked.

Chet hesitated, a frown crossing his face for a moment. "It would be better for someone to be there who can document it if you two find anything. Don't worry about the stallion. I'm still doing my investigation."

"That involves Dillon?" Cal asked.

The ranger scratched his bushy eyebrow. "I'm investigating everyone. There's too much going on with entirely too many coincidences involving the same people."

"Let me get my hat," Dillon said as she went back into the house.

Cal drank the rest of the coffee and lowered the mug to find Chet starting at him. "What's on your mind?"

"What did you find this morning?"

"Footprints in the flower bed."

"I'd like to take pictures of them."

Dillon walked out of the house then. "I would, too."

Cal took them to where he'd found the prints. All three of them took pictures with their phones. Chet studied the last impression for a long time. He laid a ruler beside it to measure the print and took more pictures. All the while, Cal tried to find any other tracks leading to or from the house.

"Anything?" Dillon asked.

He shook his head and pointed to the driveway and parking area. "My guess is he went through there."

"The arrival of all the patrol cars and everyone walking around destroyed any prints," Chet said.

Cal still took his time searching. There were so many tracks from the sheriff's deputies that it was impossible to tell whose was whose. Something urged Cal to hurry. He didn't know why, but the feeling was persistent enough that he couldn't ignore it. He glanced up to see Dusty at the barn. A look over his shoulder showed Emmett with Chet and Dillon.

Cal had told Dillon not to trust anyone, and he'd meant it. He knew in his heart that he would never have agreed to anything illegal, but he'd been so sloshed that he couldn't remember anything about that night. Had he inadvertently stepped into something? If the bartender at Ike's could be trusted, the men who had found him at the bar seemed to

know him. The only person he knew in the area was Hank—
and he hadn't told Hank where he was.

Little by little, Cal searched the ground, hoping to pick up
the shooter's trail. His father had told him that tracking was
invaluable for hunters, but Cal had never thought he would
use his skills to pursue a shooter. Hell, he'd never used them
to find a stolen animal before, either. Tracking had been his
least favorite thing about hunting with his dad, but he was
glad that he had taught Cal the skill.

He suddenly halted as he noticed an overturned piece of
gravel in the parking area. The exposed side was darker than
the others that had been bleached by the sun. He bent beside
the rock and took a picture.

"Here," Chet said as he touched his shoulder.

Cal looked over to find some small, yellow flags.

The ranger shrugged. "If we're going to be doing someone else's job, we at least want to make sure they don't destroy any evidence."

Cal grinned and accepted the flag. He stuck it in the
ground next to the rock, then looked ahead, studying the
area for any more overturned rocks. He saw nothing until
he reached the grass and spotted the bent and broken blades.
Chet was there to hand him more flags and measure the impression before snapping some photos.

When Cal stood, he glanced back and saw Dillon and
Emmett in a heated discussion. Dillon shook her head as
Emmet talked and waved his arms dramatically.

"Maybe he can convince her to stay in the house," Chet
said.

Cal snorted as he met the ranger's gaze. "Not likely. She's
got a mind of her own."

"My wife was an independent woman with an iron will.
Couldn't stand to have anyone tell her what to do. I loved that
about her. As strong-minded as she was, there was another
side she only showed to me." Chet smiled fondly, a faraway

look in his eyes. "Some might have called it a weak side. I always thought of it as soft. Vulnerable, even."

"How long were you married?"

"Forty-seven years," the ranger answered with a grin. "Some were great, some were rough, but most were good."

Cal parted his lips to answer when he spotted the first sheriff's car pulling in. "Shit."

"Ignore them. Keep going," Chet told him.

Cal briefly met Dillon's gaze. She gave him a nod, and he returned to business. This kind of tracking wasn't easy. There wasn't an entire impression of a shoe print since there was no snow, mud, or soft sand. He had to look at each small section as a whole, trying to determine if leaves had been overturned, branches on the ground broken, or blades of grass bent.

"Hot damn," he murmured when he found a partial impression of the outside of the left front of a shoe.

He and Chet measured, marked, and photographed it before Chet made notes in his small notebook. Cal found the next two tracks, allowing them to measure the person's stride.

"What's going on?" Sheriff Felps asked as he walked up.

Chet raised his head from his notebook. "Tracking the shooter."

"I have men for that."

Cal calmly looked at the sheriff. "We're helping."

"You wouldn't turn down aid now, would you, Sheriff?" Chet asked.

Felps's cheeks burned red with rage. "Shouldn't you be doing your job and looking for Ms. Young's stolen stallion?"

"It's possible they're connected," Chet replied. "Hence, why I'm here."

The angrier the sheriff got, the more Cal fought to hide his smile. But the more he thought about it, the more Cal wondered about the sheriff's motives. It could be something as simple as Felps not wanting anyone intruding on his turf. But at the same time, why not accept the help the ranger was so freely giving?

"One of my deputies will be with you to ensure that all of this is on the up-and-up," Felps stated.

Cal shrugged. "Fine by me."

Chapter 21

The day was long, hot, and exhausting, and Dillon was tense and on edge for all of it. Every sound caused her to jump. It didn't matter if others surrounded her or not. Emmett was furious at her for not staying in the house, but as she had pointed out, the structure hadn't protected her the night before.

Dillon had been ecstatic when the sheriff assigned June to follow Cal and Chet as they tracked. Dillon had known June for almost six years. They got along great. Dillon didn't mind that so much testosterone surrounded her daily, but sometimes having another woman around was good.

The sun came out early, scorching everything with its heat. The threat of storm clouds moving toward them had Cal glancing at the sky often. He didn't rush. Instead, he took the time to look at every inch of ground.

The tracks took them a little over a quarter of a mile away and through several pastures. From what Cal had told her, the shoe impressions were deeper at the fence, a telltale sign that the shooter had jumped it. Then, to everyone's shock, they'd hooked a wide left and started running back the way they'd come.

Thirty feet from the road, the first fat raindrop landed. Dillon feared the tracks would get wiped away in the rain, and the fact that Cal picked up his pace told her that he had the same concern.

Just as Cal placed the final flag, and they documented the evidence, the sky unleashed the rain. Cal took pictures of something else in the dirt beside the road. The rain dripped freely from the brims of their hats and soaked their clothes. It was a bit of a hike back to the house, but Dillon had never minded getting caught in the rain.

A honk sounded as a patrol car pulled up beside them. The four of them piled into the vehicle and returned to the house. Dillon wasn't surprised to see everyone inside her kitchen. No sooner had they arrived than Sheriff Felps wanted to know what they had found.

Dillon wasn't sure if it was because Cal had mentioned his bad feeling about the sheriff or because Felps was friends with Hank, but she didn't want to be around him. She stepped to the side but watched the sheriff carefully as Cal and Chet laid out what they had discovered to everyone inside.

"He's good," Emmett said and nodded toward Cal. "Maybe one of the best trackers I've seen."

Dillon scratched her neck before crossing her arms over her chest. "We're lucky he's here. I'm not sure the sheriff's department would've found the tracks, much less done it before the rain."

"I keep telling the sheriff they need to get some K9 units," Emmett murmured.

Morning faded to afternoon, then afternoon to evening. Sheriff's deputies stood in the rain, continuing to search, as others went back to the station to begin sifting through evidence from the night before. The rain persisted. Emmett couldn't stand to be around too many people and quickly left to get to work with Dusty.

Chet stayed for most of the day before he received a call and left. She wanted to ask him for an update, but she had to remind herself that if Chet had anything to share, he would. Dillon hated that she had to put so much of her faith in others to solve her problems.

Finally, she ushered the last of the deputies, along with the sheriff, out of her house. When she turned around, Cal was waiting for her. "What is it?"

"Something I shared with Chet. He opted not to give the information to the sheriff just yet."

Intrigued, Dillon walked to him. "What?"

"When it started raining, I saw tire tracks by the road."

"Is that what you were taking pictures of?"

He nodded. "The rain would've washed them away. It might be nothing."

"But it might be something. Like evidence. It has to help."

"Only if we can match the tread to a vehicle."

Dillon leaned back against the island. "Why didn't Chet share the information with the sheriff?"

"He told me he wanted to look into something first."

"Hank," Dillon guessed.

Cal's lips twisted ruefully. "That's my guess. If the tires match any of Hank's vehicles or anyone who works for him, Chet probably wants to talk to them first."

"Just in case Felps is helping Hank."

"Precisely."

Dillon was grateful that Cal was there. She started to tell him that but decided against it at the last second. She looked outside, shifting in the awkward silence.

"I should probably go and help Dusty and Emmett," Cal said.

She hastily nodded. "There are things I need to do, too."

They walked out of the house together and sprinted to the stables. Dillon slipped in the mud, and Cal grabbed her hand, balancing her. The touch of his hand shot warmth from her fingers all the way up her arm and then through her body.

"That was close," he said with a smile once they were inside the barn.

She nodded, unable to find words. He released her hand and turned away. Dillon watched him for a few moments before shaking herself and getting to work. She didn't stop until it had turned dark. Even then, she didn't want to halt, but she was drained.

"That's enough for the day," Cal said as he walked up. "You're dead on your feet. We'll catch up with everything over the next few days."

She didn't have the strength to argue. After the shooting and getting little rest afterward, she just wanted to curl up and sleep. Dillon looked around for Emmett and Dusty but didn't see them. At the house, she took her muddy boots off outside and made her way indoors.

"I'm going to get out of these wet clothes," she told Cal.

Except when she reached her room and stripped, her eyes landed on the bed. Her body yearned to relax. She just wanted to rest for a minute. The next thing she knew, it was morning.

Dillon rose and removed her bandages before jumping into the shower. To save time, she decided not to wash her hair. She quickly dressed and made her way downstairs to find Cal in the kitchen with two mugs of coffee.

"I heard you moving around," he said.

She smiled and accepted the cup. "I apologize for last night."

"No need," he said with a smile. "I had a feeling you wouldn't come back down. I found some bread, and your toaster survived the attack."

Dillon laughed and opened the freezer to pull out a box

of breakfast sandwiches. "I think the microwave came away unscathed, as well."

"I like your idea better."

She tossed him a sandwich for each of them. There was a comfortable silence between them as they ate their breakfast before heading outside. And for the next four days, things went back to normal at the ranch. She worked outside during the day but started the kitchen cleanup at night—and Cal was right there with her, helping.

They'd tossed broken dishes and removed the busted doors so she could get the kitchen in some semblance of order. They'd even had the window replaced so the plywood could be removed.

Despite all of that, Dillon kept waiting for someone to fire more shots. Her wounds were healing, but she would always know they were there. Cal was true to his word and was never far. If she wanted to use any kind of mechanical device, he used it first to make sure nothing was malfunctioning.

Another thing that had her wound up was that they hadn't heard from Chet in days. She had left him messages, and he had texted her that he would be in touch when he had information. But there had been nothing else from him.

Dillon walked from the stables after putting up her mare. She and Cal had moved one of the herds of cattle from one pasture to another, checking fence line along the way. She spotted Emmett rocking in one of the chairs on the porch, wearing a starched shirt—something he usually saved for church.

"You'd better hurry," he told them.

Dillon frowned and then glanced at Cal, who shrugged. "For what?"

"The dance tonight."

How could she have forgotten about it? It had always been the highlight of Dolly's year. And Dillon had to admit, she always had a good time when she attended. But she wasn't sure about this one. "No."

"What dance?" Cal asked.

Emmett smiled, his eyes twinkling with merriment. "We have an annual summer dance. It's a grand event for our fair county. Dillon always attends."

"Let's go," Cal told her.

She hesitated. "I don't know. I'm tired. It's been a long week."

"Maybe this is what you need," Cal suggested. "Get away from the ranch and the problems here. Cut loose for a night."

It didn't sound like a bad idea.

"I swear I won't drink," he told her with a smile.

Emmett stopped rocking. "Dillon, it's been four days without anyone trying to harm you. Cal will be with you. Hell, even Dusty and I will be there. You'll be surrounded by people. No one would dare to do anything."

She bit her lip, unsure of what to do. A part of her wanted to go and have fun, especially after the last week. It was the other half of her, the part that recalled the horror of being shot at, that cautioned her. Yet, would it be good to be here alone? Cal would stay, but being at the ranch would still make her an easy target. "All right."

Emmett let out a whoop. "Showers. Hurry!"

Dillon found her steps light as she traded a smile with Cal and rushed into the house to get ready. He sprinted off to do the same. She rushed through her shower so she could take her time drying her hair and putting on some makeup. Dillon then stood in her closet and let her eyes scan the garments.

She ended up choosing a long, flowy, tan lace skirt and paired it with a faded chambray button-down that she tied at her waist. She added a wide brown leather belt with large silver conchae to rest on her hips. Dillon then selected the dressy cognac leather boots Dolly had given her one Christmas.

Next, she went to her jewelry box and picked two wide

silver cuff bracelets for each wrist, silver earrings that dangled nearly to her shoulders, and a simple silver necklace with a tiny compass.

Dillon stepped back and examined herself in the full-length mirror. She usually wore one of her dress hats, but she decided against it for tonight. She turned from side to side and checked herself from every angle. Once she made sure that everything was in place, she walked downstairs.

She found no sign of anyone inside. Peeking outside, she saw Cal on the porch, sitting in a rocker. She opened the door and stepped out. Cal's head jerked to her, and his eyes widened as he let out a soft whistle.

"You look stunning," he said as he got to his feet.

Dillon smiled, pleased with his response. She took in the dark blue button-down he wore and the slim, retro vest in a pale gray that fit him like a glove. He wore dark denim and a granite gray Stetson that matched his eyes. "You clean up nice, cowboy."

His grin made her stomach flutter. "Thank you."

"I especially like the vest. Did you have that custom made?"

Cal glanced down, running his hands over the material. "It was my grandfather's."

"It fits you perfectly."

"Shall we go?"

Dillon glanced around. "Are Emmett or Dusty riding with us?"

"Both headed out separately. It's just you and me."

For some reason, that sentence made her mouth go dry. Dillon couldn't seem to catch her breath. Maybe going to the dance wasn't a good idea if she was reacting this way. But . . . how could she not? Cal had saved her like some white knight and tended to her wounds like a protective lover. Of course, her thoughts would head in that particular direction, which wasn't at all practical.

Then there was the fact that they were pretending to be a couple. Something she'd forgotten about until that very instant.

She needed to remember that they weren't together. He was her employee. Nothing more.

"Right. Nothing more."

Cal quirked a brow. "I'm sorry? What did you say?"

Dillon could've kicked herself. "Nothing. Ready?"

"If you're all right with it, I'll drive us."

She spotted his truck next to hers. Was this a date? No, this wasn't a date. He'd have to ask her out. They were simply going to a dance. Together. Dressed up. In the same vehicle. That *he* drove. While pretending to be a couple.

It wasn't a date.

Was it?

"Dillon?"

"Yes," she quickly answered. "That's fine."

He studied her for a moment before motioning for her to go ahead of him. When she reached his truck, he grabbed the handle and opened the door for her. Yeah, she could certainly get used to such treatment.

They sat in silence on the way to the dance. The only words spoken were her directing him to the location. When they reached the building, the doors were open, music wafted outside, and stringed lights hung inside and out, giving the place a romantic air.

She really needed to stop thinking along those lines. Romantic or not, he was her employee. Nothing more.

"It's going to be fine."

Her head jerked to Cal. Had he said something, and she hadn't heard? "What is?"

"I promised I wouldn't leave your side. That means tonight, as well. No one will harm you."

The sincerity in his words struck her in the chest. "Thank you."

He smiled and winked at her before climbing out of the truck. Dillon took a deep breath, wondering what the night would hold. She loved to dance. And she planned to do a lot of it tonight.

Especially with Cal.

Her door opened, and he held out his hand, his warm smile greeting her. Oh, yeah. She would definitely be dancing with him tonight.

Chapter 22

From the minute Cal walked into the building with Dillon, he felt dozens of eyes on them. He glanced down to make sure that nothing was out of place. It wasn't until they passed a group just as one song ended and another started that he heard someone whisper about them being a couple.

"Seems word spreads quickly," he whispered near Dillon's ear.

She turned her head to him, a frown on her face.

"My fib to Hank about us being together."

"Oh," Dillon said as her eyes widened.

Not that he minded. It would give him the excuse he wanted to stay near her. They didn't get too far inside the building before a group of women surrounded Dillon. He smiled as she glanced at him over her shoulder. He wouldn't go far.

Cal could watch Dillon all night. He'd never seen a woman with a more radiant smile or natural beauty. And she had no idea of how many eyes followed her. Though Cal couldn't help but wonder if one of them had been the person who'd pulled the trigger and tried to kill her.

"She has an innate charm I've rarely come across," Emmett said as he walked up.

Cal glanced at the old-timer and nodded. More people crowded on the dance floor, making him lean to the side to find Dillon again. "I've been watching everyone with her. I haven't seen anyone who appears to dislike her."

"Because they don't," Emmett replied after taking a swig of his beer and wiping his mustache. "Dolly had a lot of friends, but people didn't gravitate to her like they do Dillon. I think it's because Dolly had an objective. Dillon just wants to run a successful ranch."

"What was Dolly's objective?"

Emmett sighed, his gaze dropping to the floor. "She wanted people to treat her like they would a man. Some did."

"But most didn't," Cal guessed.

Emmett's pale brown eyes met his. "It rankled her quite a bit. She used to get very angry about it. Hated that ranching was a man's world."

"Times change."

"Not quick enough for her. Dolly tried to force the change, and that rubbed a lot of people the wrong way."

Cal snorted. "You mean it rubbed men the wrong way."

"Yeah," Emmett said with a soft laugh.

Cal's gaze returned to Dillon, seeking her through the throng of people on the dance floor. She was talking to the same group of women. Someone said something that made her laugh. He heard the beautiful sound over the music. It went straight to his gut, making his stomach clench in a way he'd never experienced before. But he liked it.

Too much, maybe. He needed to remind himself that he worked for Dillon. She wasn't just some woman on the rodeo circuit. She was different from all the others in so many ways.

"Ask her to dance."

Emmett's voice intruded on his thoughts. Cal frowned. "I will."

"Don't be an idiot and wait too long, son."

Before he could approach her, another man asked Dillon to dance. He ground his teeth together as she and the man walked onto the floor and began to two-step. It wasn't long before they passed Cal.

"I told you not to be an idiot," Emmett stated before he strode away.

The job Cal had at Bar 4 was one of the first good things he'd done in his life. Granted, he wasn't sure how he'd come to be on the property, but he would work that out eventually. All he knew was that he was happy. Truly happy. For the first time in his life.

It boggled his mind that he had continued down a path that he didn't want for so many years. The thing was, he hadn't realized that until recently. How many more years would he have wasted if he hadn't woken up on Dillon's property? How many more years would he have continued to put his body through hell?

How many more years before he ended up dead like his father?

Cal took a deep breath, his eyes locked on Dillon as she and her partner moved about the floor. She was a graceful woman and an exceptional dancer. It was obvious the man was interested, and Cal had the sudden urge to punch him in the face. Which was stupid. It wasn't as if Dillon was his. He might have saved her from a bullet, tended to her wounds, slept in her house, and watched over her, but that wasn't a relationship. No matter how much he wished it could be.

The song began to end. Cal pushed away from his spot against the wall, waiting for his chance to ask Dillon to dance. Before he could, two other men approached her and her partner as the last strings of the song died. Dillon thanked her current dance partner, spoke to the man on her right, and then turned to the man on her left when a new song started.

"If you keep the wall upright, you'll never get a chance," Emmett stated as he sauntered past.

Cal clenched his jaw again. He would get a dance by the end of the night. And if he had to knock a few heads together so he could claim his spot, no one had to know.

His thoughts halted as Dillon's eyes locked with his. She smiled at him as her partner turned her. He returned the grin, that crazy feeling in his belly happening again when she held his gaze until she was out of sight.

Cal felt something touch his arm. He looked down to see a girl about eight beside him. She had a white sash claiming her *Little Miss* . . . something he couldn't read. She wore a sparkly crown with her white hat. Her white shirt with royal blue and red accents had rhinestones on it, and she wore a large belt buckle at her waist.

"Hi," she said with a bright smile.

He took in her long blond hair that fell to her waist with perfect curls at the ends. Cal tipped his hat to her. "Hello, ma'am. What can I do for you this fine night?"

"My daddy says a lady should wait for a man to come to her. My momma says I should go for what I want."

Cal bit back a laugh by licking his lips. "Sound advice from both parents. What is it you want?"

"To dance with you."

"How could I decline such an invitation?"

She beamed and held out her hand. "I'm Dallas."

"I'm Cal," he replied as he took her hand. He glanced up and found the girl's parents not too far away. The mother smiled and waved while the father glared, not that Cal could blame him. He gave them a nod and walked Dallas onto the floor.

She wrinkled her little nose. "Perhaps I should've asked if you could dance. I don't want to be embarrassed."

"I wouldn't dream of humiliating you," he replied with a smile then put his hand on her left shoulder and took her right hand before leading her in a slow two-step.

After a minute, her smile brightened once more. "I made a good choice."

Cal couldn't hold back his chuckle. "I think you did, if I do say so myself."

"I saw you in the rodeo last weekend."

He hadn't expected that. When he looked up, he found Dillon dancing past him. She glanced at Dallas before flashing him a grin. He watched Dillon for a moment longer, then turned his attention back to his dance partner. "It wasn't my best performance."

"Bull riding is my least favorite. It's so dangerous," she stated wisely.

"You're not wrong. What is your favorite category?"

She met his gaze. "Barrel riding, of course."

"Of course. And I suppose that's what you won that belt buckle for?"

If it were possible, her smile grew wider. "It is. One day, I'm going to be Miss Rodeo USA. My momma was Miss Rodeo Texas, so she's giving me all the tips."

"I'm guessing your father is also in the rodeo?"

"He's a tie-down champion. So, I've got rodeo in my blood. It's natural that I take this route."

He twirled her as the song ended and then stopped in front of her parents. Cal tipped his hat to her again. "Thank you for the dance, Miss Dallas. I hope you get all that you dream of."

"It was my pleasure," she said with a wink before turning and strutting back to her parents.

Cal saw a woman approaching him, so he quickly maneuvered through the crowd and went to the bar to order a soda. When he turned around with the drink in hand, Hank was there.

"Coke? Really?" Hank said with disdain. "Have a real drink."

"I'm fine, thanks."

Hank took a long drink of his bourbon. "I was hoping you'd show up."

"Why is that?"

"We've not had a chance to talk."

Cal was immediately suspicious, but he also wanted answers. "What do we need to talk about?"

"The fact that you think I had something to do with the stolen horse."

"The tracks led to your property."

He chortled, shaking his head. "My land surrounds the Bar 4. Of course it led to me. I've already explained that."

"Why didn't you let me search your land?"

Hank gave him a flat look. "You're a smart man. You know why."

Cal drew in a breath and slowly released it. "What's going on, Hank?"

"I don't know what you mean."

"You know exactly what I mean. Dillon has been shot at two different times now."

Hank's nostrils flared. "You think because I wanted her land that I'm responsible for that? Is that what you think of me?"

"I think you're hiding something."

Hank moved closer so they weren't talking over the music. "You know me better than that."

"Do I?"

"Yes."

"How did I get onto Dillon's property?"

Hank shrugged, his lips twisting. "How am I supposed to know?"

The more he talked, the more Cal knew he was lying, though he couldn't prove it.

Hank glanced at the dance floor and Dillon. "With the way the men gather around her at this dance each year, I had thought she would have found a man by now. How come you're allowing all these other men to dance with her if you two are together?"

"We came together. We'll leave together."

"A woman like her needs a strong man."

"You've not found a woman," Cal pointed out.

"A woman is an accessory," Hank said. "I hire people for the things a woman claims she can do in a marriage. I've got a cook and a maid. As for female company, well, let's just say I don't have to pay women to share my bed. As I remember it, neither do you."

Cal stared at the man his father had called a friend. There were more lines around his mouth and eyes now. If his father still lived, would he have the same kind of age on his face? Cal wished he would've found out.

He leaned closer to Hank and said in a low voice so no one else could hear, "Dillon is a good woman, who is doing an excellent job of running the ranch. On her own. I'm going to do everything in my power to locate her stallion and find out who is trying to kill her and take her ranch. I hope to God you aren't party to any of it. But if you are, I'll make you regret it."

Cal leaned back and met Hank's gaze, holding it for a long moment to ensure that Hank took his words seriously. Then, Cal walked away. He had wanted a private word with Hank to see if he could determine if his old friend was involved or not. Unfortunately, he'd come away more perplexed than before. But that didn't mean that Hank was a part of things.

It also didn't mean he wasn't.

Chapter 23

Dillon begged off the next man who approached her. She searched the room for Cal as she walked to the bar for a bottle of water. She opened it and turned as she drank. That's when she saw Cal headed her way. Dillon set aside the water as he stopped in front of her.

He smiled and held out his hand. She accepted his invitation and allowed him to lead her onto the dance floor. The first strings of Hank Williams Jr.'s *Texas Women* began to play. Dillon had seen Cal two-stepping with the little girl, so she knew he could dance. But she wasn't prepared for the way it felt to move with him around the room.

"You're very popular," he said with a grin.

She smiled and ducked her head. "So are you, apparently."

His gray eyes held hers, but she looked away nervously. It felt good to be in his arms. That song ended, and another began, but he never let go of her. She hid her smile when he glared at a man who approached them.

"You're right," she told him.

He lifted his brows. "About?"

"The rumor mill is talking about us."

Cal's eyes crinkled with his smile. "There's so much attention on you right now, this is probably the safest place you could be."

No. The safest place she could be was in his arms, though she couldn't quite manage to say the words. Whether Cal knew it or not, she had leaned heavily on him these last days, but he had withstood it easily. She'd found herself wanting to have him there. Yes, she could do things herself. But that didn't mean she wanted to. She got lonely. Not to mention, life was a lot more fun if there was someone to enjoy it with.

As the second song ended, she glanced to the side and saw someone coming toward them. After being in Cal's arms, she didn't want to dance with anyone else.

"I need to cool off," she told him.

He nodded and escorted her from the floor. She hadn't totally lied. The room was stifling, even with the air-conditioning and the ceiling fans on. Dillon waved her hand in front of her face and moved the front of her shirt back and forth in an effort to get as much cool air against her skin as possible. A glance at the clock showed that the dance had been going for several hours now. She couldn't believe that time had passed so quickly.

"Better?" Cal asked.

She nodded, smiling.

"Dusty sure likes to dance," Cal said with a nod toward the floor, where Dusty twirled a woman in a short skirt and boots.

Dillon laughed. "Oh, yes. Every Friday and Saturday night, he's dancing at one of the bars."

"Come on," Cal said when he spotted an empty chair.

Dillon sank into it with a sigh. "Oh, that feels good."

"I'll get us some water."

Her gaze followed him, noting how the women sized him up. It didn't take Dillon long to find Emmett, who was at a table with several older cowboys. They were all laughing and sharing stories while watching the goings-on. Emmett and his friends were the worst kinds of gossips, but he always came back with the best stories.

Dillon's eyes continued moving about the room. Her stomach dropped to her feet when she caught sight of Hank. She had known that he would be here, but that didn't make seeing him any easier. He moved from group to group, schmoozing. She was tempted to confront him in front of everyone, but it would most likely backfire on her. As hard as it was, she remained in her seat.

Sheriff Felps was there, as well, though he wasn't in uniform. He was flirting with a young girl that was most likely underage. Dillon laughed when his wife interrupted his conversation and shooed the girl away. It was wrong to spy, but Dillon couldn't look away as Mrs. Felps gave her husband an earful.

"What's so funny?" Cal asked as he walked up and handed her a bottle of water.

She took it with a smile of thanks and drank deeply. "Felps's wife just tore him a new one for talking to some young girl."

"I bet that was fun to watch."

Dillon covered her hand with her mouth as she laughed. "It was."

"The night has gone quicker than I expected."

She nodded, knowing how he felt. "I agree."

A silence grew. Her gaze moved to the clock to see that it was past midnight. The dance could go long into the early morning hours. She wouldn't mind staying until the end if she could dance with Cal.

But she would rather be alone.

She turned to him at the same time he turned to her and asked, "Care to dance again?"

"I'd love to," she said.

Within moments, they were back on the dance floor, and she was in his arms. He pulled her closer as the first strings

of *The Cowboy Rides Away* by George Strait filled the air.
His eyes refused to allow her to look away. They swayed back
and forth as others danced around them.

They didn't speak. Cal held Dillon gently, firmly, with his
hand on her lower back. Everyone and everything faded to
nothing, leaving only the two of them, the music, and the
growing need she didn't try to ignore. It was like they were
in their own bubble. As if the night, the entire event, had been
created just for them. She stared into his eyes, seeing the
lights above them shining in them. It was, simply put, the
most romantic evening she had ever experienced.

All too soon, the song ended. She wanted to rewind things,
to have more time in Cal's arms, to stare into his stormy gray
eyes and feel the delicious things swirling within her.

He put his hand on her back and guided her silently to
the door. Others called out to her, but she didn't stop. Cal
opened the door for her at the truck and waited until she got
in before shutting it. Her hands shook as she fastened the seat
belt. He didn't look at her as he slid behind the wheel and
started the engine.

They didn't speak on the drive home. Music from the ra-
dio was the only thing that broke the silence. Dillon stared
out the passenger window as she relived their dance. Despite her many partners that night, it had been Cal who stuck
out. Because she had been dreaming of being in his arms for
some time.

Her stomach fluttered when she recalled the intensity
of his gaze and how his hand had splayed across her back,
dragging her tightly against him. She had been close enough
that she had seen the black band that ringed his irises and
the silver flecks within. Dillon replayed the dance over and
over, putting every detail to memory.

She was jerked out of her thoughts when the truck
stopped. She blinked and realized that they were at the
ranch. Dillon glanced at Cal to find him staring out the

windshield. Something had happened between them while dancing. His reaction proved it.

Finally, he turned his head to her. She only saw his silhouette in the darkness, so she couldn't tell what he was thinking or feeling. Dillon swallowed, waiting for him to say something. Instead, he got out. She released her seat belt and slid out as he came around the truck. They walked to the house together. He stood beside her beneath the porchlight as she unlocked the door. When she glanced at him, he looked behind him, his eyes moving slowly.

Dillon opened the door and stepped inside without turning on the kitchen light. Cal followed and locked the door behind him. Now was her chance. This was when she should do something. But what? Did she kiss him? Touch his chest? Tell him she wanted to do wild, erotic things to him?

All of it sounded ridiculous. Especially since she knew the worst that could happen was that he would push her away. He'd made no moves, given her no clue that he might also be interested. Staring deeply into her eyes might not mean the same thing to him as it had to her. The more she hesitated, the more she lost her nerve.

"Thank you for tonight," she whispered and walked away.

The entire walk upstairs, and as she got undressed, she silently berated herself for not taking the chance that had been there. So what if her marriage had ended in disaster? So what if she didn't have the best track record with relationships? She was alone with a gorgeous man and wanted to rip off his clothes. And he was downstairs right now. In her house.

She cleaned her face and brushed her teeth as she thought about going downstairs. What would she say? What would she do? After she'd rinsed her mouth, she looked at herself in the mirror.

"If I don't do this, I'll wonder forever," she whispered.

Dillon squared her shoulders and turned off the light as

she left the bathroom. She walked barefoot out of her room and down the hall. When she reached the stairs, she halted, shocked to see Cal at the bottom, looking up at her. His hat, vest, and boots were gone.

"Tell me I'm not crazy," he said. "Tell me you felt it."

Shivers of excitement raced over her skin. "I felt it."

He moved up one stair. "You didn't say anything."

"I was coming to talk to you."

"Talk?" he asked as he moved up two more steps.

She grinned. "There are other things we could do."

"If you only knew the things I want to do to you." He walked up a stair with every word until he was before her.

Her heart hammered wildly, her blood heating in her veins. She touched his face before combing her fingers through his hair. He groaned and wrapped his arms around her as he took the last stair and backed her to the wall.

She looked up at him, shocked and exhilarated at the desire coursing through her. Her hands were on his chest. He placed one hand on the wall beside her head and slowly lowered his until their mouths met for a brief kiss. He returned for a second, lingering longer this time. On the third, his lips moved over hers seductively, exquisitely. She sank into the kiss, into him, seeking the pleasure she knew awaited.

He pushed her against the wall, allowing her to feel his thick arousal pressing into her stomach. His tongue slid between her lips and tangled with hers. He deepened the kiss, taking her breath away. She clung to him, even as her body pulsed with need.

Dillon yanked open Cal's shirt, buttons flying everywhere. The minute her hands met warm skin, she sighed. But it wasn't enough. She pushed the garment over his shoulders, attempting to remove it. He released her long enough to yank the shirt off and toss it aside.

She was thankful the light in the hall was on, so she got to see his amazing body. Her hands moved over his firm muscles as she took in the healed wounds on his shoulders that she hadn't seen the night before. She touched every scar softly before lifting her eyes to his.

The desire in his gaze made her heart skip a beat. He cupped her face on either side and brought his head down to ravage her lips in a kiss. He left one hand in her hair, grasping tightly as his other hand traveled down her back and over her butt to cup one cheek. He ground himself against her. She grabbed his hips, holding him in place, wanting him deep inside her.

And she couldn't wait.

She reached for his pants. He lifted his head long enough to glance around, then took her hands and led her into her bedroom. She faced him, unable to believe that this was actually happening. Cal unfastened his jeans and pushed them down. When he straightened, her mouth went dry at the sight of his thick arousal jutting out.

Dillon wrapped her hand around his cock, loving the feel of the soft skin and the steel beneath. She looked up at Cal and saw his eyes darken as she moved her hand up and down his length. He groaned before claiming her lips in another fiery kiss.

Chapter 24

Cal had never craved anyone as he did Dillon. He'd never felt hunger so deep, longed so vastly.

Yearned so absolutely.

Desire had never burned this hot. The connection with Dillon was visceral, instinctual. It felt as if it had always been there, waiting until he found her to make itself known. Once it had begun to solidify, there was no backing away, no ignoring it. But he wasn't running from Dillon. He was running *to* her.

Cal moaned at the feel of her hand on his rod. He'd dreamed of her holding him in just such a way. He stared into her blue eyes and prayed that he wouldn't wake up if this was another dream. Everything felt too good, too right.

He reached between them and tugged the belt that closed her short, blush-colored satin robe. The garment fell open, giving him a glimpse of a matching gown beneath. Cal's heart thumped wildly as he gazed down at Dillon.

"So beautiful," he whispered as he gently pushed the robe over her shoulders.

She dropped her arms to her sides and let the robe pool

at her feet. Her eyes searched his as he brushed his knuckles over her cheek. He stilled when she grasped his wrist and turned her head to place her lips against his palm. Then she tugged down one thin strap of her gown, followed by the other, before shimmying her hips a couple of times and letting the slip puddle at her feet, too.

He threaded his fingers into the silky hair at the base of her neck and tilted her head back before lowering his head to hers. The instant their lips touched, desire consumed them. They were skin to skin, touching everywhere.

Cal backed her to the bed. He put a knee on the mattress and supported her with one hand at her back as he lowered her. She ended the kiss long enough to smile and move fully onto the bed before she pulled him down atop her. He moaned, his hips instinctively rocking against her.

Her nails lightly ran down his back. Cal shifted to his side and ran his hand down her body as he kissed her. Her skin was soft, her body pliable. She smelled like jasmine and heaven. He gloried in her curves as he caressed her hips, dipping in at her waist, and then moving to her amazing breasts that filled his hand.

His balls tightened when he found her nipples already hard. He rolled a turgid peak between his fingers, and hers dug into his back as she released a soft moan. He ended their kiss and gazed down at her swollen lips and the way her pulse jumped erratically at her throat. He wanted to spend hours pleasuring her.

Her eyes opened, heavy-lidded and glazed. "Please, don't stop."

"I'm not," he promised as he kissed her mouth, her cheek, and then moved to her neck, where he trailed kisses down to her breast.

Cal looked up and caught her staring at him. He held her gaze as he bent his head, wrapped his lips around her nipple and sucked. Her eyes rolled back in her head as she sighed

seductively. It was the most erotic sound he'd ever heard—
and he wanted to hear more.

He moved from one breast to the other, teasing her nipples
until she ground her hips against him, seeking release. The
need to bury himself inside her right then was so strong, he
nearly gave in. Somehow, he managed to keep control of
himself and continue learning every nuance of Dillon's
body and what made her moan.

His hand splayed over her stomach before caressing down-
ward. His fingers met the trimmed patch of hair as her legs
fell open. When he felt the wetness at her sex, his hand shook
from the force of the hunger that rolled through him.

Cal swirled his finger around her clit, slowly at first. Her
answering moan was music to his ears. He continued tanta-
lizing her, gradually increasing his speed, all the while teasing her nipple with his tongue.

A rush of hot need engulfed Dillon. She sought the pleasure
that was just out of reach, eager and impatient for it. Cal's
masterful fingers knew just how to touch her with the right
pressure. It was the most exquisite torture she'd ever endured.

And she hoped it never ended.

Her back arched, a cry falling from her lips when he suck-
led her nipple deep and quickened his finger's movements.
Just like that, he had her on the precipice of an orgasm. The
sensations coursing through her were hedonistic, decadent.
Utterly carnal.

She needed him. All of him. Inside her. She couldn't wait
any longer.

Dillon reached for him at the same time he added the
softest of pressure to his ministrations. And just like that,
pleasure surged through her with such force that it took her
breath. Ecstasy swallowed her. It wound within her, crashed
over her, rushed through her.

When she finally came back to herself, tiny spasms still

ran through her. She forced her eyes open and found Cal watching her. The need reflected in his gray eyes made her stomach flutter in excitement. He moved between her legs. Her gaze lowered to his cock, watching as he guided it to her entrance.

Then he was inside her, filling her. She dropped her head back in delight at the feel of him sliding in and out of her. She grabbed him, trying to bring him closer with each thrust of his hips. Just like his mouth and hands, he knew how to use his body to show her pleasure she'd never known.

His lips found hers, their tongues moving in time with their bodies.

Cal pumped his hips faster, pushing deeper into her each time. She wrapped her legs around his waist and rose to meet him with each thrust. Their bodies moved in a dance as old as time, but he'd never experienced anything so beautiful with another before.

He wanted to stop time. To remain in this moment for eternity—the feel of Dillon's body moving against his, her tight, wet heat clutching his cock, the way her hands moved over him. Just like with the dance, something special was happening. He couldn't see it, couldn't touch it, but he recognized that it was happening.

As he drew closer and closer to climax, he tore his lips from hers and braced his hands on either side of her head. Their eyes locked, and to his surprise, he felt her body tighten and saw her eyes widen right before she peaked. The feel of her body seizing around him shredded the last of his control. He cried out as he climaxed and buried himself deep.

Cal didn't know how long it took before he came to. He was slumped over Dillon, who traced images on his back with her fingers. He pushed himself up onto his arms to find her smiling at him.

"Well, cowboy, that was one wild ride."

He gave her a soft kiss. "I think I passed out."

"I know I did," she said with a giggle.

Cal pulled out of her and rolled to the side. She faced him, propping her head up with her hand. He moved a lock of her hair away from her face. "This may sound irrational, but I feel like I've known you my entire life."

"It's not."

"It's not?"

She shook her head, smiling softly. "I feel the same. It's . . . indescribable."

He reached over and took her hand. They threaded their fingers together. The moment was unique and amazing. He'd had his share of lovers, but no one had ever made him feel so alive.

"I've been looking for you for my entire life," he told her.

Her eyes searched his solemnly.

He glanced at their hands. "This may be the wrong time to say this, but everything about this night has been magical."

"It's not the wrong time."

Her words made him sigh in relief, but he still couldn't believe he had spoken the words. He'd never felt the need to say such things to anyone before. Then again, Dillon wasn't like any woman he'd ever known.

With her, he'd found a place that gave him hope, a way of life that eased his soul, and the stirrings of something that he feared putting into thought, much less words. He'd given up ever having a fulfilling life, and yet, here it was, waiting for him. It felt too good to be true.

His past failures made him wonder if he were worthy of seeking such a life. He wasn't exactly the epitome of accomplishment. Then again, only a fool would allow someone so precious, a woman as wonderful as Dillon, to slip through their fingers without a fight.

"What?" she asked with a smile.

He grinned and brought their hands to his lips to kiss her fingers. "I can't believe I'm here."

"I hate to tell you, but if you hadn't come upstairs, I was headed down."

"Do you always go for the things you want?"

She nodded. "Life's too short not to."

"That, it is," he mumbled, thinking of his father and the life he could've had.

She tugged on his hand. "If all of this about my ranch is too much, I understand."

"You are, without a doubt, a handful," Cal teased. Then he grew serious. "I could've walked away at any time, but I didn't. I stayed because I want to help. I can't really explain why I feel compelled to sort this out, but I do."

Dillon lowered her head to the bed. "I'm glad."

"I was thinking about my father and all the years he could've had if he'd stopped bull riding."

"You can't live someone else's life."

Cal nodded and laid his head on the bed with his arm curled underneath it. "Mom resented him for leaving her to handle things on her own."

"I can't imagine being a single mom."

He wrinkled his nose. "I didn't exactly make it easy on her."

"Did you ever call her?"

"I did," he said with a grin. "I thought she hung up on me. Turned out, she was crying."

Dillon's lips spread into a smile. "Happy tears."

"I don't think she truly believes I've given it up."

"The rodeo has been in your blood for a long time. Are you sure you *have* given it up?"

Cal thought about that for a moment. Then he nodded. "Absolutely. I'm sure you've seen the scars. A body can only handle so much before it's had enough. I've put mine through more than plenty."

"Can you tell me about the scars?"

He pointed to the one that ran from beneath his armpit to his stomach. "A bull's horn got me in my second year of riding. I didn't put my vest on properly, and the horn got between the vest and me."

"Oh, my God," she murmured.

"I've had both shoulders reconstructed. I've got pins in my left ankle from a bull landing on it and crushing it. I've lost count of how many times I've broken my collarbones. After a couple of concussions, I started wearing a helmet."

Her lips flattened. "You've not been kind to your body."

"I haven't."

"I'm sure there are more injuries, too."

He lifted one shoulder in a shrug. "I'm not sure I could remember them all."

"Yet, you still climbed on bull after bull. I'm pretty sure that's called insanity."

Cal threw back his head and laughed. "I can't disagree."

This. This is what Cal yearned for. Someone to talk to, someone to share his hopes and dreams with. Someone to laugh with.

Someone to love.

He'd finally found her, and he would be damned if someone took her from him.

Chapter 25

Hank threw his glass against the wall in a fury. Things were unraveling. He knew it.

"Calm yourself," Isaac said from the sofa.

God, how Hank detested when Isaac used that condescending voice. He wanted to turn and punch the lawyer. One day he would.

"You spoke to Cal in front of others," Isaac said. "How did you expect him to act?"

Hank spun and glared at him. "I've known Cal for years. I *know* him."

"And what is it you think you know?"

"He's not with us on this."

Isaac snorted, a bored look crossing his face. "You don't know that."

"And you don't know that he is."

"Freddy and Joshua had a long talk with him. He willingly went with them to Dillon's."

Hank fisted his hands. "He was drunk."

"Drunk or not, he agreed."

"Not if he doesn't remember it."

Isaac barked in laughter as he sat up. "Is that what this is about? You think he doesn't remember?"

"Not with how he's been acting."

"Acting. Yes, exactly. He's acting."

Hank shook his head. "You're wrong."

"I know people."

"Were you there that night?"

Isaac remained silent.

Hank felt as if he'd been kicked in the stomach by a bull.

"Oh, don't look so shocked," Isaac said with a roll of his eyes as he leaned back against the cushions. "Cal was all too willing."

"He's got innate goodness in him. Just like his father."

"Bullshit. Everyone has a price. You know that."

That rankled him. "And what, pray tell, was Cal's price?"

Isaac laughed and shook his head, glancing away. "That's between Cal and me."

"You had no right to bring him into this."

"If it weren't for me, we wouldn't be so close to getting what we want."

Hank wished he had another glass to throw. "You think we're close?" he bellowed. "We're farther away than before, all while under scrutiny from the authorities."

"Stop acting like a scared little girl. Did you kill the stallion?"

It was Hank's turn to remain silent.

Isaac's nostrils flared, his face mottling red in anger. "I told you what to do."

"No one tells me what to do on my ranch. Your people stole the fucking horse and brought it onto my land. I get to decide what to do with it. Not you."

Isaac rose to his feet. "Your idiocy will bring this plan to a grinding halt. It's just an animal. You can find another."

"You dare to get all righteous about me keeping a horse

that you stole? A theft that brought the TSCRA down on me? Shall we talk about your man, who keeps shooting at Dillon?"

"You know as well as I do that her death makes everything easier for us."

Hank drew in a breath in an effort to calm his rage. "We want the ranch. Taking a life was never what we agreed."

"I told you when I became your partner in this that we'd have to do things to speed the plan along. You readily agreed with that."

"You didn't mention murder!"

"What did you think I meant?" Isaac shouted.

Hank glared at him. "Not that."

Isaac looked away and remained silent for a moment. "You don't need to worry. Nobody will be taking any more shots at her."

"You pulled your goons away from killing her?"

Isaac chuckled. "I didn't say that."

"Who shot at her?"

With a loud sigh, Isaac turned his gaze to him. "If the authorities question you, you can't tell them what you don't know. It's better if you remain ignorant of such things."

There was truth to his words, but Hank couldn't help but feel that Isaac was leaving him out of many other things, as well—things that had nothing to do with legalities. If Isaac tried to take the entirety of Bar 4 from Hank, he'd kill the bastard with his bare hands.

"Leave Cal to me," Isaac said as he got to his feet once more. He adjusted the sleeves of his dress shirt beneath his suit jacket. "I still can't believe you go to that ridiculous dance every year."

"That get-together started over a hundred years ago."

"I don't care if Jesus himself brought it into being."

Hank crossed his arms over his chest. "What do you find so foul about it?"

"Everything."

"You sure it isn't just because you can't dance?"

Isaac's head snapped to him, his gaze shooting daggers. Hank bit back a smile. He liked when he managed to hit one of Isaac's nerves. And this one was a big one.

"Stop freaking out over every little thing. I've got this handled," Isaac stated as he walked out the door.

Hank ran his hand through his hair as he roamed his house. It was empty and silent. He hated the silence. He'd wanted to talk to Isaac, so he'd declined female company. He could still call a couple of women who were regular lovers, but he wasn't in the mood. But the longer he walked through his big, silent home, the more he hated the quiet.

He grabbed his phone and dialed a number. She answered on the second ring. "You busy?" he asked.

Chet Thompson walked into the motel room with a sigh. He was no closer to finding Dillon Young's stallion than when he'd first arrived, but his gut told him that the horse was on Hank Stephen's ranch. The problem was proving it.

He sank slowly onto the mattress, his old bones creaking. He missed his bed. More than that, he missed his wife. She would've given him a piece of her mind at what he'd been eating since arriving here. That made him smile. She had always tried to get him to eat healthily, and he did—for the most part. But it wasn't always easy during an investigation.

After removing his boots, he pushed off the bed and laid his hat upside down on the desk. He rubbed his eyes and pulled out the file that had the photos of the tracks, proving the stallion had been stolen. He compared them to the ones taken at Dillon's house after the shooting. Chet didn't know what he was looking for, but he hoped there was something there to be found.

He'd looked at the same photos every night for four days and still hadn't found anything. But years on the job told him that they were connected. He pulled out the desk chair and sank into it. Then he opened his laptop, where he kept his notes for the TSCRA that he uploaded straight to them.

Chet read over the notes covering the past few days but had nothing new to add. Still, he was restless. There was no point in going to bed because he knew he wouldn't sleep. It was better if he used the time wisely instead of staring at the ceiling.

He dug into his briefcase and pulled out a lined yellow legal tablet, writing down everything that had happened to Dillon Young over the course of the last year. One could argue that some of the minor accidents had been just that, but a closer look revealed that others had been done on purpose—like the tractor's brake line being cut.

Thanks to Dillon, he had pictures of the line, showing the clean cut and not the fraying that would occur if it had degraded on its own. While that didn't directly point to Hank Stephens, there wasn't anyone else interested in the ranch.

Then there was Cal Bennett. Chet didn't want to like him, but damn if he didn't. Cal didn't just sound and appear honest, he had been the one to come to Dillon's aid on two separate occasions—the two most dangerous ones. The problem was, Chet still didn't know how Cal had come to be on Dillon's ranch.

If he could find the answer to that question, there was a good chance it would lead to uncovering a lot more.

Chet ran a hand down his face and sat back in the chair. This is when he'd talk to his wife about it. She'd always had a way of seeing things from angles that he hadn't considered. Missing her would never get easier, no matter how many years passed.

He put aside thoughts of his wife and returned to the present issue. Hank Stephens had money and connections. He wasn't the sort of man to get his hands dirty in case things went sideways. He'd hire others.

As Chet was thinking, his gaze landed on his notes where he'd written down that Dillon had received offers for the ranch from Hank, but Stephens hadn't sent them himself. Dillon had said they had come from an attorney.

Chet sat up and shuffled through his papers. Unfortunately, he didn't have any documents stating what firm had sent the offers. He made a note to himself to get that information from Dillon in the morning. Chet tapped his finger on the desk, hating that he didn't have the information now.

Then, he suddenly had an idea. He searched local law firms to see if any might claim Hank Stephens or the Ivy Ridge Ranch as clients. It didn't take him long to find exactly what he was looking for.

"Gotcha," he said with a smile as he stared at a picture of a Latinx gentleman named Isaac Gomez.

The name sounded familiar. He pulled out the small notebook he always carried in his pocket and flipped through the pages until he found it. Cal had mentioned a man named Isaac Gomez. Based on his notes, Cal had told Chet that he'd left Ike's bar with two men and that the bartender had said that one of them worked for Gomez.

"*There's* the connection," Chet said into the room.

He wanted to know the name of the man who worked for Gomez. If they took Cal out to Dillon's ranch, then that placed them at the scene for the stallion's theft.

Chet tossed down the notebook and scratched his extended belly. He would have to tread carefully. Locating the two men who'd driven Cal away from the bar wouldn't be easy. Cal hadn't gotten their names, and it wasn't as if Gomez or Stephens would readily hand that information over if Chet asked. And he wouldn't. If he did, it would alert them, making Gomez or Stephens tell the two men to disappear.

He rose and paced the room. His ankles were swollen again. Too much salt. But how was a man to enjoy a meal if it didn't have salt? Chet missed the days when his body didn't creak and hurt. His stomach rumbled. He took out a bag of peanuts from his briefcase—salted, of course. He'd always hidden the snacks in his bag, thinking his wife wouldn't know. But she always had.

Chet smiled, even as he opened the bag and dumped the peanuts into his hand before putting them into his mouth. His mind kept tripping up when going over why the minor accidents with Dillon had suddenly escalated to attempted murder. There was a reason.

"The ranch," he said as it suddenly dawned on him.

Hank wanted the land badly enough that he had made four very generous offers, but it wasn't until after Dillon refused that the accidents had begun to happen. When that didn't cow her, they'd upped the ante by stealing Legacy. But shooting at her? That seemed out of place. Almost like two different people were after her.

"Son of a bitch," Chet mumbled.

Chapter 26

Dillon opened her eyes and smiled when she felt Cal's body pressed against her from behind. He had his arm draped over her waist. It had been a long time since she'd had someone in her bed, and she had to admit, she liked Cal there.

Her smile widened when she thought of his words from the night before. They had taken her by surprise. Then again, it wasn't every day that a handsome cowboy told her that he'd been searching his entire life for her. She sighed, remembering how tender their loving had been. How earth-shattering her orgasm. How fiery their passion.

This kind of thing didn't happen to her. She wanted to believe that it was real, but her past made her question things. It wasn't that Dillon didn't think she was worthy. It was simply that she'd never expected to feel the crazy, wonderful, indescribable emotions.

Cal sucked in a breath and pulled her tighter against him. "Good morning, beautiful."

My God. How was she to stand against his sexy voice deepened with sleep? She turned in his arms to look at him. She smiled at the growth of whiskers on his face and his half-open eyes. "Good morning to you."

"What? I don't get a *handsome* or anything?" he teased.

She laughed and smoothed locks of his dark blond hair from his face. "Good morning, handsome."

"Much better," he said with a crooked smile. He gave her a soft kiss. "No regrets?"

Dillon shook her head. "Not a one."

"Me, neither."

"The day awaits us."

He groaned and placed kisses over her face. "We could stay in bed."

"Don't tempt me."

"That's exactly what I want to do."

She pushed him back and looked into his gray eyes. "Trust me. I want a day in bed with you. We'll have it soon."

He sobered instantly. "What's on your mind?"

"I think we need to dig into what's so valuable about my ranch."

"Some would say the land is valuable enough."

She shivered as he ran his fingers slowly down her side. "I'd rather know exactly what Hank wants."

"He spoke to me last night."

That got her attention. "What did he say?"

"He tried to make me believe that he wasn't part of Legacy's theft."

"Figures," she said with a roll of her eyes.

Cal's fingers moved down to her hip. "I didn't believe him. I asked him how I got onto your land, but he said he didn't have a clue. I didn't believe that, either."

"Is that all he said?"

Cal's gaze briefly slid away. "It was—"

"Tell me," she interrupted.

He took her hand in his. "Hank made a comment that it was time you found a man, implying that a woman couldn't run a ranch properly."

"Chauvinistic pig," she spat.

"I told him you were doing a fine job."

She smiled at Cal. "Did you really?"

"Yep. Because I believe it."

Dillon leaned forward and placed her lips on his for a lingering kiss. "Thank you," she whispered.

"If you don't want me to ravish you, then you'd better get out of bed now."

She hesitated, wondering if he was serious. When he reached for her, she shrieked in laughter and rolled out of bed, his hands just missing her. Dillon ran to the end of the bed and looked back at him. Cal was on his knees, his arousal thick and hard as it jutted from between his legs.

"Don't look at me like that unless you want to be late this morning," he warned as he moved toward her.

She wanted nothing more than to have more private time with Cal, but the problems surrounding her needed to be addressed first. Then, she'd get all the time she wanted with him.

"You're still here," he said in a voice that was low and filled with need.

Dillon lifted her chin. "I wanted to give you one more look. It'll have to last until tonight."

"You minx," he said with a smile as he jumped from the bed.

She laughed and hurried into the bathroom. She tried to close the door, but he managed to push it open. Then he had her pressed against the wall, his mouth on hers as he rocked his hips against her. She was powerless to resist his kisses— or the feel of his hard cock.

Yet, it was Cal who ended the kiss. He closed his eyes, his chin to his chest, and his hands against the wall on either side of her head. He breathed heavily, and for several moments, he didn't move.

Finally, he lifted his head. "Just so you know, the minute work is done, I'm going to throw you over my shoulder and bring you up here, strip you out of your clothes, and make you scream with pleasure."

Her sex clenched just thinking about it. "Promise?"

"Yeah. And I keep my promises."

He gave her another soft kiss before pushing away from the wall and walking away. Dillon leaned her head back and closed her eyes. Maybe she was a fool for not taking the chance she had with Cal while it was there. She'd been shot at twice, yet somehow, miraculously, hadn't been struck. Nothing had happened for four days, but that could be because whoever wanted her dead was attempting to lull her into thinking it was over.

She wasn't that stupid. They hadn't given up. They would come for her one way or another. And that scared the hell out of her. It was easy to stay in the safety of Cal's arms and pretend that everything was as it should be in the world. But that was a coward's way out, and she most definitely wasn't a coward.

Dillon readied herself for the day and went downstairs. She found Cal waiting for her with a smile and an already heated breakfast sandwich and some coffee.

"Careful," she warned, "I could get used to this."

He winked at her. "Why do you think I'm doing it?"

It was bad enough that Cal was movie-star handsome. When he added his special kind of charm, she didn't stand a chance.

"I'm going to be doing some work in my office today," she told him.

Cal raised his brows. "I'll install the cameras."

She was taken aback. "Cameras? When did you get those?"

"Found them in the barn. They were in a box. Most are game cameras, but there *are* two regular ones."

Dillon chewed a bite of her sandwich and swallowed. "I had no idea. Will it be difficult to get them installed?"

"I don't foresee an issue."

"Should we tell everyone we have them?"

Cal hesitated as he finished the last of his breakfast. "If we do, that could prevent someone from coming onto the property—or at least close to the house."

"And if we don't?"

"Then we have a good chance of catching whoever is responsible."

Dillon glanced out the window. "This is going to sound horrible, but I don't want anyone but you and me to know."

"Not even Emmett or Dusty?"

She shook her head.

"Your ranch, your call," Cal said.

"You don't agree?"

He covered her hand with his. "You've been through a lot, and you have no idea who to trust. There's nothing wrong with wanting to keep this information to yourself. Though, there's one other person you might want to consider notifying."

"Who?"

"Chet."

She nodded as she considered Cal's words. "I trust him. He's not from here. But that doesn't mean Hank doesn't have him in his pocket like he does the sheriff."

"I don't think so. That's not to say I haven't been fooled a few times. But, generally, if you look hard enough, you can see a person's true colors. I think the ranger is trustworthy."

Dillon wiped her hands as she finished her meal. "Then I'll contact Chet and let him know once you have the cameras installed."

"There are six game cameras and two regulars. Where would you like them?"

She scratched her head as she moved to a window and looked out at the ranch. "The game cameras are meant to be hidden. Camouflaged, right?"

"That's right."

"One at the main entrance of the ranch and one at the back. One at the front of the house. I want the remaining three facing Hank's land. I know they won't be able to see everything, but we'll have to find the best locations."

Cal came up beside her. "And the two regular cameras?"

She turned her head to him. "One facing the barn and as much of the paddocks as possible. I want the other facing the back of the house."

"All the cameras are wireless and battery-operated, so they should go up easily. I'll still need to drill a few places for the cameras to the barn and house. The one along the fence line with Ivy Ridge will require more time."

She spotted Dusty and Emmett saddling their horses for the day. "We'll be alone here for a bit, which should make it easy for you to install the cameras. After lunch, we'll go for a ride to check the fences and put up the others."

"I won't be far," he told her. "If you see or hear anything, let me know."

Dillon smiled and grabbed his belt loop to pull him close. She gave him a kiss. "Promise," she whispered and walked away.

As she reached the kitchen door, she looked over her shoulder to find Cal staring at her, his eyes smoldering with hunger. She flashed him a smile.

"You're going to pay for that," he promised with a wink.

Dillon stopped and watched him leave the house. Her smile faded. Precautions were being taken. She just hoped it would be enough. She was glad that Cal had found the cameras, but she wished they had been discovered much earlier. High-profile ranches like Hank's had expensive security systems with surveillance everywhere. It wasn't something Dolly had ever looked into. At least, that's what Dillon had been led to believe.

She had never spoken with her aunt about such things

when Dolly had been alive. It was Emmett who had told her that Dolly had just never gotten around to such things. That didn't make sense to Dillon since she knew that her aunt had been meticulous in running the ranch. Putting up cameras would've been expensive, but they would've saved the ranch money in the long run. That was definitely something Dolly would've undertaken. Now that Cal had found the cameras, it was obvious that Dolly had taken the first steps.

But why hadn't they been put up? Why hadn't Emmett known about them?

There were too damn many questions. Dillon was tired of them. She wanted some answers. She pivoted and stalked to the office and one of two five-drawer filing cabinets in the corner. Metal squealed when she pulled open a drawer, causing her to flinch. The metal filing cabinets were old, but they did their job.

After Dolly's death, Dillon had been a bit overwhelmed with where to begin on the ranch. She had divided her time between her duties outside and inside, but she'd soon found that things were much easier when she was with the horses and cattle. Sorting through Dolly's books, files, notes, and documents on the computer was something Dillon was still doing, a year later.

Her priority had been keeping up with the accounting, and while she continued to use the CPA Dolly had chosen, Dillon was in charge of the household and ranch bills. Her aunt had kept detailed records, which made it easy for Dillon to step right in. However neat and orderly Dolly may have been, she had a habit of keeping everything.

Dillon had recycled hundreds of old magazines and newspapers that Dolly had never thrown out. As time allowed, Dillon had been going through cabinets, boxes, and such that held any papers. Anything to do with the ranch had been kept. Dillon had even kept receipts, just in case.

She recalled scanning the documents in the filing cabinet one time and seeing a file labeled *LAND RIGHTS*. Dillon pulled open drawer after drawer but couldn't locate the file. A knot formed in the pit of her stomach as she slowly closed the last drawer.

Just to be sure she hadn't overlooked it, she went through the two cabinets again—and came up empty just as before.

Dillon was sure the file had been there. With the knot growing by the minute, she spent the next thirty minutes looking through everything in the office to find it. Only when she was certain it was gone did she reach for her phone and call her lawyer in Dallas.

Les Ackers answered quickly, his Texas accent smooth and cheery. "Hi, Dillon. What can I do for you?"

"Land rights to the Bar 4. Do you have a copy of those?"

"I should. Let me see . . ."

Dillon heard papers shuffling in the background. Then keys pressed on a keyboard.

"Is everything okay?" Les asked, worry beginning to darken his voice.

Dillon licked her dry lips. "I don't know."

"Do I need to be concerned?"

"I don't know."

"That statement doesn't make me feel better about this call."

Dillon drew in a breath. "Do you have copies of the rights?"

"I do."

"Can you send a scanned copy to me immediately?"

"One sec," Les said. He covered the phone and called for his administrative assistant to give her details before getting back on the phone. "Okay. Tell me everything."

Dillon rubbed her forehead. One of the things she liked about Les was that he was respected among his peers and was there for his clients completely. He might only be in his mid-thirties, but he was one of the most sought-after attorneys in Dallas. "It's going to take a while, so get comfortable and take notes."

Twenty-six minutes later, Les let out a long sigh. "Shit. What the hell are you still doing at the ranch? Leave. Immediately. Forget the damn horse. Your life is more important."

"This is my home."

"That you won't have if these assholes succeed in killing you," he stated bluntly. "You should have those land records. Please tell me you have them."

Dillon propped her elbows on the desk and dropped her head into one hand as she held the phone with the other. "I can't find them."

"Has someone been in the house?"

"You mean has anyone broken in? No. Have I had people here? Yes. Because of the shooting. I also leave the house unlocked during the day while I'm working. Anyone who works for me has access."

"But you can't find the deeds you've seen, which leads me to believe that someone took them."

Dillon squeezed her eyes shut. Only three people had access to the house other than her—Emmett, Dusty . . . and Cal. It was possible that a stranger could've stolen them. She had been shot at, after all. But her instincts told her that it was someone she knew.

"I think I should come down there," Les said.

She sat up straight and opened her eyes. "I told you what a tangle things are. How will your arrival make it better?"

"It'd be someone else looking out for you. You need people you can trust."

Dillon thought she *had* people she could trust. Now, she wasn't so sure. Her heart was already tumbling headlong for Cal. Unfortunately, he was the only new addition to the ranch. And had come on at the same time the deeds had gone missing.

Was he a part of this?

Had his arrival been planned?

Was he here specifically to make it look as if he'd saved her so that she would trust him?

Every question made her stomach sour even more.

"You should have an email with the deed to the land." Les's voice broke into her thoughts.

She checked and found an email from Les. After she clicked on the attachments, she looked over the documents. "I own the land and mineral rights."

"That's right. Your aunt got the mineral rights to the Bar 4 about five years ago."

Dillon slowly sat back in the chair. "I know Dolly kept the same CPA, but she changed lawyers a few times. Most I've found have either been in Dallas or Houston. How would I find if she had used someone local?"

"Let me do some digging. I'll be back in touch."

"Les," she said before he could hang up, "if something happens to me, can you do anything to make sure that Hank Stephens and Isaac Gomez can't get their hands on the ranch?"

He sighed. "Regrettably, no. Once the beneficiaries of your will take over, it's out of my hands."

"Then let's change my will. I want you to have the land."

"Whoa. Hold on. Why would you do that?"

Dillon glanced out her window when she saw movement. Her gaze landed on Cal, who positioned a ladder to install a camera. "Whatever is here is apparently worth killing for. I don't want them getting their hands on it."

"Give me fifteen and I'll send over the amended last will and testament. I don't like this, Dillon. Any of it."

"Me, neither, but until I can figure out what they want to kill me for, I've got to take steps."

"Your steps should include getting your ass out of town," he retorted.

Dillon couldn't help but smile. "Thanks, Les. I'll get the revised will back to you immediately."

When the call disconnected, Dillon waited at the computer for the document to hit her inbox. She couldn't remember the last time she had looked at the land records in the filing cabinet. It had been months—possibly a year, at least. Someone could've come in at any time and taken them. It might not have been Cal.

But what if it was?

Her heart didn't want to think about what that meant. So, she pulled up the land documents again and printed them out. As she studied them, she saw a law firm in Dallas in the header.

Dillon quickly placed the call. After explaining who she was and what she was looking at, they connected her to a Walter Jessup. He answered with a slight quaver in his voice, pronouncing him as an older gentleman.

"Mr. Jessup, my name is Dillon Young. I inherited land from my aunt, Dolly Young."

Walter chuckled. "Ah, Dolly. She was certainly something. Kept me on my toes."

"She did that with everyone."

"I'm sorry to hear that she passed. Do you mind if I ask when it happened?"

"A little over a year ago."

Walter made a grunting sound. "How?"

"The coroner listed it as natural causes. They believe she had a heart attack."

Leather creaked through the phone. "I see."

Something in his tone bothered Dillon. "What's wrong?"

"It's probably nothing. What can I do for you, Ms. Young?"

"Dillon, please. I wanted to know about the mineral rights my aunt got. The land has been in the family for generations.

Why did she suddenly decide to make sure the rights were in her name?"

"You must not have seen the mineral surveys."

"What surveys?"

Leather creaked again. "Give me your email. I'll have them sent to you."

Chapter 27

Cal knew something was wrong the moment Dillon walked out of the house. He tried to talk to her, but she seemed lost in thought. He left her alone, sticking close, just in case. She spent some time with the mares and their foals until lunch.

She barely spoke during the noon meal. Cal wanted to push her to see what had happened, but he decided to leave it until they were on the ride. Whatever had happened, it had affected her greatly. She no longer had an easy smile for him. In fact, she barely looked his way.

"Did you speak to Emmett?" she asked as they walked from the house to the stables.

Cal glanced at her. "Briefly. I told him what you said we were doing after lunch. He said he and Dusty would be back around one."

Dillon nodded absently. She got her horse and brought the mare to the hitching post before brushing the black down. Cal became more worried by the minute. He chose his horse, a gray gelding, and brushed him. When he went to get a saddle, Dillon was already in the tack room.

She pointed. "Take that one. It'll fit you better than the others. It was my grandfather's."

"It's yours. I'll be okay on one of the others."

Dillon shrugged and met his gaze. "It's a bigger saddle. Honestly, it's too big for me. I use it because it was Dolly's."

Cal shrugged and grabbed a bridle as well as the blanket and saddle that sat atop it. He returned to the gray and put the saddle atop the hitching post's railing. Then he set the saddle blanket atop the gelding before putting the saddle on. The moment he did, the horse neighed and sidestepped.

Cal immediately grabbed the horse's lead rope with one hand and calmly stroked him with the other. "Easy boy," he said in a mellow tone.

"Skylar has never done that," Dillon said.

Cal glanced behind him to see her holding her saddle, watching him and the horse. "He was fine until I put on the saddle."

The horse calmed, but Cal still wasn't satisfied. He removed the saddle and blanket and walked the horse around for a bit. The gelding didn't act out again. Cal returned him to the hitching post and tried the blanket and saddle once more. This time, the horse didn't so much as bat an eye.

"That was odd," Dillon said as she cinched the saddle to her mare.

Cal shrugged. He took his time tightening the saddle and adjusting the stirrups to fit his legs. Only then did he slip the bridle over the gelding's head. Dillon was on her mare, waiting for him by the time Cal put his foot in the stirrup and swung his leg over.

No sooner had he sank down in the saddle than Skylar let out a high-pitched scream and began to buck. It was only pure instinct born of years atop bulls that kept Cal from flying off. He kept his heels down and tried to pull back on the reins to keep the gelding's head up so he couldn't buck, but the horse was having none of it. Cal knew he had to get off or chance being thrown.

Cal kicked his feet free of the stirrups and put his hand

on the saddle's pommel to protect his stomach. He used his hand on the pommel to brace himself and kicked his right leg over the back of the horse, pushing away and releasing the reins. Cal landed on his feet as Skylar continued bucking as if his life depended on it.

Dillon leaned low over her mare's neck and nudged her into a run to catch up with the gelding. She managed to get a hold of the gray's reins, but it didn't do any good. The horse continued bucking for another few moments before he finally calmed down.

Cal waited for them while Dillon led Skylar back to the stables. The first thing Cal did was loosen the cinches and remove the saddle. The gelding was breathing hard, his eyes wild. Dillon dismounted from the mare and came up on the gray's other side to try and calm him. They exchanged a worried glance before Cal lifted the saddle away. He looked the saddle over carefully before placing it on the hitching post but found nothing that would harm the horse. Then he lifted the saddle blanket to inspect it. He saw nothing against the beige material until he ran his hand down the middle of it.

"Shit," he bit out as he jerked his hand away. There, stuck in his palm was a burr.

Dillon's face paled. "Oh, my God."

Cal found three more of the prickly annoyances. He pulled them off and tossed them into a trash can before returning to Skylar. "I'm sorry, boy. No wonder you were bucking."

He led the horse to a paddock and released him. When he turned around, Dillon stood before him.

"That's my saddle."

He nodded slowly. "I know."

Her blue eyes searched his. "I didn't do this. I know it looks like it, but I didn't. I honestly thought the saddle would fit you better. I—"

"It's okay," he said over her.

"It's not." Her eyes filled with tears. "It's not okay at all. I used the saddle and blanket the other day, and it didn't have any burrs. I always use it."

He ran a hand down his face. "Then someone put them there, hoping you would be injured when you saddled your mare."

She stood there silently.

"I didn't do it." He hoped that she knew that, but he felt compelled to say the words.

She sniffed and looked away.

Cal's heart sank. "Dillon, look at me. Please," he added when she didn't comply.

Her gaze slid back to him.

"I don't know what happened in your office this morning to upset you. All I've tried to do since being here is help."

"I don't know who to trust anymore."

Cal really wanted to know what was going on. It killed him not to ask, but he knew she wouldn't tell him. He also realized how bad this likely looked for him. "And I'm the only one who's been around the barn this morning. If I had put the burrs there, I wouldn't have used the saddle."

"I want to believe you."

"Do you still want to put up the cameras?"

She glanced in the direction they had been headed. He could well imagine her thinking of doing it on her own. All Cal could hope for was that she wouldn't go out alone—not after the attempted murders and now the burrs.

"The ones by the house will have to do," she said.

"I can show you how they work."

Dillon took a step back. "I can figure it out on my own."

Cal could feel the distance growing between them, and he didn't know how to stop it. That's when he realized that she thought he was the culprit for everything. Not that he blamed her. Things had taken a dramatic turn since his arrival. Hell, if he were in her shoes, he'd think the same thing.

"And me?" he asked. "What do you want me to do? Because it's obvious you don't want me near you."

She took another step back. "I'd like you to leave."

Five words he'd prayed she wouldn't say. What the hell had happened? There was so much he wanted to say, to do. Instead, he nodded. "I'll get my things and leave immediately."

"I'd appreciate that."

Cal couldn't believe this was happening. After their night together, he couldn't understand what had gone wrong. His legs were wooden as he walked away. The entire way to the bunkhouse, he kept trying to come up with something to say to Dillon that would change her mind. He needed to be there to keep her safe. Surely, she knew that.

Once in the bunkhouse, he packed up what few belongings he had before getting into his truck and driving to the main house. Dillon stood on the porch with his toiletry bag and clothes from the night before in hand. He put the truck in park and slowly got out to walk to the porch.

"Dillon," he started.

She handed him the items and stepped back. "Good luck."

When she wouldn't look at him, he turned on his heel and tossed the items into his truck. He took a deep breath, hoping like hell this was a nightmare he'd wake from. Then he put the truck in gear and drove away. As he left, he looked in his rearview mirror to see Dusty and Emmett riding up, and Dillon going out to greet them.

Cal had thought he'd found his place at the ranch. He thought he'd found his future and so much more. But it had been yanked away from him. He was numb as he turned on the road and headed into town. He wasn't sure where to go, but he knew he wasn't leaving the area. Not yet. Not until he stopped whoever was after Dillon.

So many thoughts went through Cal's head as he drove.

He passed Ike's, and a part of him wanted to go in for a drink so he could drown his sorrows. But that was how all of this had begun. He wouldn't do that again.

Cal pulled into the motel parking lot and got a room with what little money he had left. As he walked up to his door and put the key in, he heard his name. He looked over to find none other than Chet Thompson.

"What are you doing here?" the ranger asked.

Cal looked away, not wanting to say the words because saying them would make them real.

"I see," Chet mumbled.

Cal just wanted to be alone. "Can I help you with something?"

"Actually, I believe you can."

Cal perked up. "Tell me this is about Dillon's case."

The ranger grinned. "Now that I have your attention, first tell me what you're doing here."

"I don't know exactly. Something happened this morning. Dillon was by herself in the office, and I was putting up some security cameras. She didn't want anyone else to know but me and you. Then she came outside, and she was visibly upset. She wouldn't talk about it. We had a silent lunch, then got the horses ready to put up some more cameras along the fence line near Hank's place. She wanted me to use her saddle because she said it would fit me better. I did, but someone had put burrs under the blanket, and it caused the horse to buck."

Chet crossed his arms over his chest. "You don't look any worse for wear. I take it you got off without an issue."

"It was close, but I managed to get away before the gelding could throw me."

"I'm guessing Dillon thought you put the burrs there."

Cal nodded.

Chet huffed out a breath. "Some might think she did it if she wanted you to use the saddle."

"She didn't," Cal stated.

The ranger's brows shot up. "You're that sure, are you?"

"I am. That's not the kind of person she is."

"You barely know her."

Cal shrugged. "I know what I know."

"I agree. Did she fire you?"

"In a manner of speaking."

"That might actually help."

Cal frowned in confusion. "What are you talking about?"

"Come with me, and I'll explain everything."

Chapter 28

The day dragged on, moving painfully slow. Dillon tried three separate times to saddle a horse so she could ride out and put up the other game cameras. But every time she even thought about going out on her own, the sound of the bullet ricocheting off the rock near her went through her mind. On the heels of that were the shots fired into her kitchen.

Dillon shook uncontrollably each time those memories assaulted her. She hated the fear that had nestled comfortably within her. Panic immobilized her. She feared being killed. She feared losing Cal forever. She feared his betrayal. She feared losing everything.

Worse, she found herself looking for Cal, seeking his security and the comfort she'd found in his arms.

Only to remember what had led to her demanding he leave her property—and her life.

Despite her order, she wasn't sure that he was involved. Nor could she be sure that he wasn't. He had a connection to Hank, and everything had started with Cal's arrival. It was only natural for her to blame him. She could've demanded to look through his things for the deeds, but who was to say that he hadn't given them to someone else?

Why hadn't she looked through his things? Because she hadn't wanted to know. For a short while, she had found happiness she'd never thought could be hers. Even now, she wanted to call Cal because she had felt safe with him. Yet . . . so much doubt lingered about his loyalty that it prevented her from contacting him.

Dillon had gone over all of this a million times, yet she was no closer to having an answer than when she'd gotten off the phone with Dolly's attorney, Walter Jessup. Her call to him had given her a wealth of information, the most important being that the Bar 4 ranch sat atop a blue topaz mine. When Walter told her that, she had known instantly why Hank wanted her ranch so badly.

Somehow, she'd managed to do her work, though she looked over her shoulder constantly. Everything took twice as long because terror had her in its grip. Emmett and Dusty steered clear of her, and she was thankful. The last thing she wanted was for anyone to ask her where Cal was.

It was much earlier than usual when she finally ended her day. She'd had all she could handle and sought the comfort of her home. Dillon went to each window, shutting the blinds and closing the curtains, making sure there wasn't even the tiniest of cracks to see through. Then she went upstairs to take a shower.

The moment she entered her room, her gaze went to the bed, the sheets still rumpled from her night with Cal. Anger—at him for betraying her, at herself for being so stupid as to fall for him—welled up, choking her. Dillon strode to the bed and yanked the duvet to the floor. Tears clouded her eyes as she pulled at the sheets while memories flashed in her mind of the tender, amazing night she'd spent in Cal's arms.

"Ahhhhh!" she screamed as she got the last corner of the sheet off.

She wadded up the material and tossed it toward the door, where it landed with a soft *thump*. Dillon covered her face with her hands and sank onto the bed. The more she tried to hold back the tears, the faster they came. Finally, she gave in and let the dam break.

She curled on her side, bringing her knees up to her chest as she placed one palm on the mattress, unable to hold back the memories of Cal—or the feelings that had begun to grow for him.

Was she destined to continue giving her heart to the wrong men? Had she done something in a past life to be punished in such a heinous fashion? What was it that made her fall for men who had the potential to destroy her life? Why? Why did it have to be Cal?

Dillon opened her mouth with a silent scream as the tears came faster. She thought herself a keen businesswoman, but she continued to fail at relationships. Although, was this one her fault? It had barely even begun. Besides, he was the one who had betrayed her. She'd merely managed to find out before he could do more. And to think . . . she had trusted him completely. She had even invited him into her home. Her *bed*!

She sniffed and rolled onto her back to look up at the ceiling. It didn't matter how magical the night before had been, she had discovered Cal's true colors. They had been there all along. She was the one who had chosen not to see them. She was the fool.

Dillon wiped at her eyes and parted her lips so she could breathe since her nose was now clogged. She wiped at her face, then got up from the bed and removed her clothes. After a quick shower, she drew a bath. She reclined in the water, her mind drifting from one thought to another, like frogs hopping from lily pad to lily pad. Only when her skin began to wrinkle did she rise from the water.

She toweled off, uncaring that her hair, wet from the shower, was drying without product. Dillon put on a pair of lounge pants and a tank top and left the room without looking

at the unmade bed. She turned off the lights, figuratively closing the door on Cal and the memories of their night together.

Dillon stood facing the open fridge for ten minutes, trying to find something that sounded good to eat. She gave up
and sat on the sofa, but no matter how many channels she
looked through, she couldn't find anything that held her attention. She finally gave up and tossed the remote aside, uncaring what was on the television. She reclined on the couch
and stared at the far wall until she heard her alarm the next
morning.

She leaned over to the coffee table and turned off the
alarm. Even though she told herself not to look, she checked
her texts. There was nothing from Cal, and that only made
her feel worse. Dillon dropped her head back onto the arm
of the sofa. She had only spent days with Cal. Yet, somehow,
he'd made a bigger impact on her life than the years she'd
spent with her husband. How was that even possible?

There was no way she could feel more for Cal than she
had her ex. It wasn't feasible. Sure, they might have said it
felt as if they had known each other for their entire lives, but
that was just a saying. Wasn't it?

The more she thought about it, the more unsure she was.
From the instant Cal had opened his eyes after she'd cocked
the shotgun, until he had driven away the day before, she
hadn't been able to shake the feeling that it had been predes-
tined for him to come into her life when she needed someone the most.

She had trusted him—more than Emmett or anyone.
Dillon no longer believed her instincts were reliable. How
could she after being so wrong about Cal? All this time,
she had believed that he'd saved her from being shot. Now,
she couldn't help but think that maybe it was all a setup to
ingratiate himself to her.

And it had worked.

Had he not pushed her to the side and prevented the bullet

from reaching her, she would've sent him packing. The fact that he had pulled her to safety had prompted her to hire him. That and the fact that she needed the help.

"I'm such a damn fool," she murmured and squeezed her eyes shut.

A man never would've fallen for that. But send in a good-looking cowboy with a charming smile and eyes that looked through to her soul, and Dillon had all but handed him her ranch on a silver platter.

The more Dillon thought about it, the angrier she became. After everything Dolly had sacrificed to keep the ranch. After all she had sacrificed. Dillon couldn't believe she had come so close to losing it all because of a man.

Dillon rolled to a sitting position and shoved her hair out of her face. She pushed to her feet and trudged up the stairs for clothes. Her eyes stung from the tears and lack of sleep. She made the mistake of rubbing them, which only made them burn worse. Every blink was like sandpaper. She dug through her medicine cabinet and found an old bottle of eye drops. Dillon tilted her head back and squeezed a couple of beads into each eye.

Then she stood there with her eyes closed, letting the medicine take effect. When she next opened her eyes, they felt marginally better. She blew out a breath, puffing her cheeks as she put a glob of toothpaste on her brush and cleaned her teeth. Once that chore was finished, she removed her clothes and dressed for the day. She raked her fingers through her hair and French braided it to get it off her neck.

As she walked out of the bedroom, her eyes skated to the bed. An image of her and Cal waking up the previous morning, laughing and talking, popped into her mind. She shoved it aside and hurried out of the room in a bid to outrun the memories.

The thought of food turned her stomach, but Dillon knew herself well enough to know that she needed some kind of sustenance to get through her day. She opted for some toast with peach jam. It took her longer than she wanted to get the toast down, and she used a large cup of English breakfast tea to help.

When she was finished, she dusted off her hands, put on her hat, and released a long breath. "This is my ranch. I can walk out there and do my job. I'm not afraid of anyone."

She repeated the mantra three more times. However, her hand still shook when she opened the door and walked out. She spotted Dusty near the barn. He nodded to her. Dillon returned the gesture and headed his way to start her day. She would not allow fear to control her again.

Every step was a small victory, but she knew she would have to overcome much more.

"Mornin', boss," Dusty said.

She forced a smile. "Good morning."

"Do you know where Emmett is?"

"I've not seen him this morning." Dillon checked her cell phone and saw a text from him. "He said he's on the east side of the property checking the fence."

Dusty frowned. "Without me?"

"Guess he figured he could do it alone."

Dusty shrugged and then grinned. "Guess I'm all yours today."

"You know the drill," Dillon said as she began letting the horses out of their stalls for the day.

The hours crawled by, once again. The routine helped. She continued looking around, expecting to see someone with a gun aimed at her. She thought she heard Cal's voice a few times, only to remember that he wasn't there—and why. Her anger and heartache grew each time. Her aunt had always warned her not to become a bitter person, but Dillon wasn't sure she could get past all of this. It was too personal.

She was in the middle of working with one of the foals when she heard a vehicle door close. Her head snapped up as her heart raced. She hurried to the fence to crane her neck and see the garage. That's when she spotted Chet Thompson's Ford truck. A moment later, the ranger came into view.

"Howdy," he said with a smile.

Dillon waved as her heartbeat returned to normal. "Give me a sec." She took several deep breaths and finished up with the foal before leaving the paddock to walk to Chet. "Please tell me you have some news."

"Searching Ivy Ridge will take time."

"Time Hank could have already used to move Legacy off his land and to somewhere else."

Chet stared at her for a moment. "I know you're anxious."

"I'm pissed," she stated, her hands on her hips. "He stole my horse, and he's doing everything he can to keep Legacy from me."

"I'm doing the best I can."

She glanced away. It wasn't Chet's fault that she was so furious, and she needed to remember that so she didn't take it out on him. "Anything new?"

"Not really. You claim it was Hank, and he claims you're setting him up and that you actually have the stallion."

Dillon held the ranger's gaze and said emphatically, "I would never do that."

"My gut says you're right, but I have to do my due diligence. That means I investigate every lead."

"I understand," she said and lowered her chin to her chest to kick the dirt at her feet. "You were right about Cal."

"Which part?"

She lifted her head to meet his shrewd eyes. "That I shouldn't trust him."

"What happened?"

"Someone stole the deed to my property out of my office, including the rights to the minerals on the land."

Chet nodded slowly. "It's all in your name, and I'm sure you have copies elsewhere."

"I do."

"Then whoever took it can't do anything with it."

She snorted and crossed her arms over her chest. "The point is, he took it. I trusted him. It was all a setup. He's been working with Hank Stephens the entire time to get onto my property and get close to me. It worked. Until I found the papers missing. Then there were the burrs beneath my saddle blanket yesterday."

"Where you hurt?"

Dillon shook her head. "I told Cal to use that saddle because it fit him better."

"Some might say you put the burrs there to harm Cal."

She narrowed her gaze at the ranger. "Whose side are you own?"

"The law's. I'm merely stating a fact."

"I didn't."

"But you can see how it could look."

She nodded woodenly. "But I didn't."

"What evidence do you have that Cal took the papers?"

"He was in the house."

Chet glanced at the building. "How long have the papers been missing?"

"I'm not sure," she answered reluctantly.

"In other words, you have no idea *when* they were taken."

"It was Cal. Can't you see that?" she demanded. "The shootings didn't start until he arrived. My horse was stolen the night he came. And now the deeds are gone."

Chet raised his brows. "It certainly doesn't look good, but it's all circumstantial."

"It was enough for me to send him packing. You might want to look deeper into Cal Bennett. If that's even his real name."

Chapter 29

Cal sat in a back booth of the restaurant, fighting the urge to go to Dillon. He hadn't slept at all during the night, wondering if she was safe.

And wishing he was holding her.

Cal put his elbow on the table and rubbed his forehead as he stared absently at the menu. His hat was upside down next to him. He kept glancing at the clock on the wall, waiting for the phone call. The instant he felt his phone vibrate, he pulled it out of his back pocket and saw it was Chet.

"Hey," he answered.

"Don't sound so happy to hear my voice," the ranger said, a smile in his words.

Cal leaned back against the bench and sighed. "Very funny. Did you see her?"

"I did."

"And?" Cal asked, not hiding his irritation.

Chet chuckled softly through the phone. "You've got it bad, son."

"Please. I'm dying here."

"She's unharmed. I can't say she's fine because she isn't. She thinks you took the deeds to the ranch."

"What? I have no idea what she's talking about."

Chet grunted. "She's hurt and scared, and things really got crazy when you showed up. You can't blame her for reacting."

"I don't."

"She's convinced you're a part of things with Hank."

Cal closed his eyes. "Exactly what I told you last night."

"And just like I told you, that's going to work to our advantage."

"I think you're full of shit."

"Eh, maybe. But not on this."

Cal watched as a young couple with an infant walked into the restaurant. "What if this plan of yours doesn't work?"

"It has to."

"That's not what I asked."

Chet sighed loudly. "Did you ask yourself if you would stay on a bull each time you got in the chute?"

"Of course not."

"Then don't do it now. The plan is solid."

"We have no backup. I also have no idea how deep Hank's influence is in the sheriff's department," Cal said.

The sound of a blinker came through the phone. "You've got to trust me. If you want to keep Dillon alive and save her ranch, stick to the plan."

Cal glared at the phone after the line went dead. He knew Chet was right, but that didn't mean he liked hearing it. Cal placed his phone beside him on the bench and glanced up as a plump waitress in her fifties with red hair and deep laugh lines came to his table.

"I've been waiting for you my whole life, handsome," she said with a bright smile. "What took you so long?"

Cal twisted his lips as he shrugged. "I got lost."

"That's okay, sugar." She winked. "What can I get you?"

"Um . . . what's your favorite?"

She blinked lashes that were unnaturally long and full. "Not many ask me that. My personal favorite is the Reuben. Our corned beef is the best in Texas."

"I'll take your suggestion and a sweet tea."

"A man after my own heart. I'll get that right out, hon."

He handed her the menu and drummed his fingers on the table as his thoughts immediately returned to Dillon. He hated that she thought he was in league with Hank. Cal wanted to shout from the rooftops that he was innocent, but that wouldn't get Dillon's attention. The only thing that would change her mind was proof and the truth. And Cal intended to get both.

His attention shifted to a person who stopped at his table. Cal looked up and saw a lanky cowboy with a plaid button-down, frayed at the collar and cuffs. He wore a straw Stetson and a too-bright smile.

"Sorry to disturb, but are you Cal Bennett? The bull rider?"

Cal studied the man, trying to determine if he recognized him. "I am."

"Oh, my Lord," the man said to no one in particular, his voice pitched high with excitement. "I'm all giddy. Do you mind if I sit?"

Before Cal could reply, the man slid into the booth opposite him. Cal was instantly on guard, and he surreptitiously opened his phone to record the conversation.

The man never stopped smiling. "My entire year's been made. I'm sitting with a real-life bull rider."

"Cut the shit," Cal stated, not amused by the act. "Who are you, and what do you want?"

The man chuckled and slowly leaned back. Then his voice changed, becoming deeper. "What's the matter? Don't like your ego stroked?"

"Who are you?"

"Names don't matter."

"They do to me. Tell me, or I'll end this conversation right now."

The man made a clicking sound with the side of his cheek. "Don't get your boxers in a wad. I'm Mike."

"What do you want, Mike?"

"You really don't remember me, do you?"

"This is the first time I've met you."

"Naw. We had a drink the other night."

That's when Cal had his confirmation that this was one of the men who had taken him from Ike's that night. "Then you took me to the Bar 4 Ranch."

Mike leaned forward on the table and dropped his voice low as his gaze searched Cal's. "Are you shitting me?"

"Of course," Cal said with a smile.

Mike let out a sigh and leaned back as he straightened one long leg out from beneath the table. "Damn, man. You had me going. Gomez said you weren't too drunk to make that pact."

Cal's stomach clenched in dread. "I've got to maintain my cover."

"What are you doing here then?"

"She fired me because she's sure I'm part of everything."

Mike's eyes widened as his mouth formed a big *O*. "Shit. What are you going to do?"

"Get back in her good graces. I need to know what's being planned so I can do that effectively."

Mike started to talk but clammed up with the waitress's arrival.

She shot Cal another smile as she put his order down, then she turned to Mike. "Anything I can get you?"

"I'm good, thanks," Mike replied.

The waitress put Cal's ticket next to his plate and winked at him once more before walking away.

Mike linked his fingers together and rested his arms on

the table. "The shit is about to hit the fan. They're salivating to get it."

Cal had no idea what *it* was, and he wasn't sure how to find out. He was sure he knew who *they* were, but the *it* was important. "There's a lot about that night that's fuzzy. What exactly are they after?"

"Oh, no," Mike said with a shake of his head as he grinned. "I know better than to say it out loud. And if you know what's good for you, you won't ask again in public."

"What are you afraid of?"

"You must not remember a lot about that night if you have to ask that."

Cal fisted his left hand beneath the table. "Perhaps you should fill me in."

Mike shook his head. "You want answers? You know who to go to."

"That's cryptic."

Mike's eyes narrowed into dangerous slits. "I've stayed alive this long because I'm not stupid. I don't know if you're playing me or not. If you're with us, you'll know who to talk to."

Just as quickly as he had shown up, Mike was gone. Cal didn't run after him. He stopped the recorder on his phone and stared down at his plate. Chet had been sure that someone would approach him now that he was by himself, and the ranger hadn't been wrong.

Cal had hoped he would learn more than he had, but he had more information now than when he arrived at the diner. Mike—if that was his name—had been one of the men who'd claimed to be his friend at Ike's. Had Mike driven him out to Dillon's? Cal wasn't sure.

What he did know was that he'd met with someone important. Was that someone Hank? It was possible.

Yet, the flash of fear Cal had seen in Mike's eyes made

him hesitate. Hank could be a hard-ass, but he wasn't cruel. At least not that Cal had ever noticed through the years, and he would've seen something.

Chet surmised that whoever was after the Bar 4 wasn't working alone. And that there were two different kinds of attacks. Once he had put them in writing, Cal had seen it all for himself. At least two different people were assaulting Dillon, each with the same goal. Chet had surmised that they were in a partnership. The two names that kept coming up were Hank's and the local lawyer, Isaac Gomez.

Cal took a bite of the Reuben as he recalled the bartender at Ike's saying that one of the men Cal had left with worked for Gomez. He had to be Hank's partner. If that were the case, then Cal would have to tread carefully. He had very little information, and he didn't want to tip his hand that he remembered nothing of the night he'd been drunk.

He wiped his hands and sent the recording to Chet, then saved it to the cloud before deleting it from his phone. Cal took his time eating, hoping he'd get a visit from someone else or have an epiphany. Unfortunately, neither happened.

Cal pulled some cash out of his wallet for the bill and left it, along with a tip, on the table. He rose and settled his hat on his head. It felt weird not being out on the ranch helping Dillon. He missed the heat. The aching muscles. The sweat and dirt. But most of all, he missed her.

He walked out to his truck and opened the door. As he did, a piece of paper dropped to the ground. Cal looked around before bending to retrieve it. He unfolded it and read:

COME TO THE RANCH IMMEDIATELY.
HANK

Cal glanced around once more before getting into his truck. There, he took a picture of the note and sent it to Chet with a text stating that he was headed to Ivy Ridge. Cal hadn't wanted to go to Hank's right away, but the note gave Cal the excuse he needed.

He backed out of the parking lot and turned his truck in the direction of Hank's ranch.

He wasn't leaving until he knew if his old friend had Dillon's stallion.

Chapter 30

Cal shut the door to his truck and looked at the front of Hank's house. He still remembered the first time he'd visited. At thirteen, he hadn't grown into his long legs yet, and his voice kept breaking, making those already awkward years even more embarrassing. But he'd been awed by everything at Ivy Ridge.

"You came."

Cal blinked and found Hank standing in the open front entrance. "I was remembering the first time you invited me."

Hank's face split into a wide grin. "You were all legs. Kept tripping over everything."

"Don't remind me," Cal said, chuckling at the memory.

"We had a good time that week. I could barely get you off the horse at the end of every day."

Cal shook his head. How could he have forgotten how much he enjoyed working the ranch? He'd talked about it endlessly to his mother. "It was a good week. I didn't want to leave."

"I offered for you to stay permanently."

"My place was with my mother."

Hank nodded. "Whether you believe it or not, I looked forward to your visits. I hated when they stopped. I never wanted to marry. I never liked kids. Until I spent time with you."

"You should've married and had children of your own."

"Couldn't find the right woman."

"I find that hard to believe."

Hank lifted his shoulders in a shrug. "There's the kind you fuck, and there's the kind you raise a family with."

"There's no reason a woman can't be both."

"I suppose I'm just picky." Hank motioned Cal to the house. "Come in. Please."

He walked to the door as Hank stepped aside so he could enter. Once Cal was inside, Hank closed the door behind them. Cal waited for Hank to move around him and lead the way. Somehow, Cal wasn't surprised when Hank brought him to his office. The view out the windows was second to none.

Hank had built the house atop one of the impressive hills that gave the area its name. From the vantage point five hundred feet above, Cal looked down at the awe-inspiring scenery. The barns and stables were off to the side so Hank could look at his livestock grazing in the pastures.

"You once told me you'd have an office like this," Hank said from behind him.

Cal chuckled. "Who wouldn't want this view?"

"I've worked hard for what I have, Cal. Nothing was given to me."

Cal wasn't sure if that was a dig at Dillon inheriting the Bar 4 Ranch from her aunt or not. Either way, he decided not to comment.

"I dreamed about owning the biggest ranch in Texas since I was five years old," Hank continued. "Every decision I've made, every action I took, was done to bring me closer to fulfilling that dream."

There was a creak of a chair. Out of the corner of his eye, Cal saw Hank sit in the large, leather chair at his desk. Cal watched a couple of horses running through a pasture. "You've achieved a great deal."

"I'm not the biggest in Texas. Yet." Hank's voice held a smile.

"When is enough, enough?"

"You're a smart man. You know the answer to that."

Cal turned to him. "Do I?"

"You wouldn't be here if you didn't."

Ah. Back to Dillon's ranch again. Cal should've known. He wanted to ask his questions, but he suspected that Hank would clam up and refuse to answer anything. So, Cal had to play the game—regardless of how much he hated it.

But if he had to play, he was playing to win.

"I don't remember much of the night I got drunk. I was hoping you'd fill in the gaps."

Hank studied him. "What do you remember?"

"I recollect agreeing to help once they mentioned your name. After everything you've done for me, how could I refuse?"

A muscle clenched in Hank's jaw. "First, I want you to know that I never wanted you involved. It was done without my knowledge. Had they informed me, I would've refused."

"Why? Don't you want my help?"

"Because you're moral. You're here, saying all the right things, but I can see you're struggling with it."

At least he no longer had to hide that. "I am. But, like I said, you're a long-time family friend. I couldn't refuse."

"Shit," Hank bit out as he slammed his hand on the desk. "I'm sorry, son. Real sorry."

"I think it's time you filled me in on the missing pieces of my memory. Things with Dillon are finished. She knows I'm working with you, which means I won't get any more out of her."

Hank stared at him for a long moment. "You care for her. Don't try to deny it. I saw you two at the dance."

"Whether I do or not is irrelevant. I gave my promise to help you."

"And you never go back on your word. Just like your daddy." Hank smiled sadly. "Your father was the best friend I ever had. His word was his bond, and I know he raised you right. If you were anyone else, I'd think you were here to double-cross me. But I know you too well."

Cal smiled, praying Hank didn't see the wobble in his lips.

"You'd better sit down. There's a lot to go over."

The last part of him that had prayed his friend wasn't a part of anything to harm Dillon shriveled and died. Cal hadn't wanted to believe, even when all the evidence pointed to Hank. But here was the proof. It gutted Cal. He looked at his friend, a man who had taken the place of his father and who had been a mentor to Cal in his formative years. He didn't know the man before him. In fact, he might never have truly known him.

"I want to start off by saying that I tried to do this the right way. The honest way," Hank said. "But she was stubborn."

The joy Dillon had once gotten out of the ranch was gone. And she feared she might never get it back. It was Cal's fault. All of it. He had to be charismatic and gorgeous. She had thought he was too good to be true—and she'd been right.

"Want to talk about it?" Emmett asked.

Dillon jerked her head to him as they moved a herd of cattle to another pasture to graze for a while. "No," she stated and nudged her mare into a canter.

"You can't keep things bottled up. It's not good for you or anyone else," Emmett replied as he caught up to her.

Dillon slowed her horse to a walk once more. "Talking about it doesn't help."

"It's part of the healing process."

"Drop it," she snapped. She instantly regretted her harsh tone when Emmett's expression fell. Dillon sighed. "I know you're trying to help, but please, leave it alone."

Emmett nodded. "I just want what's best for you."

"I appreciate that. Right now, I want to be able to move about my ranch without fear that I'm going to be killed."

"On the bright side, no one has tried to shoot you in almost a week."

She forced a smile at his teasing tone because she knew that's what he wanted to see. The one person she'd always been able to count on had been Emmett. He'd been there for her aunt, and he'd been there for her. "Thank you for all you do."

"It's my pleasure. Besides, I'm getting paid rather well," he replied with a chuckle.

"Can I ask something personal?"

"Shoot."

She halted her horse and dismounted as she closed and locked the gate they'd just passed through. "I always thought you and Dolly had something between you. Did y'all?"

A slow smile spread over his face, widening his full, thick mustache as he looked into the distance dreamily. "That woman was something else. She defied everybody, determined to do things her way. I loved working with her. She was as stubborn as they came, but I'd never known anyone more loyal or kind."

"Is that a yes, then?" Dillon got back on her mare and gathered the reins in her hand as she waited for his answer.

Emmett blinked and focused on her. "There was something between us briefly, but we both realized that it wouldn't work."

"But . . . why?" she asked in confusion. "You two were made for each other."

Emmett ran his thumb and forefinger along the right side of his handlebar mustache, twisting the end. "We were better in the roles we originally had."

"I'm sorry."

"It all turned out as it should. Your aunt had many men chasing her, but she was smart enough to realize they wanted the ranch, not her. It made it easy for her to keep them at arm's length."

Dillon had never heard this before. "You mean, she didn't trust anyone? She trusted you."

"To an extent, yes. It was clear that she cared for me, but there would never have been a true partnership between us. She would always run the ranch the way she wanted."

"You were her ranch manager. She took your advice all the time."

Emmett snorted. "She rarely took my advice. She asked for it, then did her own research and made decisions."

"I never knew. She always told me how important you were to the ranch."

Sadness filled his eyes. "Just never important to her, though. Right?"

Dillon parted her lips but was unsure of how to respond.

"It's all right," he said with a wave of his gloved hand.

She watched him turn his horse and nudge the animal into a trot. Dillon wished she had asked Emmett those questions long ago instead of waiting. She really wished she would've asked her aunt. Then again, there was a lot she would've asked her aunt, had she known their time was limited. Just as she started to click to her mare, her phone rang.

Dillon saw Les's name pop up on the screen and immediately answered. "Hey. Is the new will finalized?"

"It is, but that's not why I'm calling."

"What's going on?"

Les released a long breath. "Remember when I told you I'd do some digging to see if your aunt used a local attorney?"

Her stomach clenched with dread. "You found one, didn't you?"

"Pamela Stokes."

"I don't recognize that name."

"You wouldn't," Les said. "She worked for a small firm in Fredericksburg called Taylor, Otis, & Gorski. She specialized in family law but did a few things for your aunt. Apparently, she and Dolly went to school together."

Dillon thought back to all the legal papers she'd seen in the office. "I can't remember letterhead with that law firm's name."

"Dolly did business with several firms. Maybe because she didn't want one place to know all her business. I really can't guess."

"What did Pamela do for Dolly, exactly?"

Dillon heard some keystrokes. "She wrote up Dolly's first two wills. She also drafted the estate documents for your aunt. I got copies from the court."

"You make that sound ominous."

"You weren't always the one designated to inherit the ranch."

Dillon glanced to see where Emmett was. "I never thought I would get it. She didn't have kids of her own, but there were plenty of nieces and nephews to choose from. She always spoke about keeping it in the family."

"You told me that before. So, imagine my surprise when I read who had power of attorney and would own half the ranch in those documents."

She swallowed, the sound loud. "Who?"

"Emmett Perkins."

"That makes sense. He's worked this ranch all of his life, and he and Dolly had an affair."

Silence met her words.

Apprehension made her heart race. "You're freaking me out. Just tell me whatever it is."

"Those estate forms were created fifteen years ago. She had new ones drawn up two months later with no mention of Emmett anywhere."

"Coincidentally, I asked him today if he and Dolly were ever together. He said they were, but that it didn't last. He said they were better suited to their original roles. That Dolly didn't trust any man interested in her because she knew they wanted the ranch, not her. I've long thought there had been something between them. It wouldn't surprise me if she wanted to leave him a portion of the ranch."

Les made an indecipherable sound on the other end of the line. "That does shed some light on things. It could be that Dolly believed she had found someone to spend her life with and drew up the documents. Then realized she didn't want a relationship and had new ones done. Is Emmett bitter?"

"Not at all," Dillon said. "He was Dolly's closest friend. She counted on him tremendously. If he had been upset by the change, he would've left long ago."

"That's certainly true."

"Do you think he knew about the estate forms?"

"I can't answer that. His signature doesn't have to be on the forms. Dolly might have kept it a secret."

Dillon felt her body loosen from the tension. "That's more likely. Dolly never told anyone anything. I had no idea she'd named me in her will for anything."

"You know Emmett better than I do. Just thought I'd give you this information. Someone has to look out for your stubborn ass."

She smiled despite the situation. "Thanks, Les."

"You're not leaving the ranch, are you?"

"Talk to you soon," she said and hung up.

Chapter 31

"Hey, cowboy. It's time to wake up."

Cal turned at the sound of Dillon's voice. He reached for her, pulling her body against his. He ached for her, and only her. She was the other half of his soul, the missing part he'd never thought to find.

Her arms wound around him as their lips met. The kiss inflamed his already heated body until he thought he might burst. He ground against her and rolled her onto her back. She parted her legs and tugged on his hips, urging him to fill her.

Cal guided himself to her entrance and began slowly pushing inside just as the sudden sound of chirping birds grew progressively louder.

Instantly, his eyes flew open, the dream fading like smoke. Cal turned and punched the pillow before he turned off his alarm and flopped onto his back with a loud sigh. It was the second night without Dillon, and the second time he'd dreamed of her. His cock was rock-hard, but he didn't bother to relieve himself. He'd attempted it the previous morning without any luck.

He swung his legs over the bed and stood. Cal took a cold shower that eventually eased his body, but not his heart. He was in a foul mood when he dressed and left the motel for Ivy Ridge. Hank had wanted him to stay there, but he'd refused. Cal also sent Chet a text so the ranger didn't come knocking on his door. Cal had no doubt that he was being watched, especially after everything he'd learned yesterday. Even with the new information, he suspected that Hank hadn't told him everything. But what he had revealed was a doozy. Enough that Cal was truly concerned about Dillon's welfare.

At a stoplight, Cal glanced at his phone, hoping he had a response from Chet regarding his question about Dolly. Hank hadn't come out and said that Dolly had been killed, but something in his words hadn't sat right with Cal. Since he couldn't dig around, he sent the question to the only person he knew who *could*.

Even with everything Hank had shared the previous day, there were a few subjects he hadn't wanted to talk about. Dillon's stallion was one of them. When Cal arrived at Ivy Ridge, he could barely control his rage. He stalked into the house in search of Hank. When the maid pointed to the barn, Cal nodded and walked outside. On his way down the hill, Cal spotted Hank standing in the large entrance to the stables. Hank waved, and Cal forced himself to return the gesture.

"You look like hell," Hank said when Cal reached him. "I have great beds. You should've stayed here."

Cal held his gaze. "Where's the stallion?"

Hank's face mottled with rage as he grabbed Cal's arm and yanked him away from the nearby employees. "What the hell is wrong with you?"

"Answer me," Cal said as he jerked his arm away. "I know you have the animal. I also know how much it's worth."

A vein ticked in Hank's temple. "Cal, you're already in too deep."

"Exactly. I'm in. If something goes wrong, I'm going to be charged anyway. If I'm in, then I'm all in. Or I'm gone."

When Hank hesitated, Cal pushed even harder. "I have nothing to lose. I need this."

"If you need money, I can give you—"

Cal sliced his hand through the air. "You know what I mean. I'm up to my neck in this shit. I agreed because of you. I was drunk, and I could've gone to the authorities and told them I was coerced. I didn't. That should say everything that needs to be said. You told me yesterday that my word was my bond. I gave it, and you still didn't tell me everything."

"Okay, okay," Hank said softly and held up his hands. He dropped them to his sides and sighed. "You made your point. I'll say again that I didn't want you involved at all."

"Too late. Your buddy brought me in."

"There's still time for you to get out."

Cal shot him a flat look. "Maybe before you told me your plan yesterday."

"Fuck," Hank said as he ran a hand down his face and turned to the nearby fence of a corral. He rested his arms on the top rung. "If Gomez can make decisions like he has, then so can I."

Cal held his breath, hoping that his words had convinced Hank of his loyalty. If he couldn't get Hank to tell him every detail, then Cal wouldn't be able to stop the plan. He had a few names, but he knew there were more. He wasn't going to stop until he had them all.

Hank blew out a loud breath. "I have the stallion."

Cal forced his hands to remain unclenched and loose at his sides when all he wanted to do was pummel Hank.

"But it wasn't my idea," Hank said as he faced him.

"Do you still have the animal?"

"Yeah. Gomez wanted me to kill him, but I couldn't. That horse is a stunner. He's got an amazing disposition, too. If I'd known about him, I would've bought him."

Could Hank not let anyone else have anything? The more

Cal learned about him, the more he wondered how his father could've been friends with such a man. "Show me," Cal demanded.

"It's better if I don't."

"That horse is part of my payout. Show me," he said again, this time in a deeper voice.

Hank stared at him for a long moment. "I didn't believe you at first about your relationship with Dillon, but I think something developed between the two of you."

"What does she have to do with this? We're talking about a horse."

"*Her* stallion."

"I played a part, Hank. I did it well enough that I fooled you *and* her."

"And maybe yourself, as well?"

Cal swallowed, wondering if he had pushed too hard about Legacy. "I'm putting my neck on the line for you. I'm not asking for much."

Hank blew out a breath and turned to the stables. "Fine."

In short order, they were on horses and riding out. Cal no longer saw the beauty of the ranch. The greed and self-indulgence of a man he had once looked up to tainted it all. Meeting Hank's gaze was becoming harder and harder, especially after Hank had discovered that Gomez sent someone to kill Dillon and did nothing to stop it.

Hank's excuse? That it would have allowed the plan to move faster if Dillon were out of the way.

Of everything Hank had acquired—land, wealth, cars, women—nothing gave him peace. He wanted more and more and more. He could have the entire planet, and Hank would want the universe. Cal's anger churned viciously. He'd had something beautiful with Dillon, something special. A once in a lifetime something. Hank and Isaac Gomez had ruined that. Possibly forever.

But Cal would get his revenge thanks to Chet Thompson.

Hank looked over at Cal. "You sure have a bee in your bonnet this morning."

"I'm pissed because you kept things from me. Even after yesterday."

"Why didn't you say anything?"

Cal cut him a side-eye. "I gave you time to correct your mistake. The fact that you didn't trust me causes me a great deal of concern."

"I intended to do all of this on my own. I had a plan."

"You?" Cal said with a laugh. "Everyone knows your face. There's no way you could've done it alone."

Hank flashed him a grin. "Well, not everyone I employ is an upstanding citizen. Some will do anything for a price."

Cal's blood went cold as he thought of the accidents at the Bar 4. "Who did you hire?"

"You really want to know the details, don't you?"

"I had one of Gomez's goons approach me yesterday. Two of his men took me from Ike's when I was so drunk I could barely remember my name. Pardon me if I demand details."

Hank's lips twisted. "You have a point. Earl Watters is his name. He spent some time in prison. I give him a place to stay in exchange for him doing whatever I want. He doesn't ask questions, which works perfectly because I won't tell him anything."

"What has he done for you?"

"I'm not going to tell you all of my sins, son."

Cal wasn't deterred. "Who shot at Dillon?"

"And this is why I didn't tell you everything yesterday. You care for her. Hell, you might even love her."

"I made my decision."

"Have you?" Hank asked, his brows raised. "I'm beginning to wonder."

Cal pulled up on the reins to halt the horse. He might have overplayed his hand, but there was no turning back now. "I gave you my word. I don't go back on it."

"That's the only reason you're here now," Hank replied as his horse turned in a tight circle of agitation. Hank quickly got him under control. "Do you want to see the stallion or not?"

As much as it pained Cal, he refrained from pushing about who had shot at Dillon. He'd find out in time. He needed to be patient. Unfortunately, that wasn't a quality he had in great supply at the moment.

They rode on, Hank talking nonstop about his plans for the ranch. Cal listened with half an ear. They stopped near a creek, the same one that ran through the Bar 4, and let the horses drink. Cal feigned interest in Hank's conversation, though he didn't give a rat's ass about how much land Hank would need to acquire to be the largest ranch in Texas.

They rode for another hour, up and down hills. The horses knew the land well since they navigated down the steep inclines with ease. Then, finally, Cal spotted the panels of a mobile corral that encompassed a covered shelter. Standing beneath the protection was none other than a champagne-colored stallion.

Cal nudged his horse into a gallop and quickly closed the distance. He pulled up on the reins and dismounted before his mare came to a complete stop. Cal held out his hand to Legacy, but the stallion ignored him and trotted over to the mare. Thankfully, the horse looked well taken care of.

"What are you going to do with him?"

"Keep him," Hank said with a smile.

Cal couldn't believe Hank's audacity. "Even though he's been tagged as stolen?"

"I've always found it fascinating how money can buy anything."

Cal bit back his retort as Hank answered a call. The conversation lasted only a few minutes before Hank hung up and turned his horse around.

"There's an issue. Come on," Hank said before his horse leapt into a canter.

With one last look at Legacy, Cal mounted his mare. He clicked to the horse, who launched into a gallop until he caught up with Hank. Once they were even, Hank gave his mount her head, and she broke out into a run. Cal leaned lower over his horse as they gained ground quickly.

They raced over the land, maneuvering around clusters of trees and onto well-worn game paths. Ahead, Cal spotted two men near a fence with another on the other side and realized they were at the junction of Ivy Ridge and Bar 4.

When Cal spotted Emmett, elation filled him. He hoped that he'd be able to talk to him privately and see how Dillon was. Cal had to know something.

"This couldn't wait?" Hank demanded as they slowed their horses to a stop.

Emmett's gaze moved from Hank to Cal. "I had to know if the rumors were true."

"What?" Hank asked with a grin before he reached over and slapped Cal on the back. "I told you Cal's loyalty was with me. He's always been on our side."

Chapter 32

Dillon leaned against the doorway of her office, looking at the shuttered windows within while listening to the quiet house. Was this what her days would be like from now on? Was she to spend them looking over her shoulder, checking under the hood of her truck, and closing the curtains? Even when she lived in the city, she hadn't been this scared.

Then again, she had never had someone trying to kill her.

She pushed away from the doorjamb and took a drink of Chambord and club soda as she walked to her desk. She would rather be relaxing for the night. But once more, her brain wouldn't allow her to concentrate. Maybe sorting through vendor invoices might do the trick. If nothing else, it could help her fall asleep. She couldn't go another night without sleep.

Dillon sat and set aside her drink as her gaze took in the desk. The papers were in organized stacks, mostly in file folders so nothing got lost or misplaced. But the quiet of the house was too much. She called out to the smart speaker and told it to play her feel-good playlist.

She bounced her head to the upbeat music and touched her keyboard to wake up her computer. Dillon sorted through the mail and put business invoices in one stack and stuff to be shredded in another. When she'd disposed of the papers, she turned back to the computer. For the next half hour, she checked each invoice to validate that everything matched the services she'd requested or the items she'd ordered. Only then did she set them up to be paid.

When she lifted the glass for a drink, she discovered it was empty. Dillon rose to walk to the kitchen to refill her glass. On the way back to the office, she stopped to get a couple of cheese cubes and some beef jerky. It was the only thing that sounded good to eat.

Once she was back in her chair, she went through business emails before personal messages. Then, she decided to check the cameras. She hadn't gotten around to setting up those on the fence line that separated her property from Hank's yet, but she would. There had been nothing but some deer, a couple of raccoons, and a fox on the other cameras when she'd checked them the previous night.

She found it entertaining to watch the wildlife. Dillon didn't expect to find anything when she fast-forwarded through the recordings for earlier in the day. Until she saw someone approaching the house. She halted the video and rewound it. Her stomach dropped when she spotted Dusty glancing around furtively before hurrying to the house.

The camera angle didn't allow her to see where he went, but she knew he wasn't at the back door or the front. She kept watching, noting the time so she could figure out how long he had been gone. To say that she was disappointed was an understatement. Dusty had always been more concerned about his latest love than putting his all into his job, but she couldn't blame him. This was just a job, not his life. Still. It hurt that he would betray her in such a way.

He came back into the frame. She paused the recording and leaned in closer to see what he held in his hands. When she saw flowers from the front flowerbed, she busted out laughing. Why had he snuck to get them? She would've let him cut whatever he wanted. And to think, she had believed he'd betrayed her. No, it seemed that lay solely on Cal's shoulders.

"Oh, Dusty," she said with a shake of her head, still grinning.

Dillon munched on the soft cheese and the jerky as she went through the other recordings. Nothing was out of the ordinary once Dusty left for his date. She was about to turn off the video when she saw headlights flash. Dillon tried to fast-forward to determine if it was Emmett and realized that she was watching a live feed from the camera facing the back of the house and the stables.

It wasn't until the vehicle passed the camera that she saw the blue and white of Emmett's truck. It was disconcerting to know that she was completely alone on the ranch. She hadn't told Emmett or Dusty that they couldn't leave, but now, she wished she had. Dillon grew uneasy and rubbed her hands on her jean-clad thighs. With a verbal command, she halted the music. She then stood and hurried to the gun safe.

Dolly had an extensive collection of firearms, most of which had been handed down through the family. Dillon reached for her handgun of choice, an RM380. The double-action Remington handgun was light and compact with an aluminum frame and a six-round magazine. She checked the clip to make sure it was full before sliding it back into place, and then carried the gun back to the office with her.

Dillon laid it on the desk beside her. She sat back, her gaze going to the monitor. It was silly that she should be so scared of being by herself. If Emmett had stayed, he was too far away to even hear her scream, which meant that she was still by herself. But something about knowing that someone was on the property with her, someone that she could count on, calmed her fears.

Now, she was on her own. Really, she'd been alone for

much longer than this, she just hadn't realized it. Cal's arrival and her attraction to him had shown her how she had hidden away on the ranch, focusing every bit of energy she had on it. Sure, she got out to the annual dance and maybe the local fair in the fall. But for the most part, she ignored the world and everyone in it.

What had that gotten her? Absolutely nothing. Her heart had been kept safe, but she had missed out on so much. Not that she wanted to put herself on the market and let it be known that she wanted to date, but no one had asked. No one had asked because she'd closed herself off and made sure that everyone knew she wasn't available.

Cal hadn't cared. He'd busted right through the wall she'd erected. She had easily fallen for his heart-stopping smile and smooth words. When he had claimed that they were dating as a ruse for Hank, she'd actually bought into it. The two of them must have had a good laugh at how naïve and gullible she was. And all the while, she'd thought she was getting one up on Hank.

God, what a fool she'd been.

The anger and resentment that had hovered over her since she'd thrown Cal off the ranch threatened to devour her. She was angry at him for treating her in such a manner, but her rage was focused mainly on herself.

She was the one who had let him into her life, even when she knew she shouldn't. She was the one who had fallen for him instead of seeing through his disguise. She was the one who had handed her heart to him. Only one person was to blame for her predicament—herself. If she had been smarter, wiser, if she had looked past his good looks, she would've seen beyond the pretty mask he wore to the deceitful liar beneath.

Her throat clogged with emotion as tears welled in her eyes. She refused to shed them. She had already cried enough over the bastard.

"Looking for me his entire life, my ass," she mumbled to herself. She threw her hands up, rolling her eyes. "And what did I do? I fell harder for him because he said it. Ugh."

She thought about calling him and giving him a piece of her mind, but she stopped herself at the last minute. The only thing that could make matters worse would be allowing Cal, Hank, and Isaac Gomez to believe they had broken her.

"I've been through worse," she stated. "I'll survive this."

She looked at the large wooden hanging that had Dolly's favorite quote. *Strength is what we gain from the madness we survive.*

Dillon had always liked the quote, but now she understood why Dolly loved it so. All the shit Dillon was going through could aptly be described as madness. And she would survive it.

She took three long, deep breaths to center and ground herself. Gradually, her fury receded so she could think clearly once more. Dillon slowly turned and looked around the office. She thought about all the times her aunt had been in the chair she now sat in while Dillon sat on the other side of the desk. They'd shared many meaningful talks—most while Dillon filed papers since that was one chore Dolly hated above all things.

Dillon stopped suddenly, her mind centered on her aunt, and her gaze locked on the filing cabinet. She sat up straight as she remembered filing papers from a doctor in Dolly's personal file. Dillon jumped up and hurried to the cabinet, yanking the drawer open and running her fingers along the files' tabs as she read each one. When she found her aunt's personal file, she pulled it out and returned to the desk.

She sat with one leg tucked under her as she opened the file and sorted through the various documents. Most were receipts from doctors' offices. However, included in them were printouts from the doctor about what had been discussed during the visit, any tests that had been run or ordered, and medications prescribed.

Dolly had had a penchant for sweets, which had led to some excess weight, but she always appeared in good health. She had smoked when she was younger but had given that up. Her only other vise had been her nightly beer. She got all the exercise she needed by working on the ranch.

Dillon came across a visit where a Dr. T. M. Maxwell, a primary care physician, had Dolly's blood screened for troponin T three months before her death. Curious as to what that was, Dillon searched the internet and was shocked to discover that troponin T was a protein found in the heart muscle. By measuring the protein with a high-sensitivity test, it helped doctors diagnose heart attacks and heart disease.

In an attached document, Dillon found the results of Dolly's test, along with a handwritten note that said *Normal* next to the findings.

Yet Dolly had died of a heart attack. If nothing in the tests showed there was an issue, how did she die? After the attempts on her life, Dillon's mind immediately went to the idea that someone had killed her aunt. But, surely, the coroner would've discovered that.

Wouldn't he?

Dillon rubbed her head as she digested that news. She stared at the screen, wondering if she saw traitors and murderers everywhere now because of what had happened to her.

But what if she wasn't imagining this? What if it had happened?

She bit her lip and quickly researched if it was possible to kill someone and make it look like a heart attack. Just as she feared, she got results. The top one was an injection of potassium chloride. The more Dillon dug, the more repulsed she was at how many people went into detail about all the different ways to murder someone so it looked like an accident. And the more she read, the more she couldn't shake her fear that Dolly had been killed.

Dillon sat back. If her aunt had been murdered, and it had been made to look like an accident, why had someone tried the opposite approach with her? As close as Cal had gotten to her, he could've easily injected her with any number of things. Which meant that something didn't add up.

She returned her attention to the notes from the doctor and found the address and a phone number. It was well past business hours, but Dillon still called to leave a message on the machine so they could return her call first thing in the morning.

The line connected, but she didn't hear an office recording. Instead, she got a loud, abrasive voice that stated the line had been disconnected. Undeterred, Dillon looked up the doctor and discovered that T. M. Maxwell had retired.

"Shit," she said as she slumped back in the chair.

Her leg was going to sleep, so she stood and paced the office as she contemplated everything she'd learned. Then she reached for her phone and called Les.

"Dillon?" he answered breathlessly. "Is everything okay?"

"I know it's late, and there's a real possibility that I've gone off the deep end, but I need someone to talk this through with."

He grunted and whispered, his mouth away from the phone, "Don't move. I'll be right back."

Dillon grimaced as she glanced at the clock to see that it was nearly midnight. "Shit. Les, I'm sorry to disturb your night."

"It's fine. We weren't sleeping anyway."

"Eww. I don't need to know that."

He chuckled. "You call in the middle of the night, you get the details of my sex life."

Dillon laughed, the action bringing much needed clarity. "Fair enough."

"Now. Let's have it."

"As I said, I might be seeing things that aren't there."

"Dillon," he said calmly. "Tell me everything."

She cleared her throat and resumed her seat at the desk. Then, with a deep breath, she began.

Chapter 33

Chet threw his phone onto the bed. He still hadn't heard from Cal. And his investigation at Ivy Ridge had wrapped up without any sign of Dillon's stallion. Despite that, Chet knew the horse was there. The challenge was proving it.

He'd hoped that Cal would find something and report back so he could arrest Hank. It wasn't only that Cal hadn't texted or phoned, but he hadn't been seen, either. Chet had spoken with the motel clerk and learned that Cal had checked out earlier that day.

His head whipped around when his phone rang with a call. He grabbed it and looked at the number but didn't recognize it. He answered all the same. "Hello?"

"I'm looking for Special Ranger Chet Thompson," a woman said.

"You've found him. Can I ask who this is?"

"My name is Wanda Bennett. Cal is my son."

Chet sank onto the corner of the bed. "Have you heard from him?"

"I have. The call was short. I didn't get much out of him other than that he's at Hank's," she said.

"How did you know to call me?"

She chuckled softly. "It's no secret that I've never been a fan of my son's chosen profession. I was overjoyed when he told me that he'd quit and was working at a ranch owned by a woman. I could tell by his voice that there was something between them."

"That there is."

"I didn't hear from him again until the night he left the ranch, after you stayed up planning. He told me everything. That's when he gave me your number and said that if he ever mentioned the horse my husband gave me that I should immediately call you."

Chet blew out a long breath. "Then things aren't going well."

"I've always known that Hank couldn't be trusted," she said, her voice laced with anger. "He once tried to convince Cal to come live with him. Hank told me he could give Cal a better life than I could. I informed the bastard that money wasn't everything. To which he laughed and said that of course I'd say that because I'd never had money."

"He's a slippery one. That's for sure," Chet replied.

Wanda asked, "What about Dillon? Who is there to watch her?"

"Her ranch manager, Emmett, and another employee."

"Can they be trusted?"

"As far as I know."

She sighed. "I've never understood what my husband saw in Hank Stephens as a friend. Cal gravitated to him because Hank was a link to his father. But I never trusted him. I lost my husband, Mr. Thompson. I don't want to lose my son."

"Ma'am, I'm going to do everything I can to ensure that doesn't happen."

"I'm only a few hours away. I can drive down in the morning."

Chet winced. "I'm not sure what your presence could do."

"I could stay with Dillon."

"She believes Cal betrayed her. She wouldn't accept his mother's aid."

Wanda made a sound with her lips. "I suppose you're right. What about talking to Hank?"

"Cal's involvement is contingent on Hank thinking that Cal is working with him. If you show up, it might disrupt that."

Cal stood at the window in his bedroom at Ivy Ridge and watched the big orange ball rise from the horizon, chasing back the darkness of night. He'd waffled between rage and shock ever since yesterday, when he'd discovered Emmett's involvement.

He still couldn't believe it. Emmett had looked after Dolly and then Dillon. Why had he turned against them? It explained how all the accidents had happened to Dillon at the ranch, though. Yet, that made Cal worry about her safety even more.

He rubbed his eyes. He'd managed to doze for a few hours, but his mind was too rattled to truly rest—and he wouldn't until Dillon was safe. He turned on his heel and walked from the room, pausing long enough to grab his Stetson and turn the light off behind him.

The house was quiet as he made his way downstairs. The cook and maid hadn't even arrived yet. Cal went to the alarm and used his code to turn it off. He couldn't stand to be in the house one more second. He walked outside, softly closing the door behind him before making his way to the stables.

Ranch workers moved about, and Cal greeted them as he passed. When he reached the stables, he found the wheelbarrow and rake and began mucking out the stalls from the horses that had already been let out.

"Um . . . that's my job."

Cal glanced up to see a teenage boy with bad acne staring at him. "It's your lucky day. I'm going to do it."

"You won't hear me complain," the kid said with a smirk and walked away.

The mindless chore allowed Cal to expend the pent-up energy he had while also allowing his mind to work through the problem. His father had often preached that there was an answer to every problem. Cal just had to find it.

He finished the stalls and returned the wheelbarrow and rake to their places when he saw Hank leaning against one of the stalls, watching him. Cal dusted off his hands. "What?"

"You know you don't have to do that, right?"

Cal shrugged. "I needed to do something."

"You're still upset about Emmett, aren't you?"

"Yeah." There was no point in lying.

Hank pushed away from the stall and walked to Cal. "All that money we're set to make? I wouldn't know about any of it if it weren't for Emmett."

"Once more, you left something out yesterday. Is there anything else you aren't telling me?" Cal demanded angrily.

Hank twisted his lips. "I told you about the blue topaz deposits. I just didn't tell you who told me about them."

"And the survey you showed me? That came from the Bar 4, didn't it?"

"Dolly had it done," Hank replied with a nod.

Cal shrugged as they started walking. "Why did Emmett tell you about the topaz?"

"Dolly refused to give him any of the profits."

Cal didn't mention that it was her land, and it was her prerogative to do whatever she wanted with it. "He turned on a boss he'd worked years for. You trust someone like that?"

"I do," Hank said plainly. "Emmett put us in a position to have the ranch."

"But you didn't get it from Dillon."

Hank smiled. "Catch up, Cal. I'm talking about Dolly."

"What?" he asked, his stomach dropping to his feet.

"That was all out of my hands, I swear. I had no idea what the plan was until Emmett took care of her."

Cal's mind reeled. Dillon and the others all believed that Dolly had died from a heart attack. But if Hank could be believed, then Emmett had killed her. Somehow, Cal wasn't surprised. He had suspected as much already.

"Like I told you the other day, we thought she would leave the ranch to someone who wanted to sell and profit. Then, Dillon upended our plans."

"And you couldn't have two deaths so soon, so that's why you offered for the ranch."

Hank held his gaze. "Exactly."

"That didn't turn out like you wanted."

"Nothing has. Dolly was gone quickly. We expected the same from Dillon, but she's a fighter. Unfortunately, things are out of my hands."

Cal halted and spun to face him. "What does that mean?"

"It means, son, that decisions were made last night."

"What decisions?"

"You have a stake in this, Cal, but you aren't a main player. There's no reason to run everything past you."

Cal fought to compose himself. "You told me that no one else would be shooting at Dillon."

"And no one is."

"Then what?" he demanded, searching Hank's eyes.

Hank glanced away. "She's a complication, son. She already suspects you, me, and Gomez. She brought in the ranger. If any more outside authorities come in, then everything will fall apart, and we could be arrested. I won't go to prison."

"You said the ranger's investigation wrapped up. We know he didn't find Legacy. You're free and clear."

"Not until he's gone from the area. He'll stop by Dillon's today and inform her of what he's found—or hasn't found.

She'll pitch a fit. But, ultimately, nothing can be done. She'll then make a call to her insurance agent and get the money for the stallion. Meanwhile, I'll be able to bring the stallion out of hiding."

Cal frowned. "What if Dillon sees the horse?"

"She won't."

"How can you be sure?"

Hank slapped him on the back. "Because we're going to pay her a visit."

Cal watched him walk away, a yawning pit of fear and trepidation growing within him. He couldn't call Chet because he was being watched. Hank said that he trusted him, but the fact that he'd forced Cal to move to the house and had left him out of conversations last night said otherwise. It was obvious that Emmett wasn't convinced of Cal's loyalty.

Calling Dillon was out of the question. Not to mention, she wouldn't believe a word he said. As for his mom, he didn't want to involve her any more than he already had. If he did, it would be just like her to drive to Hank's and give him a piece of her mind. And that would only create more of a mess. The men he was dealing with were dangerous.

Cal had to come up with a plan to stop Dillon from being killed. The problem was, he didn't know who all was involved or who would do it. He was one man without any backup, going up against an unknown number. Those odds didn't spell victory.

Chapter 34

"You can't be serious." Dillon stared in shock at Chet Thompson as they stood in the stable. "Hank stole my horse."

The ranger sighed as he briefly looked at the ground before returning his gaze to her. "I've searched every inch of his property."

"You're one man. Did you really think you could find Legacy on your own? Of course Hank was moving him around so you *wouldn't* find him."

Of all the shit that had gone wrong over the last couple of weeks, this was one that Dillon honestly believed would be resolved in her favor. Then again, that was when she'd thought that Cal was on her side. It seemed that life hadn't done enough to her. But it seemed it wasn't just going to kick her when she was down.

It planned to stomp all over her.

"Wait," she said, suddenly remembering something that Chet had said. "I thought you told me you weren't out here alone. That you had help."

He nodded once. "I do."

"And?"

"We found nothing."

Dillon threw up her arms and turned, taking a few steps before letting them slap against her legs. "He can't get away with this."

"If he has the horse, he'll never be able to sell him."

She rolled her eyes, her hands on her hips as fury simmered. "Oh, that makes me feel so much better."

"I'm sorry, Dillon. I really am."

She couldn't even look at him.

Chet cleared his throat. "I've submitted my report. My advice is to call your insurance agent and get things rolling with that."

Dillon already figured that with the insurance money and drawing some out of her savings, she would be okay. But for how much longer? If she bought another stallion, would Hank steal that one, too? Would she be fighting him for the rest of her life? The ranch was her sanctuary. She didn't want to lose it. But she didn't have the wealth to go up against Hank and his cronies.

However, all of that hinged on whether she was alive to fight him.

"Have you heard anything from the sheriff's department regarding their investigation into who shot at you?" Chet asked.

Dillon shook her head. "I'm sure the evidence will lead nowhere, and it'll become a cold case. Up until they *do* manage to kill me."

"I think I know the answer, but why don't you sell?"

She turned to look at him. "This is my home. I shouldn't be bullied—in any fashion—to sell what is legally mine, all because some wealthy jackass wants it. Someone has to stand up to him."

"And that has to be you?"

"Who else will do it? Hell, even you're leaving."

Chet's chest deflated. "If you ever need anything, don't hesitate to call me."

Dillon didn't respond. The ranger had been the one person she could trust, and now he was leaving. She was irate with him for not locating her stallion, and incensed with Hank for everything else.

"Take care of yourself, Dillon," Chet said as he touched the brim of his hat and walked away.

She didn't move until his truck was down the lane. She looked around, trying to figure out what to do next. Her gaze went to Legacy's empty stall. Then she walked to Cupid and rubbed her hand down his forehead to his velvety nose. She rested her cheek against the sorrel stallion's head as tears threatened.

"Good news for you, boy. You won't have to share the mares with anyone now."

She stayed like that for a moment more and then lifted her head. Cupid's soulful dark eyes watched her. She got the feeling that he recognized the myriad emotions within her and was offering what comfort he could.

"This is why I prefer animals to people," she said and kissed his cheek.

She gave him a scratch behind his ears, his favorite, before heading to the house. Dillon didn't say anything to Dusty or Emmett when she spotted them. She wasn't in the mood for anyone that morning. The last thing she wanted to do was get on the phone with the equine insurance company, but it was better to get that out of the way and move forward. Especially when there was no other place for her to go.

Thirty minutes later, she hung up the phone and sat back in her chair. She wasn't motivated to do anything. Unfortunately, the ranch didn't care about her emotional or mental state. Just as she was about to get up, her phone rang. The instant she saw Les's name pop on the screen, she answered.

"Tell me you found Dr. Maxwell," she said.

"Hi, yourself."

Dillon lifted her face to the ceiling and clenched her free

hand. Then, she lowered her head and calmly said, "Hey, Les. How are things this morning?"

"I found her."

"Her?" Dillon asked with a frown. "Dr. T. M. Maxwell is a woman?"

"Yep. Her final month of practice was the month that Dolly went in. Terry retired to Cabo San Lucas right after that."

Dillon blew out a breath. "But you got ahold of her?"

"I did. We just got off the phone. When I told her how Dolly died, she thought the call was a practical joke from one of her friends. Apparently, they play some pretty wild pranks on each other often. Anyway, once I made her understand that my call was serious, she wanted to see the medical examiner's death certificate. I emailed it to her. She wasn't happy that an autopsy hadn't been done."

Dillon placed her elbows on the desk. "Emmett was with Dolly when it happened. He saw her collapse and called the ambulance. They pronounced her dead once they arrived."

"And the medical examiner noted on her report that the cause of death was natural, giving no need for an autopsy."

"What did Dr. Maxwell say to all of that?"

"She said that had she known about this, she would've demanded an autopsy. She went on to say that tests and screenings can't find everything, but she had discovered nothing that would've suggested your aunt was in poor health."

Dillon swallowed. "People die all the time."

"Are you trying to convince me, or yourself?"

"Emmett told me she died of a heart attack."

"Without an autopsy, the ME couldn't have determined that. Only an external examination was done, and no toxicology tests were administered. The ME made their ruling of natural causes and a heart attack based on what they discovered."

Dillon began to shake from fear or anger or a combination,

she wasn't sure. "Is there a chance that Dolly was murdered?"

"No one could make that determination without an autopsy."

"But?" Dillon prodded.

Les sighed heavily. "It can't be ruled out, either. If Hank wants the ranch, chances are he tried to buy it from Dolly before you inherited the land."

"There won't be a record of that."

"Sadly, no. Not unless he made a formal offer as he did for you. But my guess is he didn't."

Dillon slammed her fist on the desk. "I know less than I did yesterday. I feel like the walls are closing in on me."

"Get out. Right now. Don't even pack a bag. Just leave, Dillon."

She loved the ranch, the animals, and the house. But was it worth dying over?

As if sensing her indecision, Les said, "I'll make sure you don't lose the land. There are some legal things we can do. I'll go over all of them with you. First, you need to get to safety. Because I don't know about you, but I don't think you can trust anyone there. I'm scared for your welfare."

"I know." Her gaze moved around the office. She couldn't help but feel that if she left, she would never return. Yet, she could only fight for her ranch if she was alive. "I'm getting in the truck as soon as I hang up."

"Oh, thank God," Les said, relief in every word. "Don't say anything to anyone. Just get in your vehicle and get on the road."

"Where do I go?"

"Come to Dallas. My girlfriend is moving in with me. You can stay at her place."

Dillon had to admit that it sounded like a good idea. "I never thought it would be my lawyer who saved my life."

"Hey," Les said with a chuckle, "we can be heroes, too."

"I'll call you from the road."

"I'll be waiting."

She hung up and glanced at the desk. Dillon briefly thought about putting things in a locked drawer, but if someone came in, they'd just bust the lock. She turned to the computer, intending to set the password so they couldn't get into that, at least, when she spotted Cal on camera.

"What the hell?" she murmured.

Cal didn't want to be here, but he had no choice. Ever since Hank had informed him at breakfast where they were headed, Cal had been trying to figure out how to get in touch with Dillon to warn her.

He hadn't been given a moment alone to text or call anyone. His stomach churned. He couldn't look at Hank or Isaac. They were no longer human beings to him. They were monsters. That was the only explanation for men who could so coldly and callously plan someone's murder.

They fact that they were smiling and laughing about the riches that would soon be theirs as they rode in Hank's truck to the meeting spot with Emmett only confirmed to Cal the greedy, demented men they were.

"You're quiet," Isaac commented to him from the front seat.

Hank looked over his shoulder at Cal in the back seat as he drove. "He's thinking of all the things he'll be able to do with his share of the money. Wouldn't surprise me if he got himself a ranch of his own."

Isaac chuckled. "We've waited long enough for our payday. It's about time we got it."

Thankfully, Cal didn't have to reply as the two stroked each other's egos, talking about how great they were to have put such a plan together. It made Cal sick. It also caused dread to settle uncomfortably within him—a feeling he feared wouldn't leave anytime soon.

Cal's hands were clenched in anger when they arrived at the same section of fence line that he had tracked Legacy to that first day. Emmett was there, waiting with the UTV. The old cowboy didn't wear a smile as he watched them alight from Hank's truck. His expression was stern, his gaze hard as he ordered the three of them to get into the UTV.

"You don't need to tell us to hurry," Hank said with a laugh. "I didn't sleep at all last night I'm so excited about this day."

Emmett said nothing as he started the vehicle and put it in drive.

Cal's mind raced, trying to find an opportunity to get word to Chet or someone else for help. Then he thought of Dillon's other employee. "What about Dusty? We don't want witnesses."

"Don't worry about him. He's on the southwest portion of the ranch. He'll be too far away to see or hear anything," Emmett replied.

Cal inwardly grimaced. His last hope had been Dusty. He wouldn't give up, though. He couldn't. Dillon's life was on the line.

"Where is she?" Isaac asked.

Emmett glanced at the lawyer in the back seat beside Cal. "She's been in the house ever since the ranger came this morning."

Isaac rubbed his hands together. "Everything is going as planned."

"Of course, it is," Hank replied, his chest puffed up with vanity. "Enough things have gotten in our way. There will be no more obstacles after today."

All too soon, they arrived at the barn. Emmett parked behind it so the vehicle couldn't be seen from the house. Cal reached for the handle and opened the door, slowly pushing it wide as he thought about making a run for the house to alert Dillon. He stepped out and found himself standing before Emmett. They stared at each other silently.

How had he not seen Emmett's true nature? If Cal had discovered the man's involvement sooner, then Cal might have been able to stop things from reaching this point. He didn't want to go to the barn. Didn't want to do anything but run to the house and pull Dillon into his arms. Cal wanted to stop the madness, but he hadn't figured out how yet. It would be just him and Dillon against Emmett, Hank, and Isaac. The odds were stacked against him every way he looked.

"Here I thought I was the master of deception," Emmett said.

Cal shrugged, doing his best not to pound the old man into the ground and send him to Hell as he deserved.

Emmett smirked, his mustache tilting slightly. "You don't remember me from that night, do you?"

"Nope." No use lying. Hank had offered very little to fill in the blanks of the night Cal had gotten drunk. It was better if he didn't try to pretend otherwise.

Emmett snorted and walked even with him. "You're a cold bastard to have gotten Dillon to fall in love with you." He smiled. "Good going. You fooled even me."

Cal's heart dropped to his stomach the minute he heard that Dillon was in love with him. He spun around and watched Emmett walk to Isaac and Hank. The three men stared at him, observing him carefully. Cal realized that they were trying to determine if he was really with them.

That's when he knew. If they thought for even a second that he wasn't on their side, they would kill him. That couldn't happen. He had to be able to help Dillon.

He shoved aside his fear for the woman he loved and went to them. "What now?"

"Open all the gates," Hank ordered.

Cal didn't argue as he walked past them and through the

stables. He didn't go to the paddock nearest him. Instead, he walked across the lawn, where he knew the camera was and headed to the gate farthest away. All Cal could hope for was that Dillon had the screen up on the computer and saw him. If she was smart, she'd call Chet for help. Hell, even the sheriff's department. No one could make a 911 call disappear.

"Come on, darlin'. Come and find me so I can get you to safety before the psychopaths find you," Cal whispered as he opened the first gate.

Chapter 35

Dillon cocked the shotgun and brought it up to her shoulder as she stared down the barrel at Cal. He halted in his tracks, his hands lifting skyward slowly.

"Don't shoot," he said and gradually turned to face her.

"I thought I made it clear that you were never to return."

He glanced toward the stables. "I understand you're upset."

"You know nothing. What are you doing here? How did you get on my land? Oh, wait. Let me guess. You cut the fence and came from Ivy Ridge."

He licked his lips, looking remorseful. "Actually, the fence that was cut when Legacy was stolen still isn't fixed."

She frowned, not wanting to believe him. Emmett promised that he had fixed that days ago. How would she know for sure, though? It wasn't as if she had ridden out to see for herself.

Because she was too scared.

Anger that had been simmering began to bubble furiously. She stared into gray eyes that she had thought kind and trusting. It might have taken her a bit, but she finally saw Cal for who he really was. Her heart was broken, but the only thing that kept her going was the knowledge that she would win this battle. Somehow.

"Whatever you're doing, you're leaving now," she told him. Dillon then motioned with the gun for him to start walking.

"Dillon," he started.

"Don't," she stated over him in a firm voice. "Get moving. Or I'll shoot."

He glanced at the ground. "No, you won't. Because you're a good person."

"Care to test that theory?" To affirm her statement, she put her finger on the trigger, ready to pull it.

"I do."

Dillon's heart skipped a beat at the sound of Hank Stephens's voice behind her. She glanced over her shoulder to see that Hank had a gun pointed at her. When she looked at Cal, he couldn't meet her gaze.

"Take the shotgun," Hank ordered Cal.

Dillon ordered herself to pull the trigger. It was her only play that gave her any kind of an advantage. No matter how many arguments she gave herself, she couldn't shoot Cal. And if she did, Hank would shoot her. How could she fight for the ranch then?

As if sensing her decision, Cal lowered his hands and walked to her. He pushed the barrel away from him and wrapped his fingers around it. His gaze held hers.

"Asshole," she said as she released her grip on the gun and shoved it at him, causing him to stumble back a step.

Hank laughed behind her. "Oh, you don't know the half of it. Come on. We're going for a little walk. I've been waiting for this day for a long time."

Dillon pivoted to glare at him. "No."

"Come on," Cal said and took her arm.

She yanked it from his grasp and cut him a scathing look that he didn't seem to notice. "Don't you dare touch me."

He held up his free hand, fingers splayed. "Suit yourself. But you need to walk."

"Where?" she demanded, looking from Cal to Hank.

Hank jerked his chin toward the stables. "There."

Dillon studied her options. The problem was, she didn't have any. Les was expecting her in Dallas, but that was a good four-hour drive. He wouldn't start searching for her until then. Chet was already gone, and she hadn't seen Emmett or Dusty since Chet had been there a few hours earlier. There was no telling where they were on the ranch.

Hank pointed his gun at her. His gaze told her he wanted her to give him a reason to pull the trigger. Before the day was up, he would most likely do just that. But she needed to give herself time for Dusty or Emmett to arrive for help. So, she started walking. Hank lowered the gun and continued on.

So much for her getting to Dallas to be safe. She hadn't even made it to her truck. Dillon wished she had brought the handgun with her, too. She could've hidden it and given herself a bit of an advantage. Even a knife. Why hadn't she thought ahead?

Cal stayed just behind her while she followed Hank to the stables. The entire time, she thought of all the various ways she hoped the two of them would die for what they were doing to her. When they reached the stables, she wasn't surprised to find Isaac Gomez leaning against a stall. Dillon looked around for some type of weapon, but unfortunately, there was nothing close.

"Stop," Hank ordered her as he halted next to Isaac.

She halted and faced the three men. So, this was where she would die. Funny, but she never imagined she would go out in such a fashion. Then again, she hadn't expected to be betrayed in such a manner, either.

Isaac reached into his back pocket and produced folded

documents and a pen. "We're going to need you to sign the rights to the Bar 4 over to us."

"Go to hell," she told them.

Isaac's brown eyes shone with malice so deep that her heart dropped to her stomach. "It wasn't a request."

"No." Despite her fear, she lifted her chin, daring him.

Hank sighed and raised his gun. "One way or another, we're going to get your signatures on those documents."

Cal almost smiled when Dillon lifted her chin, radiating defiance, and stated, "No."

"Yes!" Hank bellowed, spittle flying from his mouth as he lost his temper. "I've waited long enough to claim what's mine."

"What's yours?" Dillon asked with a snort. Her eyes raked over him with pure disdain. "This land isn't yours."

"It ought to be."

She rolled her eyes, seemingly unconcerned that she faced two men wishing to do her harm. "Wanting it doesn't make it so."

Hank stalked indignantly to her until he towered over her, attempting to intimidate her. "I always get what I want. Always."

Cal shifted, not liking how close Hank was to her. In the next second, Dillon jerked up her leg, slamming her knee into Hank's balls. He let out a strangled cry, grabbing his crotch with his free hand as he dropped to his knees. He let out a keening sound of anguish as his hand holding the gun lowered to the ground to keep himself upright.

Before Cal could react, Isaac was before her in two strides. He backhanded Dillon so hard she spun around, catching hold of the stall door to keep herself standing. Cal gripped the shotgun tightly, ready to lift it and fire at a moment's notice. If Dillon wasn't so close to either Hank or Isaac, he could have the two at gunpoint already.

"You bitch," Hank ground out as he slowly climbed to his feet. His face was flushed as he glared at her. "I'm going to make you pay for that."

Everything in Cal wanted to reach for Dillon and pull her against him so he could comfort and protect her. She wouldn't accept his help, and he couldn't fight her and the others. Which meant he had to wait to make his move. Cal hated to admit it, but he wasn't sure there was a way out. He didn't want to kill anyone, but he would do it to save Dillon.

Her hair covered her face. She tried twice to get her feet firmly under her before she could stand on her own. When she finally faced them, her left cheek was bright red. Cal slid his gaze to Isaac and thought about lifting the shotgun right then.

Hank raised his gun and pointed it at Dillon. "Sign the fucking papers."

"No," she said once more.

"Sign or die," Hank threatened. "I'm not going to tell you again."

She shook her head, standing defiant and resilient. "You're going to kill me anyway. Why should I make things easy for you? Oh, and I should warn you, that if I die, you'll never get this ranch. Ever."

"What?" Hank asked in shock.

Isaac chuckled, unfazed by her words. "Don't listen to her. She can't keep us from getting the ranch."

"I've waited too fucking long," Hank said as he kept the gun trained on her. "I'm not waiting any longer."

Dillon crossed her arms over her chest.

Hank took a step toward her. "Sign the papers."

"Go to hell," Dillon said.

Dillon had never been so terrified as she was staring down the barrel of the gun aimed at her head. She wanted to run and hide, but she had to take a stand. They were going to kill her anyway, and that was the only reason she was able to keep somewhat calm.

"You did this all wrong," she told them. "If you wanted me to sign easily, then you should've made me believe I was going to live. For all your planning, y'all suck. I mean, did you really think I wouldn't find out what was in the ground? Did you really think you could take it from me? It's not going to happen. I can promise you that."

Hank's smile was pure evil. "I'm going to make you suffer. I tried to be nice. I tried to be fair, but you just wouldn't take the hint and leave."

"I'd sign if I were you," Isaac said.

Dillon noticed that Cal didn't have the shotgun pointed at her. He hadn't said anything, which concerned her. She didn't think for a second that he was having second thoughts about helping his cronies. He might not have the gun raised, but she wouldn't underestimate him, either. He'd stolen her heart easily. He could take her life just the same.

Isaac's nostrils flared, anger darkening his eyes. "Sign."

"No."

"I'm going to make you sign one way or another," Hank said and took a step toward her.

"No, you aren't," Cal replied.

Dillon was unsure why Cal would suddenly speak up. The fury that flashed in Isaac's eyes made her wonder if the three were as tight as she had thought. Then she saw something out of the corner of her eye. When she turned and spotted Emmett, hope flared within her. She shouted his name. But what little optimism she felt faded when Emmett didn't even look her way as he walked to the men.

"I told you how to handle her," Emmett said. "Now, this will be harder than it had to be."

Dillon started shaking. This couldn't be happening. Not Emmett. She had trusted him above all others. She stared at him, willing him to face her. And the truth struck her—something she hadn't wanted to see. "You killed Dolly."

He ignored her.

"You killed my aunt, you bastard!" she shouted.

Emmett finally turned his head and looked at her. "So?"

"Why?" she asked, shocked that he had admitted it. "Dolly was good to you."

"After all the work I'd done for her, she wouldn't share any of the profits with me. There was more than enough."

Dillon had never hated anyone as she did at that moment. "Having a secure job wasn't enough, huh? Having a home, friends, someone you could count on wasn't enough."

"If it wasn't for me, Dolly never would've known what she had. If I hadn't found the stone and shown her, she wouldn't have called the surveyor and had it confirmed. There is a fortune beneath our feet, and she wouldn't share it. I've earned my share."

"Because it was her land," Dillon stated calmly.

Isaac held out the paper and pen again. "And it'll soon be ours."

"You're kidding." Dillon looked at the four of them. "Y'all think you can trust each other? I wonder who will kill who first."

Hank pressed the gun to her head. "Do you ever shut up? Just sign."

"I said no," she reiterated, meeting his gaze.

Emmett sighed dramatically and turned on his heel. "I know how to get her to sign."

Dillon glanced at Cal, who was holding her shotgun as if he were about to raise it, but his gaze was locked on Hank. She wasn't sure what to make of that. There had been plenty of opportunities for Cal to help her, and he hadn't. He likely wouldn't do anything in the future, either.

Her head swung around at a loud neigh of fear from one

of the horses. Then the sound of hooves reached her. She gasped in outrage as Emmett led one of the foals into the stables. The mother continued neighing loudly, seeking her baby. The little filly responded and tried to return to its mother, but Emmett's hold on the halter was firm.

"Sign the papers, Dillon. I'm only going to say it once." He then drew a pistol and pointed it at the foal. "Or I'll shoot her."

Dillon knew Emmett would kill every animal on the ranch to get her to sign. His greed wouldn't let him stop until he had what he wanted. Dillon's revulsion grew. She could no more allow the foal to die than she could any of the horses on the ranch. And Emmett knew it. It had hurt when Cal had fooled her, but she was devastated by Emmett's betrayal.

She held out her hands to Isaac. Hank lowered the gun and backed up a few steps. Once the papers were in her grasp, she couldn't help but wonder how long it would take for the authorities to find her body. If they ever found it. Les wouldn't give up until he knew the truth, but she would probably be in a shallow grave somewhere long before then.

Dillon unfolded the papers and skimmed the first document. The legal jargon made her eyes cross, but the gist was that she willingly signed over all rights to the ranch for the sum of three-point-five million dollars. All of which was bullshit. She wouldn't get a penny of it. No doubt there was already a plan in place to state that they wouldn't be able to transfer the money for one reason or another. They'd likely covered all the bases. She was the only weak link they had to shore up.

She glanced at the foal, who still struggled and cried to get back to its mother. The mare screamed, and Dillon heard the horse running back and forth to get to her child. If the filly wasn't returned soon, the mare could bust down the fence and harm herself.

How had it come to this? How had everyone she knew betrayed her? How had she been so blind to all of it?

"Ticktock," Emmett said to hurry her along.

She shrugged, her mind racing with a plan that was more foolhardy than anything. But a chance was a chance. "I need to sign this on something."

Isaac let out a long-suffering sigh and turned his back to her before bending over. "Use my back."

Dillon had hoped that one of them would do exactly that. She propped the paper on his back and clicked the pen. Instead of signing, she raised the pen and plunged it into Isaac's neck. He let out a scream as she shoved him aside and rushed Emmett, knocking up his hand that held the gun. He fired, the sound scaring the filly so that she reared, flailing her hooves, one of which struck the arm that held her.

The foal bolted. Dillon spun around in time to see Hank raising his weapon at her. A loud boom sounded. Dillon jerked, but she felt nothing. She looked down at herself, but there was no entry wound. Then she looked back at Hank to see a huge red stain spreading over his chest. He turned his head and looked at Cal, disbelief on his face. Dillon saw the end of her shotgun smoking in Cal's grasp.

Isaac was on his hands and knees, screaming in pain. Cal looked at her, then his face went white as he looked past her. Dillon spun and found Emmett on his knees with his gun aimed at her. She heard the retort as he pulled the trigger. Saw the flash of the bullet as it left the barrel. Everything moved in slow motion. There was no time to move, no time to duck. There was a blur of something in front of her and then the *thwack* as the bullet met flesh. Her eyes dropped to find Cal. The world returned to normal like a punch to the gut when she realized that Cal had taken a bullet for her.

She wanted to go to Cal, but her gaze jerked to Emmett when she realized that he still held his gun. His smile was pure evil and sent chills down her spine. Just as his finger curled around the trigger, a figure came from the side of the stables and pressed a rifle against Emmett's back.

"Drop it," Dusty demanded of Emmett.

Dillon let out a sigh when she saw Dusty.

Emmett's lips lifted in a sneer. "You weren't supposed to be here."

"Did you really think I didn't notice what you were doing?" Dusty demanded.

She dropped to her knees as Cal rolled onto his back with a moan of pain, blood everywhere. She tore open his shirt to see where the wound was, but there was so much blood. Her gaze lifted and met his.

"I . . . tried to . . . warn . . . you," he said.

She shook her head. "Shh. Save your strength."

Cal smiled. His face was pale from the pain. "I wasn't going to let them hurt you. Dillon—"

She shook her head at him. "Stop talking. You need to save your strength."

"But I have to tell you something."

Tears gathered when he closed his eyes and grew still. About that time, the sound of sirens filled the air as cars came to a halt on the gravel drive. In seconds, sheriff's deputies and Chet Thompson swarmed the stables.

"Help! I need an ambulance!" she yelled.

EMT personnel moved Dillon aside and began to tend to Cal. They put him on a gurney and rushed him out of the stables. She jumped to her feet to follow, only to have a deputy stop her.

Cal lifted his head and looked at her as he mouthed, "*I love you.*"

Her mouth parted in shock. The doors of the ambulance slammed shut, and she watched it race away.

"Dillon."

She turned to see Chet. Her knees gave out when she realized that the nightmare was over. The ranger caught her, holding her firmly as he walked her to one of the patrol cars. He opened the back door and helped her sit.

"I need to know if he's going to be okay," she told the ranger.

He nodded and motioned to one of the nearby deputies. "They'll keep us posted. Is all that blood Cal's? Or is some of it yours?"

She looked at her hands and saw they were covered in blood, as was the front of her shirt. "It's his. He saved me. How did you know to come?"

Chet got a towel from someone and handed it to her so she could wipe her hands. "Dusty is a volunteer for the TSCRA. Usually, volunteers only work the auctions, but he had a lot of information about what was going on here. I did tell you that I wasn't here alone. Cal was also working with me."

She shook her head. "But I thought he . . . You mean he didn't betray me?"

Chet shook his head. "They tried to bring Cal in the night he was drunk, but he was so inebriated that he didn't remember anything. He never would've agreed to anything while sober. Once you sent him away, we used that as a ploy to get him to discover all the details. But you can rest easy now. It's all over."

She watched as the deputies led Emmett and Isaac away in handcuffs. Isaac had a huge white bandage on his neck and blood staining his shirt. Hank was on a stretcher, a white sheet covering him as they casually loaded him onto another ambulance.

"Did you hear me?" Chet asked. "It's over."

She looked at him. "I know."

Chapter 36

Cal slowly came to. The pain radiating through him made him wonder what injury he had now. He couldn't remember what bull he had been on. Then it all came back to him.

Dillon. Hank.

The gun.

His eyes fluttered open, and he blinked against the harsh light of the room. He tried to swallow, but his throat was dry and scratchy.

"Cal? Oh, God, Cal."

He turned his head at the sound of his mother's voice to find her rushing to his side. He spotted the chair near his bed that she had been sitting on, reading one of her favorite romance authors, Sawyer Bennett.

She gently touched his face, her watery smile proof that she had been worried. There was happiness mixed with tears in her gray eyes. "Are you in pain? Do you need anything?"

He tried to lick his lips, which was a mistake. He attempted to swallow once more—another mistake. "Water," he croaked.

"Oh," she said, flustered and turned around. A moment later, she had a cup in her hand with a bendable straw.

He pulled the liquid into his mouth and let it sit before

swallowing. After two more such drinks, he waved it away, knowing from experience that he shouldn't take too much at once.

"You scared the hell out of me," his mother said.

Her chin-length pale brown locks were in disarray. She had a habit of running her hands through her hair when she was anxious. Cal used to tease her about it often when he still lived at home.

"I'm okay," he told her.

She gave him a heavy dose of side-eye as she took his hand in hers. "Here I thought I wouldn't have any more hospital visits once you quit rodeoing. What you did was crazy. Heroic, but crazy."

"It worked." Cal glanced around the small room, hoping he might find Dillon.

His mother patted his hand. "You're lucky. The bullet missed your heart by an inch. The doctor got it out, but your recovery will be long."

Cal's mind replayed the scene where Emmett had lifted the gun toward Dillon. Cal hadn't hesitated to dive in front of her. He could still hear the sound of the gun's retort, deafening him for a second.

Then the impact of the bullet entering his body, taking his breath as he plunged to the ground.

"You're on a heavy dose of antibiotics as well as painkillers," his mother said.

Cal drew in a breath, grateful for her voice that pulled him from his mind. "I can tell."

"Are you up for a visitor?"

He immediately perked up. The beeping of his heart monitor caused his mother to glance at the machine, then back at him. It would be just like Dillon to wait in the hall so he and his mother could have some private time.

Cal held her gaze, fighting back the smile at the thought of seeing Dillon. "Yes."

His mother turned and walked to the door. She opened it a crack and said something he couldn't hear. The door then opened wider and a body filled the doorway, but it wasn't Dillon. Instead, he found himself meeting Chet Thompson's gaze.

"How you doing, son?" the ranger asked.

Cal's disappointment was profound. Dillon couldn't still think he had betrayed her, could she? He thought he had told her why he'd been there, but he wasn't sure. His pain had been great, and he'd been fighting to stay awake. Surely, Chet had told her everything. But if he had, then where was she? He hadn't imagined the feelings between them. They had been real and amazing, something he'd never experienced before.

Something he knew he would never feel with another person.

Dillon's absence made him face the possibility that she didn't feel the same for him. Or maybe she wasn't ready for what was between them. Neither scenario made him feel better, though.

"Cal?"

He blinked and focused on Chet. "Yes?"

"I asked how you were doing."

"Hurting. But alive."

The ranger's lips curved into a crooked smile. "You did what you set out to do. You stopped Hank and saved Dillon."

The mention of her name was like rubbing salt in his wound. Cal forced a smile as he glanced at his mother. "Anyone who knows us Bennetts knows how muleheaded we are."

His mother smiled, but her eyes were sad.

"So," Chet said and cleared his throat, "a lot has happened since you were rushed to the hospital. Emmett has been charged with attempted murder against Dillon, horse theft for stealing Legacy, and several other things I can't remember. Dolly's body is being exhumed, and a pathologist will run some tests after Emmett admitted to murdering her.

Isaac Gomez has also been arrested and will be charged with a myriad of things."

"Did you find the stallion?" Cal asked. "I know where he is."

Chet's smile was wide. "Hank's employees willingly revealed Legacy's whereabouts, and he was returned to the Bar 4, where he belongs."

"Good. That's good."

"I've alerted the Texas Rangers about Hank. If he was willing to kill to get land, then it might be wise for them to take a look at his other dealings and associations—especially those he had in his pocket like Sheriff Felps."

That made Cal grin. "Please tell me the Rangers will dig into his dealings, even though he's dead."

"They will. The county is about to get upended. It might take some time to sort things out, but all dirty laundry gets aired out eventually. I suspect Hank's and Isaac's is particularly dirty."

"Thanks for updating me."

Chet started to turn away when he paused. "One more thing. A body was found just outside of town. The remains were a male with a gunshot wound to his head. The ME identified the man as Freddy Miller, who was known about town as having worked for Isaac Gomez. He had a wife and two young children who reported him missing a week ago. He was found with a .22 rifle. Forensics identified that one of the slugs pulled from Dillon's cabinet matches a bullet fired from Freddy's rifle."

"Damn. Do you think Gomez killed him because Freddy didn't get Dillon?" Cal asked.

Chet shrugged. "Could be. We'll likely never know. Right now, the authorities are trying to see if they can determine who killed Freddy. If it's Gomez, he'll be charged for murder."

"Let's hope they find what they need."

The ranger looked at Wanda and tipped his hat to her. Then he slid his gaze to Cal. "Good luck, son. If you ever want a job with the TSCRA, let me know."

Cal smiled as Chet walked from the room.

"I'll be right back," his mother said and hurried after the ranger.

Cal leaned his head back against the pillow. The pain in his left side throbbed with every beat of his heart. He tried to shift and clenched his teeth in pain. Instead of subsiding, it intensified. He fisted his right hand and squeezed his eyes closed as he battled the brunt of the agony.

Dimly, he heard the door open. He didn't want to look up and have his mother see him in such a state. No doubt she'd drag every doctor in the hospital to his room to have a look at him. Slowly, the pain began ebbing enough that he could relax. It was only then that he realized that someone had spoken, and it wasn't his mother.

Cal snapped his eyes open, and his gaze landed on Dillon. She stood at the foot of his bed, her wavy, dark locks flowing freely. She had changed and now wore a black dress that looked like a long T-shirt with slits on either side to show off her gorgeous legs.

"Hi," she said nervously.

He swallowed, so happy she was there that he could hardly contain himself. "Hi."

"It seems I owe you an apology."

"You don't."

"I accused you of stealing the deeds."

"I would've done the same in your shoes, I'm sure. Besides, it allowed me a way in with Hank so I could learn all the details I wouldn't have known otherwise."

She tucked her hair behind an ear, her gaze dropping to the floor. "You saved my life a second time."

"I'd do it again in a heartbeat. Always."

"I'll never be able to repay you."

Cal smiled. "Sure, you can."

"How?" she asked with a frown.

"Kiss me."

She quirked a brow and gave him a flat look. "A kiss for a life? That hardly seems fair."

"It's what I want."

Dillon stared at him for a moment longer before she walked to him and leaned down to gently place her lips on his. Cal reveled in her taste before she pulled back.

"Is that it?" she asked. "We're even now?"

He shook his head. "Not exactly. I want a kiss a day for the rest of my life."

"Oh, really?" she asked with a chuckle, her lips curving into a smile. "You're really pushing things now."

"I think it's fair. I did take a bullet for you."

Her face sobered. "You did."

"Don't," he said and took her hand in his good one. "I wasn't lying. I'd do it again."

She looked down at their joined hands before returning her gaze to him. "You mouthed something when they put you in the ambulance."

"I sure did."

"Say it again. Please?" she asked in a soft voice.

Cal looked into her powder blue eyes and said, "I love you."

"I love you, too," she replied with a slow smile.

"Now you'll never get rid of me," he joked.

She leaned down for another kiss and whispered, "That's what I was hoping you'd say."

Epilogue

Two months later . . .

Cal rocked on Dillon's porch in the evening air, his left arm in a sling. He was getting stronger every day, but it would be a while before he was at a hundred percent. Dusty stood at the grill, tapping his toes to a country song. Dillon, his mother, and Arizona—Dusty's latest girl—filed out of the house carrying food they set on the table.

"Is it almost ready, honey?" Arizona called to Dusty.

He glanced at them. "You can't rush perfection."

Everyone chuckled, including Cal. They'd all recently learned that Dusty loved to grill as much as he loved ranching, and he took both seriously. Especially with the black apron he wore with big, white letters that said: *Grill Master.*

Arizona strutted down the steps in her short dress to stand by Dusty. He gave her a quick kiss and wrapped his free arm around her as they talked.

Dillon came to sit beside Cal and handed him a sweet tea. "What a day."

"You can say that again," his mother said as she joined them.

Cal blew out a breath. "I'm glad it's over."

"I wouldn't say it was over," Dillon said.

He glanced at her and chuckled. "I still can't believe Hank left me Ivy Ridge."

"I'm not surprised," Wanda said. "He thought of you like a son."

Cal took a long drink of tea. "The whole ranch, though."

"What are you going to do with it?" Dillon asked.

Cal felt Dillon's and his mother's gazes on him. He looked into the distance. Ever since he'd learned that Hank had left him the ranch, Cal had been considering what to do. "I figure there are a couple of options. I can run it while you run yours," he told Dillon.

She nodded. "That's an option."

His mother snorted and looked away to take a drink of tea.

Cal shook his head at her. "I could sell it."

"You could," Dillon said, wrinkling her nose.

His mother snorted even louder.

"The option I'm leaning toward is dividing it. We take as much as we want and incorporate it into the Bar 4. The rest, we divide into sections and sell."

Dillon's eyes brightened. "I have to admit, I like that idea the most."

Cal looked at his mother to find her smiling.

"What about the house?" Dillon asked. "It's much bigger and nicer than mine. The location atop the hill is rather amazing."

Cal reached for her hand with his right one. "I personally prefer your place, but I'll live anywhere you are."

"Really?" she asked with narrowed eyes.

He chuckled. "Really."

"Then I'd like to stay here."

His mother let out a big sigh. "Thank God. I don't know if I could walk into the other house even if you two lived there. Now, tell me. When's the wedding?"

"Mom," Cal said with a glower. "We're getting to that. In our own time."

Dillon laughed and leaned forward to see Wanda. "He's made it plain that he wants to be able to use both arms before then."

"Oh, I see," his mother said with a chuckle before bringing the glass to her mouth for another drink.

Cal rolled his eyes. "You two."

"Hey," Dusty called to them and held up his phone. "Did y'all see?"

Dillon shook her head. "See what?"

"Dates for Emmett's trial as well as Isaac's have been announced."

Cal looked at Dillon. "I can't believe both are going to leave it to a jury to determine their fate."

"I don't want to talk about them," she said with a smile. "I'd rather continue talking about our future."

He tugged her out of her chair and onto his lap. "You are one special woman."

"I know. Aren't you lucky to have me?" she teased with a smile as she ran her hands through his freshly cut hair.

There was no laughter in his eyes when he said, "More than you could possibly imagine. I love you, darlin'."

"I love you, cowboy," she whispered and placed her lips on his.